GALAXY'S EDGE
CREATED BY MIKE RESNICK

ISSUE 57: July 2022

CONTENTS

Lezli Robyn, Editor
Lauren Rudin, Assistant Editor
Z.T. Bright, Slush Reader
Taylor Morris, Copyeditor
Shahid Mahmud, Publisher

Published by Arc Manor/Phoenix Pick
P.O. Box 10339
Rockville, MD 20849-0339

Galaxy's Edge is published in January, March, May, July, September, and November.

Please check our website for submission guidelines.

ISBN: 978-1-64973-123-4

SUBSCRIPTION INFORMATION:
Paper and digital subscriptions are available (including via Amazon.com) . Please visit our home page: www.GalaxysEdge.com

ADVERTISING:
Advertising is available in all editions of the magazine. Please contact advert@GalaxysEdge.com.

FOREIGN LANGUAGE RIGHTS:
Please refer all inquiries pertaining to foreign language rights to Shahid Mahmud, Arc Manor, P.O. Box 10339, Rockville, MD 20849-0339. Tel: 1-240-645-2214. Fax 1-310-388-8440. Email admin@ArcManor.com.

EDITOR'S NOTE by Lezli Robyn   3

THE LAND AND SEA MUST NEEDS SHARE by Kimberly Unger   3

TIN SOLDIER by Angela Slatter   9

STILL CITY by Mica Scotti Kole   16

TRAVELS WITH MY CATS by Mike Resnick   19

SIZED by Elaine Midcoh   29

MEN OF GREYWATER STATION by George R.R. Martin & Howard Waldrop   40

A FLYING ARK FOR THE GHOST DOLPHINS by Antony Paschos   57

GALAXY'S EDGE INTERVIEWS WESLEY CHU by Jean Marie Ward   66

RECOMMENDED BOOKS by Richard Chwedyk   73

THE SCIENTIST'S NOTEBOOK *(column)* by Gregory Benford   78

TURNING POINTS *(column)* by Alan Smale   84

LONGHAND *(column)* by L. Penelope   86

ACT ONE *(serialization)* by Nancy Kress   88

G000067493

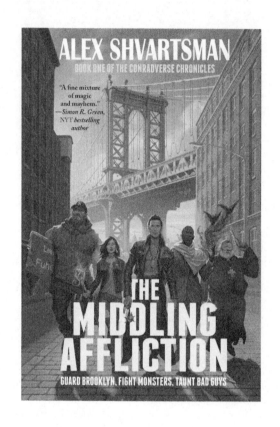

EDITOR'S NOTE

by Lezli Robyn

Arc Manor Publishers, along with its imprint CAEZIK SF&F, and *Galaxy's Edge* magazine, was absolutely delighted to go to Balticon last month and share our new issues and books with our writing and reading community. Regular fiction contributor Alex Shvartsman, spent a lot of time at our tables, launching his new novel, *The Middling Affliction*. While we are biased, all the incredible reviews attest to what an intelligent, witty read it is. An urban fantasy set in Brooklyn, no less!

Speaking of Brooklyn.... I was staying in that borough ahead of Balticon, touring New York and sharing the sights. And yet, it was only when I turned up at the convention that someone decided to share Covid-19 with me, which has then led to pneumonia and quite a significant infection in my teeth, because apparently I am not Wonder Woman, and my editor pen can't erase this virus from my own existence.

Consequently, this editorial will be short and sweet. We're absolutely thrilled that Jean Marie Ward was able to interview Wesley Chu, again pulling back the curtains of creativity to share the heart and mind of a wonderful author. We also welcome a new columnist to the magazine, Alan Smale, who will intrigue us with all the Turning Points in science, history and life, and how these pivotal topics can impact or inform authors while they write. I had the pleasure of editing his novel, *Hot Moon*, which is absolutely wow-ing science fiction geeks, Apollo fans and reviewers alike! It releases this month, and given that the author is an astrophysicist who works for NASA, you can imagine how accurate the science is. Not only that, but the characters are so rich. I could go on, but this is meant to be a short editorial.

Also in this issue, we have new-to-my-editing-pen authors, Elaine Midcoh, Kimberly Unger and Antony Paschos, and regular favorites, Mica Scotti Kole, Nancy Kress, Mike Resnick, Angela Slatter, and George R. R. Martin—the latter in collaboration with the venerated Howard Waldrop, whom I am delighted to have bought another two foundational pieces of fiction from, to feature in upcoming issues!

Be well. Stay safe. And, as always, happy reading!

Kimberly created her first videogame back when the 80-column card was the new hot thing. This turned a literary love of science fiction into a full-blown obsession with the intersection of technology and humanity. Today she spends her day-job building ecosystems for XR, occasionally lectures on the intersection of art and code for game design, and writes science fiction about how all these app-driven superpowers are going to change the human race.

THE LAND AND SEA MUST NEEDS SHARE

by Kimberly Unger

The research ship bucked in the current, engines churning against the brine. The tide did it's best to keep them from the boundary between the shore and the deep, holding the line between land and sea. The big fusion turbines did their work well, inexorable in their own way, and for a time the balance held. The ship hung suspended between two worlds. Diplomatic permissions had been exchanged; the ship would be allowed to pass unrestricted to the release grounds. All that remained was the acceptance of the tide.

The escort appeared on the sonar when they finally passed the invisible boundary. The monsters hung outside the circle, patiently awaiting their turn.

The wind off the sea was cool and crisp. It did nothing to alleviate his pain; it failed to dry the sweat that peppered his brow, the salt speaking to salt and both turning against him. He was having trouble breathing. In and out—short, sharp breaths. He ignored the bindings at his wrists, the sweet-sharp pain in his head. *It's just like childbirth*, they said. *A perfectly natural response to a natural process.* The tinny voice through the speaker by his head held no real comfort. A natural process for the deep-seekers, perhaps, but the psychic link between parent and child was an entanglement that the human heart was not prepared to let go of so easily. He didn't think it would hurt this much.

He'd been warned, of course. The warnings had never stopped coming. Feed him this, don't feed him that; limit his time in the ocean, limit his time watching television; make sure he milks his poison glands; give him lots of fatty foods, no sugar; don't let him sleep after sunrise…. Every moment of parenting came with warnings dire and not so dire, impossibly contradicting one another. Somehow they'd both managed to survive without completely understanding them all. Somehow his son would have to survive the next steps alone.

Roger was born for this, he reminded himself in those rare in-between moments when he still retained some sense of himself, when he knew who he was. Those rare moments now when the memories were not being flensed, divided between conjoined souls that were peeling apart like the halves of an unripe orange.

☼

"Kappa! Kappa!"

It was summer, bright and the kind of sea-salt sticky that only popsicles and lemonade could rightly address. His son was there, pale haired and pale skinned but never managing to catch a sunburn. Roger caught his hand, dragging him towards the rough and tumble surf, past the rip-current flags and posted warnings to swim at one's own risk.

"Let me show you, Kappa! You stay there. Tim showed me how to bodysurf, but you get sand in your shorts, so don't be mad if I get sand in the car, okay?" And he was off, not forging a path through the water, but embracing it, moving as one with the tide until only Roger's straight blond hair bobbed above the wrack as he waited for the next surge.

Roger was seven in this memory, gill slits showing only as sketches underneath the pale skin at his neck, the barest sprinkling of pre-scales like freckles across his shoulders, slightly webbed fingers and toes—absolutely at home in the salt water the way a lizard takes to sand. The riptides were his favorite because then the seas were clear, the tourists bunched up on the sand and out of his way.

☼

The knowing, the father realized, does nothing. In the face of the moment, the fact that you know this separation was inevitable made not one damn bit of difference. All children must leave somehow or they stay children forever. *It's a process. What's done is done. The point of no return is fast approaching.*

What if it *could* be undone? This twisting and thrashing of the soul as memories are so un-gently prized apart, separated into one-for-me-and-one-for-you by a biological process he had no control over. If they had never bonded, if Roger had stayed with mother rather than father, the memories would be his and his alone to cherish, to hold close. Those memories would be colder, warmer, different. *Lonelier.*

How can you judge the worth of a memory that might have been?

☼

When Roger was born, the room had been filled with doctors from both sides of the family. Specialists, tanks, machines, cameras, recording devices. *This is monumental*, they told him. Medical students had been sending requests for copies of the video, for access to the records, permission to attend. A birthing room had been changed to a birthing theatre and the press of bodies filled the space. Blonde haired, blue skinned, fins, flair, green eyes, yellow eyes, they had formed a colorful bohemian backdrop to the only thing in the world that mattered to him in that moment.

A quiet bubble had descended over his mind, over the scene at the center of the room where his wife twisted and turned, framed by the wires that fed the recordings. Cleverly laid out so as not to impede her progress, she'd thrashed in her tank, spilling salt water that sought the drains in the cold concrete floor. The action empowered her contractions, and he'd missed the moment in the blur of motion and waves. Doctors leaned in with the catch-net in case the soft-shelled egg-case broke too soon or too late, releasing the tiny body into a world it would be ready for in moments.

That first cry he felt with more than his ears. It rattled in his chest, his bones. A psychic pulse of betrayal and *why have you abandoned me to this?* He saw it move through the crowd, the more sensitive doubled over, clutching at their chests, their hearts. The doctors tipped the angry wet ball from the catch-net into his hands, careful not to touch—careful that the very first skin to skin contact was between father and son.

4

✿

The man inhaled, exhaled, flexing his bound hands, counting the moments between breaths. He tried to retain sense of self, to retain some kind of rational thought. The memories he took, the memories that Roger took, would shape them both going forward. He was the parent, he was the decision maker—but only for a little while longer. He had to make good choices.

This is why, he realized, doctors ask for a plan, they ask for decisions made ahead of time. Decisions you don't want to think about, that feel wrong when addressed without the immediacy of the moment. But She was there, just off the side of the boat, directing the doctors and deciding for him the same way he had decided for Her when Roger had been born. All he had to do was focus on the memories and She would take care of the rest. All he had to do was let go. All he had to do was trust the process. All. All. All. It was all a failure—his failure, he knew. A deep-seeker could have managed letting go; it was ingrained, it was a part of who they were. Instead, he was compelled by his land-borne nature to fight, to retain every moment he could cling to, every memory as if it were his alone. It took an effort of will and pain to let them go.

Make good choices.

Less than five feet away, in a glass-sided tub filled with salt and foam, his son fought the same fight.

✿

"Roger has a life here, he has a home. His college scores are fabulous—all the universities want him. There's a place for him here if he never makes the leap." His father remembered how cold the beach had been that night, the frost-rimed surf pushing against the sand, smoothing it and reclaiming the detritus cast up by the storm the night before.

"You know why. He has to grow, he has to become his own man." She'd answered him from where she lolled, half in and half out of the tide on the beach where they'd first met, first fell in love. "If he survives the passage, he will have a home in the sea." Her legs were locked together in the semblance of a tail, long fins and streamers moving hypnotically with the back-and-forth of the water. Her visit this time was out of concern—concern that Roger hadn't yet begun to call to the sea.

He sighed and sat down in the waves beside her. He had considered simply not answering her call, had waited behind the heavy wood door and the heavy glass panes until his conscience had got the better of him. It was a discussion he didn't want to have, but her presence was compelling. "Maybe he's different. Just because every child has returned to the sea so far, doesn't mean every child *has* to. I'm still looking for ways to fight it." He reached out a hand and she twined her fingers in his. "Is that so wrong? He's not just your son, but our son. He could stay here, be happy here."

"It will hurt less if you do not fight it," she said somberly. "Less for you and less for Roger. He may be staying for you now, but he will not be able to stay forever. It is the nature of children to leave their parents. It is the nature of deep-seekers to leave a wreckage behind and for that I am sorry. Whatever you choose, this is a fight you *cannot* win. Roger needs you to lose." The emphasis caught his attention. He turned his gaze to her and found himself lost in her great luminous eyes. Under her influence his worry grew less, his fear for the life of their son subsided. Her gentle calm suffused him. Roger was born for this. He would make it through the hazards.

✿

That memory he got to keep, a brief respite from the stripping and loss, a moment of intermingled joy and sadness.

✿

"I HATE it. Why do they even call them math TEACHERS. They ought to just call them math GIVERS because all they're doing is giving me homework and not TEACHING me how to do it in the first place!" The balled-up homework paper hit the edge of the mantelpiece, teetered, then fell towards the fireplace, saved only by the rush of hot air from the closed fire grate.

The man found himself staring at his son, the uncharacteristic outburst ringing off the walls of the small room. "I thought you were doing well in math…"

"I was doing just FINE until the TEACHER said nothing at all about how to handle the negative numbers. NOT ONE THING." The skin over his gill-slits rippled in frustration, Roger's all-too-human eyebrows pulled together into a tight and angry frown.

"Maybe you missed that bit, but we can look it…"

"I SHOULDN'T HAVE TO LOOK. I SHOULD HAVE BEEN TAUGHT. ALL TEACHERS ARE GARBAGE." The pencil followed the paper, point shattering when it hit the stone mantel. Roger stormed down the hallway, slamming the bedroom door hard enough to rattle the glass.

Outside the house, the sea turned and roiled, surf and seagulls warning of an impending storm.

A deep breath, then a second. He recognized Roger's frustration, the shame at being caught out on a topic that usually flowed as easily as water. He resisted the urge to shout back, to bring down the heel of discipline down. Roger would be back once he calmed down and they would be able to talk through the assignment together. The math wasn't the problem, or the learning; the schoolwork was never the problem. The school's counselor had called again. The bullies had been after Roger, laughing at the turtlenecks and scarves he wore to conceal the gills that betrayed his inner feelings.

✧

He realized, abruptly, that there were memories he didn't want to keep. Moments of anger, of the cruelty of children, of the injustice of people who just didn't quite get how big and dark the world really was. But to burden Roger with only those, to keep the good memories for himself, would be worse. He couldn't save himself and damn his son. That was how the monsters were made.

✧

"So many fathers try to keep only the happy memories," she'd murmured to him as they lay in the surf, naked bodies entwined in the moonlight. "And so many try to keep all the bad memories to themselves, to send the children ahead with only the best and brightest thoughts in their head. You shared in creating those memories, you have to share them still—strike a balance of light and dark."

"It doesn't seem fair, to have to burden him with my memories. He ought to be making new ones."

"Memories have two sides, sometimes more. He will need them. He will need your experience to survive the passage."

✧

On the outside it'd seemed so simple. On the inside, every memory—good or bad—shone like a pearl in his consciousness, making letting them go much harder. Separation meant they would each only be the sum of the memories they contained.

"It's okay, Dad."

He opened his eyes to find Roger regarding him from his tank on the deck of the ship. His body rocked, the motion of the bath trailing the motion of the ship just enough to engender seasickness.

"I need those too, okay. I got stronger—I can handle them. I need the bad and sad ones too if I'm going to make it through."

The approximation of Roger's voice crackled through the speaker by his head, his son's lips moving underwater in time with the words. The boy had lost his voice weeks ago, when he'd still been in denial. He'd plied his son's throat with menthol and honey, trying to coax forth a voice that had no hope of return; the change had already begun. He felt like a fool now, that he hadn't been able to see it. He'd held out hope that maybe, just maybe, it would be different for them. That somehow Roger would be something new. More of a hybrid who could live in both worlds.

✧

Roger's hands clenched, nails he could never quite keep filed down digging into palms that were always too dry, always rough; the skin catching, snagging on the soft surfaces his Dad's people loved so much.

✧

His Dad's people.

It wasn't the father's memory. It was Roger's, shared back along the link that bound them. When did his son stop thinking of himself as part of the family? *When did "my people" become separate from "his people" in his mind?" How did I become an outsider to my own child?*

Sadness came, sharp and keen. A memory that had been unshared—a solitary moment had been given and he wasn't sure if it would be, could be, taken back.

✿

Roger stared around the darkened living room with it's mix of hard and soft, smooth and slick with warmth and contrast. He remembered lying on the cold wood floors as a child, pretending he was floating in an ocean under the chill of a sky filled with stars. The house was a jumble of things that made no sense, but felt of love and completeness. To unfamiliar eyes the mix appeared to be nonsensical, that the owner should choose one or the other and be satisfied.

Somehow, Roger thought, *somehow they all work together anyway. They make a whole greater than the pieces. Why does it work when their very natures should be fighting, when they are all so very different in form and material?*

Roger pulled off his turtleneck and flipped on the living room lights. His reflection stared back at him from the mirror over the mantel, gills rippling under the skin, eyes black and luminous.

✿

"Men used to go mad all the time," she'd said. "It wasn't that they were pining for us when we left them; they were only after a quick roll in the surf anyway. It was giving up the children that did it."

"*I'm* still here," he pointed out.

She chuckled, bubbles coming up through the orange fringe of her gills with the sound. "Well, my love, you and I—we are a little bit weird. But listen, letting go is never easy. I brought him into this world, but you're the one who will have to free him in the end."

"Weird?" he responded with mock outrage. "You're a fish-girl from another world and I'm a hairless ape with aspirations beyond my station, trying to co-parent a teenager across biomes. How on earth could anyone see us as weird?"

✿

Dad startled him as Roger came through the front door. He'd been standing in the jumbled conflict of the living room, using the long mirror over the mantel to see, to properly look at the new buds and changes he'd been denying for months: the orange frill that had appeared along the edges of his gill-lines, the organs that had been deemed vestigial by the human doctors beginning to blossom, to show crenellations and colors through skin now as thin as paper. They fluttered as fear caught in his throat.

He turned as his father stopped in the doorway, arms laden with groceries. Roger was laid bare, the changes in his physiology writ large in the revealing light. He opened his mouth to say something, but his father got there first.

"Well, shit. I don't think the schools in Atlantis are gonna accept your SAT scores."

Roger had counted off seconds of stunned silence, waiting for the words to come to him. It began as a chuckle, a laugh of relief at his father, at his own burgeoning fear, his body, the world—the creeping horror of a future now laid bare before him as a certainty rather than a fairytale.

Then the laughs devolved into sobs as his father set the groceries carefully on the floor and crossed the room to embrace him, soft parts and hard parts all mismatched.

So many possibilities died in that instant, as they should. A thousand land-borne versions of Roger's future self cried out and vanished, replaced by a ticking clock that neither of them could hear just yet.

✿

"You're doing just fine," the nurse told him, patting his wrist with her warm fingers. "We still have time. Roger's changes have slowed a little. We think the final push is coming up."

He was struck by a moment of sheer, blinding panic. In a crazed moment he thrashed, reaching for the wires that bound him to his decision. If he could just get free—if he could just get Roger and get out of here, away from the sea—he could save his son, he could protect him from the future that was coming. They had no roadmap, no experience for what came next. Everything the man could offer, every experience he had of a life lived on land and among the cities didn't apply here. He had nothing to offer to shield his son, to chart a new course. If he could take Roger back, he could protect him, could make sure he turned out all right.

"Dad"

Roger's voice cut through the panic. He turned his head to find luminous, alien eyes staring from within Roger's tank.

He has his mother's eyes.

"Are you ready, Dad? This is it. I can feel it." The gill slits along his throat had blossomed like coral on the tide, finally tearing free of his human masquerade.

He has his mother's gills too.

He realized, in the truth of that moment, that there had never been a point of no return. That moment had come and gone when he'd fallen in love with a fish-maiden by the edge of the sea and agreed to father her child, to protect him until he was ready to return to the ocean.

But he couldn't protect him any longer.

"Ready." The words didn't need to pass his lips. The psychic bond they'd been unraveling so torturously still connected them by the thinnest of threads. A bond that, had he been born of the sea, would have vanished like sea foam in the rain. It popped and began to tear, memories flowing through the gaps like water.

☼

Roger lying at the bottom of the pool, the chlorine making his eyes and skin burn, holding his breath until his lips turned blue as he tried to force his gills to work.

Checking every incoming trawler at the wharf until he'd been able to return home with two bags of those black striped zebra shrimp that Roger said tasted like candy.

His dad trying to show him how to pin a corsage on his date and Roger stabbing himself in the thumb with the pin, drops of red blood so different in hue and thickness from his own.

Roger's glossy green fingernails being filed down again because one of the parents at the school had expressed a "concern" for her little bully's safety, even though Roger had never lifted a finger to retaliate.

☼

Some memories flowed to Roger, some stayed. Some vanished and he wasn't entirely sure where they'd ended up. Every single one hurt as they passed. He hoped he'd got the balance right. It became clear now that the moment was approaching where the memories became the only thing he had to arm Roger with. The one last gift he had to give.

"HE'S GOOD! DROP THE TANK!"

The bereft man could hear the commotion, the clank and slide as the tank was shoved to the side of the boat, levered up into position by the hydraulic lift.

Wait. I'm not ready for you to go.

But it was out of his hands. The advisors and doctors from both sides of the family held the reins now and, with a final tearing that momentarily deprived him of reason, the familiar presence that was Roger was gone.

The cheer that went up could be heard both above and below the waterline. Someone shook his hand, shouting congratulations over the noise, but he was too weak to make sense of it. A bubble of quiet calm descended in the midst of the chaos and he was alone. Eighteen years of a shared life, of memories in two parts and—like a lightning strike—it was over.

Thank you. It was Roger's voice, his real voice. One last wisp of connection popped and flew free.

"C'mon, up you go." Rough, unfamiliar hands fumbled and undid the restraints binding him down, catching arms now freed and hauling him to his feet. The salt air was cold, drying the sweat on his face, in his hair. He didn't want to move, didn't want to break the bubble that held the memories he'd been left with, the last illusions of closeness and safety.

She'd had it right, he realized. It was the leaving that drove men mad. Black depression loomed, waiting for its chance to envelop him, to grind at the newfound aloneness in his soul.

They led him to the railing, propped him up.

"Wave goodbye, dad," someone prompted him, nudging his elbow. He raised an arm automatically. As he gazed out over the waves, his depression ebbed, soothed as it always was at the sight of the sea.

A webbed hand broke the surface. Roger's hand, a final farewell before moving towards another life, another home. His mother would be waiting at the end of his journey, if he survived the passage.

He turned away before the shark fins broke through the surface. He would return to the little house by the sea. He would lie with Her in the surf at high tide and hear her reports of their son. Maybe he'd remember to call his old man once is a while.

Copyright © 2022 by Kimberly Unger.

Angela Slatter (also writing as A.G. Slatter) is the multi-awarded Australian author of All The Murmuring Bones *(Titan Books), followed by* The Path of Thorns *in June 2022. Both are gothic fantasies set in the world of the Sourdough and Bitterwood collections. Angela has recently signed another two-book deal with Titan for the novels* The Briar Book of the Dead *(2023) and* The Crimson Road *(2024), and she is the author of the supernatural crime novels from Jo Fletcher Books/Hachette International:* Vigil *(2016),* Corpselight *(2017) and* Restoration *(2018),*

TIN SOLDIER

by Angela Slatter

"He asked for you."

I hadn't set foot in Tenby Hall for six years, I hadn't seen Harry Vander in seven, and I'd neither seen nor spoken to Worth de Havilland in nine. All in all, it was a bit of a shock to the system, with so many ghosts floating around me. The hall hadn't changed, its interior was the same not-quite-right white, the lights a bit too bright, a preponderance of shiny metal and tasteful furniture, milque-toast artworks, the strange slippery carpet they'd created so that gurneys and wheelchairs could run along it but footsteps would still be muffled. And it strictly speaking wasn't a hall—it was a tower, but just about everything was a tower nowadays and the CCR Board wanted a name that stood out. Tenby Hall was a cross between a hospital, a research facility and a guinea pig hutch, no matter how much money they threw at it or what the nameplate said. Situated in the middle of a field in Hampshire, it stuck up like a big finger directed at the sky.

Harry was grayer, in both hair and face. Looking at him made me glad I'd gotten out when I did. His eyes were tired and sad, a bit suspicious. He'd put on some weight—he'd once been greyhound thin, now there was just a little paunch billowing under his suit, and the lab coat looked tight across the shoulders. Was the tarnished gold band on his left hand a sign that his wife or husband could cook, or that there were too many takeaway meals on his dance card? I wondered if there were any little Harrys running around, and calculated how old he was: ten years older than me, so nudging fifty-two, fifty-three. I'd been thirty when I'd first started at Tenby, the baby, the prodigy, the *enfant terrible*—no one else had been under forty. I was a girl to boot. Imagine the fun.

"He asked for you," Harry repeated. "We suggested his family but he got very agitated. It wasn't worth having him hurt himself."

"Did he say why? Why me?"

Harry shook his head, shaggy hair needing a cut. "He was adamant. And he's still important. It took us a while to find you. You did a good job of disappearing."

"Bollocks, Harry, you searched the iDirectory and had my number in about two-point-five seconds. Only the poor have any real chance of disappearing in today's world."

"Well, you took a long time about returning my call," he grumbled, and I had. Two weeks in fact. I could tell from his expression that he thought I might have bothered to dress up a little, too, something better than jeans and a t-shirt, leather jacket and boots. Instead he said, "You need to prepare yourself, Faith. He's … well, not to put too fine a point on it, he's a fucking mess."

I nodded, said nothing, felt the sense of unease that had been steadily building since I got Harry's message throb and expand. It sat at the back of my throat, malignant, making it hard to swallow. We stopped outside a frosted glass door and Harry pulled a swipe card from his pocket, ran it through the reader, then pressed his thumb deeply into a gel pad beneath. The lock clicked and the door slid aside.

We stepped into a vestibule, empty but for a long bench running along the floor-to-ceiling glass wall in front of us. On the bench, stainless steel, were bottles of pills, paper towels, syringes, antiseptics, bandages, white towels, bags of saline, kidney trays, all manner of medical paraphernalia. Through the glass, though, that's what caught my eye, the man in the wheelchair.

If Harry hadn't told me who he was, I wouldn't have recognized him. Even then I was prepared to call Harry a liar and walk out, not look back. In the end the only thing that convinced me were the eyes, when he seemed to sense us and turn around. It had to be the eyes, because nothing else was the same, nothing else was right.

There were no legs below the knees, just rough red-looking stumps; only one arm remained, the right, the other ended just above the elbow. His left ear was gone, sheared off at the skull, making his head look lopsided. The mouth was crooked, lips strangely thin, and a nerve ticked irregularly just above his left temple. Under the white hospital gown, he seemed smaller, thinner, his muscle mass wasted. Shaved off, his hair was a black shadow across the skull broken only by scars, some long, some jagged, some simply dots, one almost a perfect square; his face was clean-shaven too, but the blue stain of a beard darkened his chin and thin cheeks.

It was the eyes, though, so blue, so large, with lashes like an alpaca and brows straight and fierce. The expression in them was the same, as if something always vaguely amused him. And when he smiled, or gave an approximation of one, the lift at the corner of his mouth was identical, the little quirk that said *Well, you and I are okay, but the rest of this world? Fucking nuts!* And it made you think you were the only two who counted, that it was your little club. His face lit up and he knew it was me, so I guessed his brain was intact even if the rest of him looked like Picasso had taken to an Action Jackson doll with a hatchet.

The lump in my throat flipped over and over. I felt sick. I wanted to run.

All these years and he asked for me, no one else.

"What have you told his family?"

"That he's still on a black op, linked with the American forces in Saudi."

"Why did he ask for me?"

"Ask him yourself." He pressed his thumb into another gel pad and the door to inner room gaped like a chasm. "We fitted him with a temporary voice box when we knew he was going to live. It's just a stop-gap measure until we could get you … get a specialist to step up."

That should have made me nervous but I wasn't really listening. All I was thinking about was fleeing. I took four steps backward, stopped, tried to make myself move in the opposite direction, couldn't, looked at Harry, shook my head. "I can't. I can't,

Harry. It's too much, too long ago. I …" I didn't bother to finish the sentence, turned on my heel and walked as fast as I could without actually breaking into a run.

Once I got on the M3 I set the car on auto and slept most of the way back to London. Sleep, though, was no escape. I dreamt of Oxford back in 2195, and of Worth de Havilland the first time I saw him.

There'd always been a university regiment and an Officers Training Corps, but for a long while that had mostly been about students playing at soldiers. Only some of them took it seriously as a career move, most were just marking time until their degrees were done and they could join Daddy or Mommy's firm in the city, or wait for an inevitable inheritance as soon as some rich uncle or aunt dropped off the twig. They were never *real*, not in those days; at least not until a nifty Act of Parliament had decreed Oxford not merely to be a place of higher learning, but also a military academy. The never-ending road show of wars the government subscribed to needed not just new flesh, but new training grounds. New College was colonized by men and women who took their service seriously; now soldiers played at being students.

They weren't all moneyed thugs, but that was a large chunk of their population. They acted as though they owned the place, played rugby on the quadrangle, hassled students both male and female, and God help you if you weren't white. For fun and practice, they abseiled down the facades of buildings that had resisted the depredations of Henry VIII, the Roundheads, World War II bombing raids, the Irish-Islamic bombing campaigns of 2070 and 2080. They dislodged medieval gargoyles, broke stone rosettes, scrawled graffiti on the walls of the All Souls, and in the chapels broke stained glass windows older than their family names. Those without a bloodline, but the right degree of aggression went along for the ride.

The curious anarchy of an undercooked, undisciplined military held sway until the vice-chancellor had had enough. He called a general strike and was supported not just by his crusty old dons, but also by the majority of students, who'd found their studies interrupted and made damned-near impossible by the tramp of jackboots and general thuggery.

My family was incredibly poor, so poor, we still lived in a house. Well, a shack, still one step up from the camps on the Welsh Border; only the truly indigent couldn't afford a place in one of the meanest tower blocks. My older sisters married as soon as they were legally able, just to get out, not caring that they left us behind, just to be able to move into one of the tower blocks at the very outskirts of London. I was an accident, ten years after my parents thought they were done, and I had a brain, a fierce, questing mutant of a brain that dragged me upwards. It pulled me through scholarship exam after scholarship exam, it got me into Oxford. Eventually it got me to Tenby Hall where, due to the new, freer laws about work done by individuals for corporations, I was able to patent my research and trademark my designs. Tenby Hall still has to pay me for anything they do using technology I created. My parents and Gran live now in a penthouse apartment atop one of the towers on the site of Old Buckingham Palace. My sisters don't starve or want for anything, but they live where they married; I'm petty like that.

An education was the only way out for me and, in the early days, the military bloc was playing havoc with that. Like a lot of other students I was pissed off and we were spoiling for a fight. I was one of a group who wrote and circulated a protest flyer. Nothing quite says "civil disobedience student-style" like a scrappy yellow piece of paper. Rather than risk detection by using electronic means of communication and dispersal, we'd typeset it every Friday afternoon, then four or five of us would wander the campus, looking for unattended copy machines, then bang off as many prints as we could. We'd pass them along to other students who acted as couriers, walking streets after dark, slipping the roughly folded pages into mailboxes, under windshields, hastily taping them to poles and pub doors, and trying like hell not to get discovered.

If you *were* caught, the least you had to fear was a beating; the worst was expulsion, loss of scholarship, blacklisting for the rest of your life so you could never, ever expect a job better than that of a mudlark. Not as a result of university action, but of the influ-ence of rich and powerful parents of military gorillas pretending to be students. Though rumors had begun circulating that the Home Secretary was going to intervene, we'd believe when we actually saw it; too many promises like that had disappeared like smoke on the breeze. We kept writing, kept printing, kept dissenting.

I got caught. Of course I did.

I'd left the Bodleian with a couple of hundred yellow sheets buried at the bottom of my satchel. Someone had either seen me making copies, or they'd been suspicious for a while, and watched me. At any rate, I found myself dragged into the space between two buildings by three men in camouflage-patterned clothing, who proceeded to empty the contents of my bag into a puddle of muddy water. When they found the flyers I was slapped until my ears rang, was spun around and had my face pushed against the rough brick of the wall so blood seeped from abrasions. I stayed quiet, determined not to show fear, until busy, greedy hands began to pull at my belt; then I started to scream.

Which was when it all stopped.

He was beautiful: raven's-wing black hair, dark blue eyes, long lashes, full lips, olive skin, broad cheekbones, square jaw, broad shoulders, deep chest, wearing army greens. Tall and straight. Powerful. He pulled the ringleader away from me and threw him down, giving him a kick so vicious that I heard ribs break. The other two dispersed, dragging the injured one with them. They all seemed afraid of him and it made me glad.

He helped me back to my college room, washed the blood off my face and sprayed an antiseptic bandage over the seeping graze.

"Okay?" he asked.

I nodded. "Okay. Thanks."

He was gone, then, no names exchanged, nothing. And it took a while before I worked out he was the one sent in by the Home Secretary—Edward de Haviland's own son—but he found me again and again. In the library, at lunch, in the pub, at my lectures, in my favourite spot by the river. Somehow, he was always there.

"Are you following me?" I demanded one afternoon as I sat propped against a tree, and heard the soft footfall of boots.

"Yes. I was wondering when you'd notice."

"I'm teaching you a valuable lesson."

"Which is?"

"Anything you get too easily, you don't appreciate."

That was the first time he kissed me, there by the river, with the warmth of the sun on our skins, the lap of the water, the murmur of passing students. He was loyal and funny and smart. He was steadfast.

And I'd run from him.

☼

In my Hampton Tower apartment, the phone kept ringing: I recognized Harry's number and ignored it. For a while he kept hanging up, trying again, but he should have remembered that I could always out-stubborn him. Eventually he left a message, saying my name had been left at the hall security desk along with a temporary swipe card and he'd arranged for my old security clearance to be resurrected; a dorm room would be set aside for my use if required. Just in case.

Just in case.

It was three am by the time I got back to Tenby. I was beyond sleep. Driven to return.

I stepped through the vestibule into Worth's room which, now that I was paying attention, was more than comfortable: still white with a state-of-the-art hospital bed, but otherwise furnished a bit like a drawing room, two over-stuffed chairs, a bookshelf, a table with impossibly carved legs, a chaise longue worth more than my watch (a vintage twentieth century Rolex). It was a little cold, but they'd drawn the blankets up over him. The pale yellow of a night-light glowed in a corner.

In his sleep, he looked almost as I remembered, as if slumber smoothed away the aches of waking hours. The long lashes resting on his olive cheek, the lips fuller in repose, his lack of limbs hidden. I sat gently on the edge of the bed, reached out to touch his face. His right hand snaked up to grab my wrist, still dangerously fast. In the weak light we stared at each other. I leaned in and kissed him and found that I still responded to the touch of him as I always had. My eyes stung. I wanted to talk, to tell him I was sorry, but if I had tried I knew the only thing that would come out of my mouth would be a long, low howl of grief that would remind him of all

he'd lost, of all that was gone. So, instead, I filled my mouth with the taste of him so that we might both forget for a time.

☼

The War on Terror was entering its one hundred and ninety-ninth year; big celebrations were planned for the bicentennial. They couldn't make any more soldiers than they already had—military programs had sprung up across the Western world sponsored by the so-called allied powers, those on the side of good. At least, they were allies as long as they toed the line—in the past, alliances and allegiances had shifted—if a nation disagreed with the US-led, British-backed coalition, there was a good chance said nation would find itself added to the blacklist of "evil" nations. New Zealand had gone that way—only the North Island remained, the South had the consistency of charcoaled toast. Similarly, Tasmania (with the consent of the Australian Mainland Parliament) had been flattened; as had Japan, the Netherlands, a large chunk of Indonesia, Switzerland (greatly affecting the world's supply of watches and chocolate); Belgium got lightly fried and the Court of International Justice in the Hague was the target of a surgical strike on Valentine's Day in 2085.

The military had always promised those at the bottom of life's ladder—orphans, kids from poor families, the uneducated, the poor—a chance to improve their lives. If they didn't get killed, then once they'd served their tours, they could make a fresh start with more money than they otherwise might have ever seen. Some people figure it's worth it, the PTSD, the insomnia, the strange illnesses and rashes, the suicidal urges, the marriage breakups. And just like the soldiers, the terrorists—or freedom fighters, depending on who you spoke to—didn't disappear. They kept breeding, they had belief, they had faith, they had nothing else to lose.

So in Britain, the government decided that if we couldn't breed more and we couldn't make more, then we had to be able to repair very effectively and very efficiently the ones we did have. Hence, the Cybernetics Cooperative Research program at Tenby Hall, which had always been the site of some military hospital or other. During World War One, it was those affected by mustard gas; in World War

Two those suffering shell shock; after the first Gulf War it took care of those with the strange diseases no one could account for, from medical experiments neither the Americans nor the British would admit to carrying out; the second Gulf War—which basically had never really ended—saw Tenby enlarged and turned into a plastic surgery facility, specializing in replacing amputated limbs. Cybernetics was the next step in the medical evolutionary chain.

I started working on my specialty at Oxford, did my PhD on melding flesh and bone with inorganic materials, on getting the atomic structures to mesh together meat and metal. I created an organic alloy that mimicked the growth of a living being. Harry developed an artificial skin that would work with my cybernetic limbs. They sent us the worst injured soldiers, those taken apart by mines and explosions and guns and weapons that should never have been turned against human flesh. They sent us those who should not have lived, who had nothing to lose and who didn't care whether we put them back together or not. We called it the Humpty Dumpty Ward, between ourselves and our patients. The first year, we lost fifty percent of our intake. By the third year, we saved ninety-five percent. We were drunk on achievement; *I* was drunk on playing God. I'd patented all my creations and it made me rich, sickeningly, petrifyingly rich. Almost as rich as the bastards that kept sending us to war.

I thought I was sending those soldiers home to new lives, to a rest they'd earned by the sacrifice of their limbs, of their peace of mind. But after a while I started recognizing faces, scars; I found men and women I'd already put back together coming across the table again and again, torn and ruined over and over.

I left Tenby Hall when I realized that they using my work to *recycle* humans so they could be sent back into war zones to be broken again. All that work, all that pain and sorrow, and they would simply keep sending them back until their bodies couldn't be patched up any more, and they had to be scrapheaped. They still haven't managed to make robot soldiers—of all things, that still eludes us, robots are no more than toys, laughable things that kids play with—and we've never managed to make robot servants or robot hookers or a robot that thinks in-dependently. We've never made a facsimile of a human that presents a greater danger to us than we do to ourselves. But the cybernetics? That's where we've excelled ourselves. The melding of injured flesh with a living, healing metal, with networks of artificial neurons that can imitate the workings of a human body, replace what's been lost. Even the skin, though it doesn't feel quite like the real thing—there's a smoothness to it that's almost plastic-y—but it doesn't feel awful, not totally wrong.

And here was this man, who'd once been everything to me, waiting, wanting me to put him back together again.

"Worth, I don't do this anymore. I haven't done it for years. There are people here who *can*, I trained them." We both lay on the bed, he under the covers, I on top, shivering a little.

"I don't want them," the voice was not just metallic, it was *metal*, hard and cold. "No one else knew me—before."

So there was the heart of it: I was to rebuild my lover, from remembrance, on his hope that *my* memory of him would match *his* memory of himself. Memory: the worst thing in the world, an unreliable tool, and he wanted me to remake him in the image in my head.

"Why did you leave?" Three months down the track and his robotic voice box had been replaced by a new organo-cyber one that Harry and I had created between us. "Why did we break up?"

I looked at him, confused.

He shook his head. "Only I can't remember. I can't remember anything about that part of us. I have blank spots, that's one of them."

I was working on an ankle joint, checking the connections before I spliced the nerves with those of the foot we were going to attach and let grow. The left leg had been working perfectly for a couple of weeks, so it was time to finish the right. Worth's left arm was a little stiff, but with the exercises we had him do it was loosening up nicely. Harry had him on a course of fish oil, of all things, but it seemed to be doing the trick. I stayed bent over the limb, not wanting to answer him. My eyes burned.

"Faith, look at me."

I did, blinking.

"Whatever it was, it doesn't matter now." He smiled. "I'll forgive you anything."

"That's big of you, Worth, but I'm not the one needs forgiving." My voice was rough, a film coated the back of my throat, acrid and stubborn. His face clouded. It hadn't occurred to him that *he* might have been the one in the wrong.

"What did I do?"

"Worth, trust me, some things are best forgotten." I stood up. "I can attach the foot today; I'll tell Harry to prep for surgery this afternoon."

I turned away. He grabbed at my wrist: he had regained his strength, in fact, his right arm had become stronger after we'd augmented the musculature. I could feel the circulation slowing in my forearm. I wiggled my fingers to show he was hurting me. He loosened his grip but didn't let me go.

"Tell me what I did."

I sat next to him, took a deep breath. "You remember how we met?"

He smiled, nodded.

"Two years after that, there was the Siege of Magdalen College. In spite of what your father did, in spite of your work there, the military still wasn't popular. There were more and more student protests against the war. Magdalene was the centre of it all, where they gathered, discussed, dissented. The university's governing body tolerated it, encouraged quietly. The government was getting tired of it. You and I—it was the only thing we used to fight about; it was the reason we broke up. There was a protest, a huge protest march from Oxford to London. Got so much attention, the world saw it wasn't just lazy hippies, grubby student or the rent-a-mob protesting; it really stirred things up.

"So they sent in soldiers against Magdalen—students barricaded themselves in. We were there for a week—I was with them. You were brought in as a negotiator. There were more important people than me there but none of them could be risked. I agreed to talk to you outside, thought you might stay your hand because of our relationship." I swallowed hard.

"What did I do, Faith?" He was desperate now.

"I went to talk to you, and you hit me. You knocked me out and from what I heard later you carried me behind the barricades and left me safe with a doctor. Then you went back and led the attack." I leaned forward, elbows on knees, head in hands, feeling waves of nausea break over me. "One hundred and forty-seven students were killed. Anyone not taken out in the rocket attack was shot when they tried to crawl from of the wreckage and look for help. That's what you did. That's why I left."

He was silent for so long that I wondered if time had stopped around us, but when I looked up he was examining his left hand, staring at the places where the skin was still a little thin, where he could still see the workings of the things I'd made for him, grown for him. The things that would see him walk free into a life of privilege once more: Worth de Havilland wouldn't go back to the fighting, not this time. His father, Prime Minister now, had finally been advised of his location, of his condition, and he was determined his only son would never be at risk again.

"Worth?" I said. How much difference would this knowledge make to him? He'd lived with what he'd done for nine years. How much had it bothered him then? Or was he comfortable with the idea he'd just done his duty? Now that this memory had been returned to him, would it matter at all?

"I would give anything," he said, meeting my eyes at last, "to make it up, to pay for all those lives I don't remember."

☼

He looked as good as new. I think maybe he was a little taller and he joked about that. The scars were mostly gone. His hair had grown back, wild and curly and I hadn't let them cut it.

"How do I look?"

"Perfect. No one would know you're a tin soldier."

We stood on Westminster Bridge, ignoring the Houses of Parliament and Big Ben, hunched and leaning into each other to try to ward off the cold breath of the coming winter.

He was warm and tender and there had been moments in the past eight months when I forgot everything bad that had ever happened between us. When I could ignore the remembrance of rebuilding him, of having so much of his blood on me that my scrubs turned dark, of reconstructing him like he was a doll I'd taken apart to play with. There were times when I could forget who he was and what he came from and everything he had done.

When he'd knocked me down and kept me safe behind the barricades, he'd given me the worst nightmare I would ever have: the thought that I survived just because he loved me, and in that one afternoon he had helped to murder almost all of my friends. Sometimes I still dreamt of him walking the bloodied halls of Magdalen, pistol in hand, pumping a Teflon-jacketed bullet into brains that should have been used to help heal the world, not to decorate a wall. I wondered if he'd remembered other things about that day, although we'd not spoken of it since I gave that part of his memory back.

"The old man's trying to pass an Act today. No one knows about it so far, he's kept it very quiet."

My heart beat with an irregular rhythm for a few painful moments. I *knew*. I had overheard Worth's father on one of his visits. "Oh?"

"He wants to extend the Tenby program—replicate it across the country. More Tenbys, more soldiers back to the field. It's all about the bodies," he said bitterly. "I'm going to meet him for lunch. I don't think you should come, Faith."

He moved his hands across my belly. Even though it was still flat, somehow he knew. And somehow he knew something else. "I don't know how else to stop them. They'll never stop, Faith."

"I love you."

"I love you. I never stopped." His face against mine, my hands in his, I could feel the subtle difference between the real skin and the false. He kissed me slowly, sadly. "For what it's worth, Faith, I'm so sorry."

He didn't even give me time to say that I was sorry, too; he turned and walked away, across the bridge toward the House of Parliament, a tall, dark figure in the crowd, his coat billowing around him in the wind, people stepping out of his way.

In my handbag was a small black metal box, an old fashioned key safe, which now seemed impossibly heavy. Inside was a detonator, only two inches long by half an inch wide. It was keyed to the system I'd planted inside Worth—all the components, all the cybernetics to make him walk and work were also a small integrated bomb. I knew enough people who remembered the Siege of Magdalen, who'd lost children and friends, siblings and lovers. People

who could make or get me what I'd asked for when I made my decision.

I would give him ten minutes, let him walk into the House of Lords, time to get inside, time to sit down with his father, with all the lords of destruction within range as they sat down to their meals. Then, with my hand on my belly, I would press the switch.

My tin solider would be steadfast to the last.

Copyright © 2016 by Angela Slatter. First published in Dark Discoveries Magazine, *Aaron J. French (ed.) Issue #35, Summer 2016, JournalStone Publishing, July 2016.*

Mica is a ghostwriter, developmental editor, and Writers of the Future winner. She's currently pursuing traditional publication with a virtual-reality novel about a kid stuck inside a video game boss—all while making an Actual Living as a ghostwriter on the side. She grows too many plants, brews her own beer, and makes googly noises over her goofy husband and one-too-many cats. She once wrote 25,000 words in one day.

STILL CITY

by Mica Scotti Kole

On the day her world ends, Samantha sleeps on the couch. She doesn't have to; she volunteers. If she goes upstairs, she'll try talking to Garrett—but he says the time for talking is past.

Instead, Sam shares that last night with her cat. The Himalayan lies to the right of her head, purring loud enough to echo. The walls are so bare, they reverberate. She took all the pictures down, but the memories still hang.

She scratches the cat behind his ears, pulling his warmth a little closer. "Don't worry, Bubs," she tells him. "You'll be coming with me."

The cat does nothing. Sam sighs and listens for her husband's snores, but the empty house crackles with silence. It is cold—too cold for August. The warmth of their love has gone one-sided, and it is not enough.

I wish I could skip tomorrow, she thinks. She doesn't want to squabble over who gets the dryer. She just wants her husband to stay.

Sam shivers and glances at the thermostat. Had Garrett turned up the A/C?

She frowns and thinks, *That can't be right.*

It is the last thing she'd think for the next hundred years.

Samantha wakes without lingering, from a wide screaming void.

It is not a nightmare. Sam sees the screen.

It glares down at her face, concave and bright, bolted to a ceiling that's much, much too low. Two words scroll across in letters with no pixels. The screen tells her to STAY CALM.

Next, she feels yawning terror, as blank and ceaseless as her hundred-year sleep. Samantha tries to move, but she is bound by her thighs and her wrists and her shoulders. Samantha opens her mouth, and she screams.

Next, there is a poke in her neck, a slowing-down, a stillness. Her heart is a thud: *Kadump. Kadump.*

"Welcome, Samantha Jennings."

It is a cheerful female voice. It resonates from all around her. Her eyes roll toward the white walls on both sides, the pressing closeness of the plastic.

I'm in a coffin, she thinks.

"We realize this will be very jarring," says the voice, "but do try to bear with us, if you can. You have been cryogenically frozen, and you have just woken up in the future."

Blearily Samantha registers this. "What?" she says, her voice grating.

"You were a victim of a terrible accident in a cryogenic facility," the voice goes on. "You may have known the company as Icer Incorporated, located at twelve-twelve Belton Street in Plymouth, Michigan. The explosion radius was about one-point-two-six miles, and included your home and the homes of thirty-six others. Other victims include the hundred-and-eighteen employees of Icer Incorporated and its neighboring businesses."

Samantha feels something slip off her arm, and she knows that she can raise it. The effort nearly drains her as she reaches up to the screen.

The message changes with the brush of her fingertips.

WELCOME TO THE YEAR 2122.

✿

"It hasn't changed, has it?" says Garrett a month later, after they'd been through a rehab process that would have made a cyborg flinch. The strange orb-shaped tanks of the Cryogenic Reconditioning Center had cured everything but their balance, but both of them could stand if they leaned on something. On their front porch now, they lean on each other, but they both still feel the cold.

"They said it's a street stuck in time," Samantha says, staring down the familiar road. The brick houses hadn't been altered on the face of things, but the doors were painted brighter, the plants all swapped out, and the brick shone as if they'd shellacked it. Somewhere along the way, a fund had been raised, to preserve the town for when its people woke up.

Garrett nods at the sign at the end of their street. It reads "Dingman Street," but it used to say Harvey.

He says, "The hospital told me what happened to Jeff. Icer Inc. tried to restore him."

She clings to him a little tighter. She'd heard the story too.

"But the restoration didn't work," he went on, his voice wavering. "That's why they left the town frozen until we thawed on our own. They didn't want to lose us, like Jeff…."

Tears burn in her eyes; the comfort of Garrett can't stop them. Jeffrey Dingman used to get their mail by mistake. He'd bring it over, call her pretty. Garrett used to call her *gorgeous* and *stunning*. But he never called her pretty.

"They're all dead," she says. "My mother and father. My sister… and *her.*"

He nods as a vehicle passes by overhead. It's not a flying car, but something else—slick and silent and sneaking.

Garrett sighs. "Let's go back inside."

Samantha nods. She follows him.

But inside, she is still cold.

✿

At least the realtors haven't changed. They still walk in, still give things the once-over, still indicate all the curious nooks and crannies. The only difference, in Still City, is that buyers want owners present; Samantha and her neighbors are novelties.

One potential buyer, dressed in what looks like three raincoats, sees Garrett's flat-screen smart TV and declares it to be "*so twenty.*" Samantha waits for her to go, sitting by the base of the stairs. Garrett thinks the questions are funny—*what does this do? It's a coffee maker*—but Sam just wants Bubs back. Some pets made it through the icing, but some could not manage. The flourishing yard, curated by strangers, is made barren by his grave.

She thinks of that night, of pulling him close. Of that small and final warmth.

Looking out through the window, she sees the vehicles, a trail of them hover-parked at the curb. They look fast and wide, and her house is the opposite, too snug and far too still.

✿

Later, the buyers offer asking. Nostalgia on a whole other level: she and Garrett tripled their money.

"Half and half?" Garrett asks. Samantha signs the papers. They leave the dryer behind.

✿

"We shouldn't have sold it," he says a month later. They are sitting at a Beijing outdoor café beneath a shuttle service that offers "moon cruises." Garrett eyes the huge tower nervously, wincing as an advertisement swings over its panels. *Everything has a screen now*, she muses. WELCOME TO 2119.

"It was a good deal," he elaborates, turning back to her. The people who stayed in Still City had become tax-exempt for life.

Samantha sips her tea and watches him. "I don't know. I think the moon would be fun."

Garrett's paper cup dents as he squeezes it. She knows it's recycled, but otherwise there's no change. The coffee doesn't float in midair, or come in pill form, or anything. It's almost disappointing.

"The moon, Sam? Are you crazy?"

He's got a weird wild-eyed look to him. It makes her heart thump. *Kadump kadump*, like she's back in that coffin.

The feeling passes, and Sam fingers the order screen set into the table. A robot will deliver whatever she chooses, the money deducted through the translation of fingerprints. She selects a pineberry scone, something genetically modified. The food in the future is completely to die for. She can't say the same for the fashion.

"Sam," Garrett says, "I'm talking to you. You'd really trust that technology? I mean, *the moon?*"

She responds with a pointed statement: "I've never been on a cruise."

Garrett winces again. They'd bought tickets for a cruise the month before they were frozen. He'd screenshotted the flight info, and she'd tried to find it. Instead of the itinerary, she found something else, right there in the photo gallery on his phone.

His shoulders sag. He had said he was sorry. He reaches out to take her hand.

"How about the Nile?" he says. "I looked it up. They still run ships there, on the water. We could visit the Pyramids, see an oasis. Get the cold out of our bones."

As he talks, he runs a finger over her knuckles. He hasn't done that since their wedding. She smiles at him, takes her scone to-go. Back at the hotel, they make love like newlyweds.

But afterward, Sam looks at the moon.

✿

A week passes, and Sam gets sick of room service. They still haven't gone to the Pyramids.

"I'm going out," she tells Garrett. He's in the vision nook. Television has changed, but it's still a time killer. She wonders what adult films are like now.

She turns to leave, but Garrett cuts her off. "When will you be back?"

Sam frowns as she turns. He's stepped out of the nook. "I don't know. Do we have plans?"

Garrett looks around the hotel room as if he's watching a fly and trying to see where it will land. Their room is an expensive suite, but only because it's so retro—*so twenty.*

His face brightens. "They've got karaoke tonight, in the lounge. It's been so long since I heard you sing."

Sam doesn't roll her eyes, but she wants to. The lounge is just downstairs.

"I'll be back in two hours," she tells him.

It is now her turn to lie.

✿

Sam takes two hours. Then she takes four. There's so much to see and do. Art installations fashioned from heat, holograms that make you hallucinate when you touch them. Some shops sell memories, others prosthetics, and still more sell nanomites. Even the advertisements are an adventure, a web of blinking fiber-optics, strung across the city by drones.

She's staring up at the ads, at the stars past their glimmer, when a woman says, "You got a smoke?"

This is another thing that has not changed. Sam drops her gaze, and freezes.

"Sorry, mim. You got a smoke?"

This time, Sam blinks. She overreacted. The woman's nose is too long. She has an accent. Her skin is paler. It's not *her.*

"Sorry, no," Sam says, and the woman moves on, while Sam herself does not. In her head, she scrolls through the photos again. The purr echoes off the walls.

Sam glances across the street; she's made her way back to Garrett; the hotel looms overhead like a gatekeeper. She turns around to find herself in front of the shuttle service, its transparent entry field rippling back at her.

She watches as people waft through the false wall, excited, on their way to the moon.

Her two hours are six. Her thoughts are still.

STAY CALM, she thinks, and takes a step.

She's never been on a cruise.

Copyright © 2022 by Mica Scotti Kole.

Mike Resnick, along with editing the first seven years of Galaxy's Edge *magazine, was the winner of five Hugos from a record thirty-seven nominations and was, according to* Locus, *the all-time leading award winner, living or dead, for short fiction. He was the author of over eighty novels, around 300 stories, three screenplays, and the editor of over forty anthologies. He was Guest of Honor at the 2012 Worldcon.*

TRAVELS WITH MY CATS

by Mike Resnick

I found it in the back of a neighbor's garage. They were retiring and moving to Florida, and they'd put most of their stuff up for sale rather than pay to ship it south.

I was eleven years old, and I was looking for a Tarzan book, or maybe one of Clarence Mulford's Hopalong Cassidy epics, or perhaps (if my mother was looking the other way) a forbidden Mickey Spillane novel. I found them, too—and then the real world intruded. They were fifty cents each (and a whole dollar for *Kiss Me Deadly*), and all I had was a nickel.

So I rummaged some more, and finally found the only book that was in my price range. It was called *Travels With My Cats*, and the author was Miss Priscilla Wallace. Not Priscilla, but Miss Priscilla. For years I thought Miss was her first name.

I thumbed through it, hoping it at least had some photos of half-naked native girls hidden in its pages. There weren't any pictures at all, just words. I wasn't surprised; somehow I had known that an author called Miss wasn't going to plaster naked women all over her book.

I decided that the book itself felt too fancy and feminine for a boy who was trying out for the Little League later in the day—the letters on the cover were somehow raised above the rest of the surface, the endpapers were an elegant satin, the boards were covered with a russet, velvet-like cloth, and it even had a bookmark which was a satin ribbon attached to the binding. I was about to put it back when it fell open to a page that said that this was Number 121 of a Limited Printing of 200.

That put a whole new light on things. My very own limited edition for a nickel—how could I say no? I brought it to the front of the garage, dutifully paid my nickel, and waited for my mother to finish looking (she always looked, never shopped—shopping implies parting with money, and she and my father were Depression kids who never bought what they could rent cheaper or, better yet, borrow for free).

That night I was faced with a major decision. I didn't want to read a book called *Travels With My Cats* by a woman called Miss, but I'd spent my last nickel on it—well, the last until my allowance came due again next week—and I'd read all my other books so often you could almost see the eyetracks all over them.

So I picked it up without much enthusiasm, and read the first page, and then the next—and suddenly I was transported to Kenya Colony and Siam and the Amazon. Miss Priscilla Wallace had a way of describing things that made me wish I was there, and when I finished a section I felt like I'd *been* there.

There were cities I'd never heard of before, cities with exotic names like Maracaibo and Samarkand and Addis Ababa, some with names like Constantinople that I couldn't even find on the map.

Her father had been an explorer, back in the days when there still *were* explorers. She had taken her first few trips abroad with him, and he had undoubtedly given her a taste for distant lands. (My own father was a typesetter. How I envied her!)

I had half hoped the African section would be filled with rampaging elephants and man-eating lions, and maybe it was—but that wasn't the way she saw it. Africa may have been red of tooth and claw, but to her it reflected the gold of the morning sun, and the dark, shadowy places were filled with wonder, not terror.

She could find beauty anywhere. She would describe two hundred flower sellers lined up along the Seine on a Sunday morning in Paris, or a single frail blossom in the middle of the Gobi Desert, and somehow you knew that each was as wondrous as she said.

And suddenly I jumped as the alarm clock started buzzing. It was the first time I'd ever stayed up for the entire night. I put the book away, got dressed for school, and hurried home after school so that I could finish it.

I must have read it six or seven more times that year. I got to the point where I could almost recite parts of it word-for-word. I was in love with those exotic faraway places, and maybe a little bit in love with the author, too. I even wrote her a fan letter addressed to "Miss Priscilla Wallace, Somewhere," but of course it came back.

Then, in the fall, I discovered Robert A. Heinlein and Louis L'Amour, and a friend saw *Travels With My Cats* and teased me about its fancy cover and the fact that it was written by a woman, so I put it on a shelf and over the years I forgot about it.

I never saw all those wonderful, mysterious places she wrote about. I never did a lot of things. I never made a name for myself. I never got rich and famous. I never married.

By the time I was forty, I was finally ready to admit that nothing unusual or exciting was ever likely to happen to me. I'd written half of a novel that I was never going to finish or sell, and I'd spent twenty years looking fruitlessly for someone I could love. (That was Step One; Step Two—finding someone who could love me—would probably have been even more difficult, but I never got around to it.)

I was tired of the city, and of rubbing shoulders with people who had latched onto the happiness and success that had somehow eluded me. I was Midwestern born and bred, and eventually I moved to Wisconsin's North Woods, where the most exotic cities were small towns like Manitowoc and Minnaqua and Wausau—a far cry from Macau and Marrakech and the other glittering capitals of Priscilla Wallace's book.

I worked as a copy editor for one of the local weekly newspapers—the kind where getting the restaurant and real estate ads right was more important than spelling the names in the news stories correctly. It wasn't the most challenging job in the world, but it was pleasant enough, and I wasn't looking for any challenges. Youthful dreams of triumph had gone the way of youthful dreams of love and passion; at this late date, I'd settled for tranquility.

I rented a small house on a little nameless lake, some fifteen miles out of town. It wasn't without its share of charm: it had an old-fashioned veranda, with a porch swing that was almost as old as the house. A pier for the boat I didn't own jutted out into the lake, and there was even a water trough for the original owner's horses. There was no air-conditioning, but I didn't really need it—and in the winter I'd sit by the fire, reading the latest paperback thriller.

It was on a late summer's night, with just a bit of a Wisconsin chill in the air, as I sat next to the empty fireplace, reading about a rip-roaring gun-blazing car chase through Berlin or Prague or some other city I'll never see, that I found myself wondering if this was my future: a lonely old man, spending his evenings reading pop fiction by a fireplace, maybe with a blanket over his legs, his only companion a tabby cat …

And for some reason—probably the notion of the tabby—I remembered *Travels With My Cats*. I'd never owned a cat, but *she* had; there had been two of them, and they'd gone everywhere with her.

I hadn't thought of the book for years. I didn't even know if I still had it. But for some reason, I felt an urge to pick it up and look through it.

I went to the spare room, where I kept all the stuff I hadn't unpacked yet. There were maybe two dozen boxes of books. I opened the first of them, then the next. I rummaged through Bradburys and Asimovs and Chandlers and Hammetts, dug deep beneath Ludlums and Amblers and a pair of ancient Zane Greys—and suddenly there it was, as elegant as ever. My one and only Limited Numbered Edition.

So, for the first time in perhaps thirty years, I opened the book and began reading it. And found myself just as captivated as I had been the first time. It was every bit as wonderful as I remembered. And, as I had done three decades ago, I lost all track of the time and finished it just as the sun was rising.

I didn't get much work done that morning. All I could do was think about those exquisite descriptions and insights into worlds that no longer existed—and then I began wondering if Priscilla Wallace herself still existed. She'd probably be a very old lady, but maybe I could update that old fan letter and finally send it.

I stopped by the local library at lunchtime, determined to pick up everything else she had written. There was nothing on the shelves or in their card file. (They were a friendly old-fashioned rural library; computerizing their stock was still decades away.)

I went back to the office and had my computer run a search on her. There were thirty-seven distinct and different Priscilla Wallaces. One was an actress in low-budget movies. One taught at Georgetown University. One was a diplomat stationed in Bratislava. One was a wildly successful breeder of show poodles. One was the youthful mother of a set of sextuplets in South Carolina. One was an inker for a Sunday comic strip.

And then, just when I was sure the computer wouldn't be able to find her, the following came up on my screen:

"Wallace, Priscilla, b. 1892, d. 1926. Author of one book: *Travels With My Cats*."

1926. So much for fan letters, then or now; she'd died decades before I'd been born. Even so, I felt a sudden sense of loss, and of resentment—resentment that someone like that had died so young, and that all her unlived years had been taken by people who would never see the beauty that she found everywhere she went.

People like me.

There was also a photo. It looked like a reproduction of an old sepia-toned tintype, and it showed a slender, auburn-haired young woman with large dark eyes that seemed somehow sad to me. Or maybe the sadness was my own, because I knew she would die at thirty-four and all that passion for life would die with her. I printed up a hard copy, put it in my desk drawer, and took it home with me at the end of the day. I don't know why. There were only two sentences on it. Somehow a life—any life—deserved more than that. Especially one that could reach out from the grave and touch me and make me feel, at least while I was reading her book, that maybe the world wasn't quite as dull and ordinary as it seemed to me.

That night, after I heated up a frozen dinner, I sat down by the fireplace and picked up *Travels With My Cats* again, just thumbing through it to read my favorite passages here and there. There was the one about the stately procession of elephants against the backdrop of snow-capped Kilimanjaro, and another about the overpowering perfume of the flowers as she walked through the gardens of Versailles on a May morning. And then, toward the end, there was what had become my favorite of all:

"There is so much yet to see, so much still to do, that on days like this I wish I could live forever. I take comfort in the heartfelt belief that long after I am gone, I will be alive again for as long as someone picks up a copy of this book and reads it."

It *was* a comforting belief, certainly more immortality than I ever aspired to. I'd made no mark, left no sign by which anyone would know I'd ever been here. twenty years after my death, maybe thirty at most, no one would ever know that I'd even existed, that a man named Ethan Owens—my name; you've never encountered it before, and you doubtless never will again—lived and worked and died here, that he tried to get through each day without doing anyone any harm, and that was the sum total of his accomplishments.

Not like her. Or maybe very much like her. She was no politician, no warrior queen. There were no monuments to her. She wrote a forgotten little travel book and died before she could write another. She'd been gone for more than three-quarters of a century. Who remembered Priscilla Wallace?

I poured myself a beer and began reading again. Somehow, the more she described each exotic city and primal jungle, the less exotic and primal they felt, the more they seemed like an extension of home. As often as I read it, I couldn't figure out how she managed to do that.

I was distracted by a clattering on the veranda. *Damned raccoons are getting bolder every night,* I thought—but then I heard a very distinct *meow.* My nearest neighbor was a mile away, and that seemed a long way for a cat to wander, but I figured the least I could do was go out and look, and if it had a collar and a tag I'd call its owner. And if not, I'd shoo it away before it got into the wrong end of a disagreement with the local raccoons.

I opened the door and stepped out onto the veranda. Sure enough, there was a cat there, a small white one with a couple of tan markings on its head and body. I reached down to pick it up, and it backed away a couple of steps.

"I'm not going to hurt you," I said gently.

"He knows that," said a feminine voice. "He's just shy."

I turned—and there she was, sitting on my porch swing. She made a gesture, and the cat walked across the veranda and jumped up onto her lap.

I'd seen that face earlier in the day, staring at me in sepia tones. I'd studied it for hours, until I knew it's every contour.

It was *her.*

"It's a beautiful night, isn't it?" she said as I kept gaping at her. "And quiet. Even the birds are asleep." She paused. "Only the cicadas are awake, serenading us with their symphonies."

I didn't know what to say, so I just watched her and waited for her to vanish.

"You look pale," she noted after a moment.

"You look real," I finally managed to croak.

"Of course I do," she replied with a smile. "I *am* real."

"You're Miss Priscilla Wallace, and I've spent so much time thinking about you that I've begun hallucinating."

"Do I look like a hallucination?"

"I don't know," I admitted. "I don't think I've ever had one before, so I don't know what they look like—except that obviously they look like you." I paused. "They could look a lot worse. You have a beautiful face."

She laughed at that. The cat jumped, startled, and she began stroking it gently. "I do believe you're trying to make me blush," she said.

"*Can* you blush?" I asked, and then of course wished I hadn't.

"Of course I can," she replied, "though I had my doubts after I got back from Tahiti. The things they *do* there!" Then, "You were reading *Travels With My Cats*, weren't you?"

"Yes, I was. It's been one of my most cherished possessions since I was a child."

"Was it a gift?" she asked.

"No, I bought it myself."

"That's very gratifying."

"It's very gratifying to finally meet the author who's given me so much pleasure," I said, feeling like an awkward kid all over again.

She looked puzzled, as if she was about to ask a question. Then she changed her mind and smiled again. It was a lovely smile, as I had known it would be.

"This is very pretty property," she said. "Is it yours all the way up to the lake?"

"Yes."

"Does anyone else live here?"

"Just me."

"You like your privacy," she said. It was a statement, not a question.

"Not especially," I answered. "That's just the way things worked out. People don't seem to like me very much."

Now why the hell did I tell you that? I thought. *I've never even admitted it to myself.*

"You seem like a very nice person," she said. "I find it difficult to believe that people don't like you."

"Maybe I overstated the case," I admitted. "Mostly they don't notice me." I shifted uncomfortably. "I didn't mean to unburden myself on you."

"You're all alone. You have to unburden yourself to *someone*," she replied. "I think you just need a little more self-confidence."

"Perhaps."

She stared at me for a long moment. "You keep looking like you're expecting something terrible to happen."

"I'm expecting you to disappear."

"Would that be so terrible?"

"Yes," I said promptly. "It would be."

"Then why don't you simply accept that I'm here? If you're wrong, you'll know it soon enough."

I nodded. "Yeah, you're Priscilla Wallace, all right. That's exactly the kind of answer she'd give."

"You know who *I* am. Perhaps you'll tell me who *you* are?"

"My name is Ethan Owens."

"Ethan," she repeated. "That's a nice name."

"You think so?"

"I wouldn't say so if I didn't." She paused. "Shall I call you Ethan, or Mr. Owens?"

"Ethan, by all means. I feel like I've known you all my life." I felt another embarrassing admission coming on. "I even wrote you a fan letter when I was a kid, but it came back."

"I would have liked that," she said. "I never once got a fan letter. Not from anyone."

"I'm sure hundreds of people wanted to write. Maybe they couldn't find your address either."

"Maybe," she said dubiously.

"In fact, just today I was thinking about sending it again."

"Whatever you wanted to say, you can tell me in person." The cat jumped back down onto the veranda. "You look very uncomfortable, perched on the railing like that, Ethan. Why don't you come and sit beside me?"

"I'd like that very much," I said, standing up. Then I thought it over. "No, I'd better not."

"I'm thirty-two years old," she said in amused tones. "I don't need a chaperone."

"Not with me, you don't," I assured her. "Besides, I don't think we have them anymore."

"Then what's the problem?"

"The truth?" I said. "If I sit next to you, at some point my hip will press against yours, or perhaps I'll inadvertently touch your hand. And …"

"And what?"

"And I don't want to find out that you're not really here."

"But I am."

"I hope so," I said. "But I can believe it a lot easier from where I am."

She shrugged. "As you wish."

"I've had my wish for the night," I said.

"Then why don't we just sit and enjoy the breeze and the scents of the Wisconsin night?"

"Whatever makes you happy," I said.

"Being here makes me happy. Knowing my book is still being read makes me happy." She was silent for a moment, staring off into the darkness. "What's the date, Ethan?"

"April 17."

"I mean the year."

"Two-tousand and four."

She looked surprised. "It's been that long?"

"Since … ?" I said hesitantly.

"Since I died," she said. "Oh, I know I must have died a long time ago. I have no tomorrows, and my yesterdays are all so very long ago. But the new millennium? It seems"—she searched for the right word—"excessive."

"You were born in 1892, more than a century ago," I said.

"How did you know that?"

"I had the computer run a search on you."

"I don't know what a computer is," she said. Then, suddenly: "Do you also know when and how I died?"

"I know when, not how."

"Please don't tell me," she said. "I'm thirty-two, and I've just written the last page of my book. I don't know what comes next, and it would be wrong for you to tell me."

"All right," I said. Then, borrowing her expression, "As you wish."

"Promise me."

"I promise."

Suddenly the little white cat tensed and looked off across the yard.

"He sees his brother," said Priscilla.

"It's probably just the raccoons," I said. "They can be a nuisance."

"No," she insisted. "I know his body language. That's his brother out there."

And sure enough, I heard a distinct *meow* a moment later. The white cat leaped off the veranda and headed toward it.

"I'd better go get them before they become completely lost," said Priscilla, getting to her feet. "It happened once in Brazil, and I didn't find them for almost two days."

"I'll get a flashlight and come with you," I said.

"No, you might frighten them, and it wouldn't do to have them run away in strange surroundings." She stood up and stared at me. "You seem like a very nice man, Ethan Owens. I'm glad we finally met." She smiled sadly. "I just wish you weren't so lonely."

She climbed down to the yard and walked off into the darkness before I could lie and tell her I led a rich full life and wasn't lonely at all. Suddenly I had a premonition that she wasn't coming back. "Will we meet again?" I called after her as she vanished from sight.

"That depends on you, doesn't it?" came her answer out of the darkness.

I sat on the porch swing, waiting for her to reappear with the cats. Finally, despite the cold night air, I fell asleep. I woke up when the sun hit the swing in the morning.

I was alone.

☼

It took me almost half the day to convince myself that what had happened the night before was just a dream. It wasn't like any other dream I'd ever had, because I remembered every detail of it, every word she said, every gesture she made. Of course she hadn't really visited me, but just the same I couldn't get Priscilla Wallace out of my mind, so I finally stopped working and used my computer to try to learn more about her.

There was nothing more to be found under her name except for that single brief entry. I tried a search on *Travels With My Cats* and came up empty. I checked to see if her father had ever written a book about his explorations; he hadn't. I even contacted a few of the hotels she had stayed at, alone or with her father, but none of them kept records that far back.

I tried one line of pursuit after another, but none of them proved fruitful. History had swallowed her up almost as completely as it would someday swallow me. Other than the book, the only proof I had that she had ever lived was that one computer entry, consisting of ten words and two dates. Wanted criminals couldn't hide from the law any better than she'd hidden from posterity.

Finally I looked out the window and realized that night had fallen and everyone else had gone home. (There's no night shift on a weekly paper.) I stopped by a local diner, grabbed a ham sandwich and a cup of coffee, and headed back to the lake.

I watched the ten o'clock news on TV, then sat down and picked up her book again, just to convince myself that she really *had* lived once upon a time. After a couple of minutes I got restless, put the book back on a table, and walked out for a breath of fresh air.

She was sitting on the porch swing, right where she had been the night before. There was a different cat next to her, a black one with white feet and white circles around its eyes.

She noticed me looking at the cat. "This is Goggle," she said. "I think he's exceptionally well-named, don't you?"

"I suppose," I said distractedly.

"The white one is Giggle, because he loves getting into all sorts of mischief." I didn't say anything. Finally she smiled. "Which of them has your tongue?"

"You're back," I said at last.

"Of course I am."

"I was reading your book again," I said. "I don't think I've ever encountered anyone who loved life so much."

"There's so much to love!"

"For some of us."

"It's all around you, Ethan," she said.

"I prefer seeing it through your eyes. It was like you were born again into a new world each morning," I said. "I suppose that's why I kept your book, and why I find myself re-reading it—to share what you see and feel."

"You can feel things yourself."

I shook my head. "I prefer what *you* feel."

"Poor Ethan," she said sincerely. "You've never loved anything, have you?"

"I've tried."

"That isn't what I said." She stared at me curiously. "Have you ever married?"

"No."

"Why not?"

"I don't know." I decided I might as well give her an honest answer. "Probably because none of them ever measured up to you."

"I'm not that special," she said.

"To me you are. You always have been."

She frowned. "I wanted my book to enrich your life, Ethan, not ruin it."

"You didn't ruin it," I said. "You made it a little more bearable."

"I wonder …" she mused.

"About what?"

"My being here. It's puzzling."

"Puzzling is an understatement," I said. "Unbelievable is more the word for it."

She shook her head distractedly. "You don't understand. I remember last night."

"So do I—every second of it."

"That's not what I meant." She stroked the cat absently. "I was never brought back before last night. I wasn't sure then. I thought perhaps I forgot after each episode. But today I remember last night."

"I'm not sure I follow you."

"You can't be the only person to read my book since I died. Or even if you were, I've never been called back before, not even by you." She stared at me for a long moment. "Maybe I was wrong."

"About what?"

"Maybe what brought me here wasn't the fact that I needed to be read. Maybe it's because you so desperately need someone."

"I—" I began heatedly, and then stopped. For a moment it seemed like the whole world had stopped with me. Then the moon came out from behind a cloud, and an owl hooted off to the left.

"What is it?"

"I was about to tell you that I'm not that lonely," I said. "But it would have been a lie."

"It's nothing to be ashamed of, Ethan."

"It's nothing to brag about, either." There was something about her that made me say things I'd never said to anyone else, including myself. "I had such high hopes when I was a boy. I was going to love my work, and I was going to be good at it. I was going find a woman to love and spend the rest of my life with. I was going to see all the places you described. Over the years I saw each of those hopes die. Now I settle for paying my bills and getting regular check-ups at the doctor's." I sighed deeply. "I think my life can be described as a fully-realized diminished expectation."

"You have to take risks, Ethan," she said gently.

"I'm not like you," I said. "I wish I was, but I'm not. Besides, there aren't any wild places left."

She shook her head. "That's not what I meant. Love involves risk. You have to risk getting hurt."

"I've *been* hurt," I said. "It's nothing to write home about."

"Maybe that's why I'm here. You can't be hurt by a ghost."

The hell I can't, I thought. Aloud I said: "*Are* you a ghost?"

"I don't feel like one."

"You don't look like one."

"How *do* I look?" she asked.

"As lovely as I always knew you were."

"Fashions change."

"But beauty doesn't," I said.

"That's very kind of you to say, but I must look very old fashioned. In fact, the world I knew must seem primitive to you." Her face brightened. "It's a new millennium. Tell me what's happened."

"We've walked on the moon—and we've landed ships on Mars and Venus."

She looked up into the night sky. "The moon!" she exclaimed. Then: "Why are you here when you could be there?"

"I'm not a risk-taker, remember?"

"What an exciting time to be alive!" she said enthusiastically. "I always wanted to see what lay beyond the next hill. But *you*—you get to see what's beyond the next star!"

"It's not that simple," I said.

"But it will be," she persisted.

"Someday," I agreed. "Not during my lifetime, but someday."

"Then you should die with the greatest reluctance," she said. "I'm sure I did." She looked up at the stars, as if envisioning herself flying to each of them. "Tell me more about the future."

"I don't know anything about the future," I said.

"*My* future. Your present."

I told her what I could. She seemed amazed that hundreds of millions of people now traveled by air, that I didn't know anyone who didn't own a car, and that train travel had almost disappeared in America. The thought of television fascinated her; I decided not to tell her what a vast wasteland it had been since its inception. Color movies, sound movies, computers—she wanted to know all about them. She was eager to learn if zoos had become more humane, if *people* had become more humane. She couldn't believe that heart transplants were actually routine.

I spoke for hours. Finally I just got so dry I told her I was going to have to take a break for a couple of minutes while I went into the kitchen and got us some drinks. She'd never heard of Fanta or Dr Pepper, which is what I had, and she didn't like beer, so I made her an iced tea and popped open a Bud for me. When I brought them out to the porch she and Goggle were gone.

I didn't even bother looking for her. I knew she had returned to the *somewhere* from which she had come.

☼

She was back again the next three nights, sometimes with one cat, sometimes with both. She told me about her travels, about her overwhelming urge to see what there was to see in the little window of time allotted us humans, and I told her about the various wonders she would never see.

It was strange, conversing with a phantom every night. She kept assuring me she was real, and I believed it when she said it, but I was still afraid to touch her and discover that she was just a dream after all. Somehow, as if they knew my fears, the cats kept their distance too; not once in all those evenings did either of them ever so much as brush against me.

"I wish I'd seen all the sights *they've* seen," I said on the third night, nodding toward the cats.

"Some people thought it was cruel to take them all over the world with me," replied Priscilla, absently running her hand over Goggle's back as he purred contentedly. "I think it would have been more cruel to leave them behind."

"None of the cats—these or the ones that came before—ever caused any problems?"

"Certainly they did," she said. "But when you love something, you put up with the problems."

"Yeah, I suppose you do."

"How do you know?" she asked. "I thought you said you'd never loved anything."

"Maybe I was wrong."

"Oh?"

"I don't know," I said. "Maybe I love someone who vanishes every night when I turn my back." She stared at me, and suddenly I felt very awkward. I shrugged uncomfortably. "Maybe."

"I'm touched, Ethan," she said. "But I'm not of this world, not the way you are."

"I haven't complained," I said. "I'll settle for the moments I can get." I tried to smile; it was a disaster. "Besides, I don't even know if you're real."

"I keep telling you I am."

"I know."

"What would you do if you *knew* I was?" she asked.

"Really?"

"Really."

I stared at her. "Try not to get mad," I began.

"I won't get mad."

"I've wanted to hold you and kiss you since the first instant I saw you on my veranda," I said.

"Then why haven't you?"

"I have this … this dread that if I try to touch you and you're not here, if I prove conclusively to myself that you don't exist, then I'll never see you again."

"Remember what I told you about love and risk?"

"I remember."

"And?"

"Maybe I'll try tomorrow," I said. "I just don't want to lose you yet. I'm not feeling that brave tonight."

She smiled, a rather sad smile I thought. "Maybe you'll get tired of reading me."

"Never!"

"But it's the same book all the time. How often can you read it?"

I looked at her, young, vibrant, maybe two years from death, certainly less than three. I knew what lay ahead for her; all she could see was a lifetime of wonderful experiences stretching out into the distance.

"Then I'll read one of your other books."

"I wrote others?" she asked.

"Dozens of them," I lied.

She couldn't stop smiling. "Really?"

"Really."

"Thank you, Ethan," she said. "You've made me very happy."

"Then we're even."

There was a noisy squabble down by the lake. She quickly looked around for her cats, but they were on the porch, their attention also attracted by the noise.

"Raccoons," I said.

"Why are they fighting?"

"Probably a dead fish washed up on the shore," I answered. "They're not much for sharing."

She laughed. "They remind me of some people I know." She paused. "Some people I *knew*," she amended.

"Do you miss them—your friends, I mean?"

"No. I had hundreds of acquaintances, but very few close friends. I was never in one place long enough to make them. It's only when I'm with you that I realize they're gone." She paused. "I don't quite understand it. I know that I'm here with you, in the new millennium—but I feel like I just celebrated my thirty-seecond birthday. Tomorrow I'll put flowers on my father's grave, and next week I set sail for Madrid."

"Madrid?" I repeated. "Will you watch them fight the brave bulls in the arena?"

An odd expression crossed her face. "Isn't that curious?" she said.

"Isn't what curious?"

"I have no idea what I'll do in Spain … but you've read all my books, so *you* know."

"You don't want me to tell you," I said.

"No, that would spoil it."

"I'll miss you when you leave."

"You'll pick up one of my books and I'll be right back here," she said. "Besides, I went more than seventy-five years ago."

"It gets confusing," I said.

"Don't look so depressed. We'll be together again."

"It's only been a week, but I can't remember what I did with my evenings before I started talking to you."

The squabbling at the lake got louder, and Giggle and Goggle began huddling together.

"They're frightening my cats," said Priscilla.

"I'll go break it up," I said, climbing down from the veranda and heading off to where the raccoons were battling. "And when I get back," I added, feeling bolder the farther I got from her, "maybe I'll find out just how real you are after all."

By the time I reached the lake, the fight was all but over. One large raccoon, half a fish in its mouth, glared at me, totally unafraid. Two others, not quite as large, stood about ten feet away. All three were bleeding from numerous gashes, but it didn't look like any of them had suffered a disabling injury.

"Serves you right," I muttered.

I turned and started trudging back up to the house from the lake. The cats were still on the veranda, but Priscilla wasn't. I figured she'd stepped inside to get another iced tea, or perhaps use the bathroom—one more factor in favor of her not being a ghost—but when she didn't come out in a couple of minutes I searched the house for her.

She wasn't there. She wasn't anywhere in the yard, or in the old empty barn. Finally I went back and sat down on the porch swing to wait.

A couple of minutes later Goggle jumped up on my lap. I'd been idly petting him for a couple of minutes before I realized that he was real.

✿

I bought some cat food in the morning. I didn't want to set it out on the veranda, because I was sure the raccoons would get wind of it and drive Giggle and Goggle off, so I put it in a soup bowl and placed it on the counter next to the kitchen sink. I didn't have a litter box, so I left the kitchen window open enough for them to come and go as they pleased.

I resisted the urge to find out any more about Priscilla with the computer. All that was really left to learn was how she died, and I didn't want to know. How does a beautiful, healthy, world-traveling woman die at thirty-four? Torn apart by lions? Sacrificed by savages? Victim of a disfiguring tropical disease? Mugged, raped and killed in New York? Whatever it was, it had robbed her of half a century. I didn't want to think of the books she could have written in that time, but rather of the joy she could have felt as she traveled from one new destination to another. No, I very definitely didn't want to know how she died.

I worked distractedly for a few hours, then knocked off in midafternoon and hurried home. To her.

I knew something was wrong the moment I got out of my car. The porch swing was empty. Giggle and Goggle jumped off the veranda, raced up to me, and began rubbing against my legs as if for comfort.

I yelled her name, but there was no response. Then I heard a rustling inside the house. I raced to the door, and saw a raccoon climbing out through the kitchen window just as I entered.

The place was a mess. Evidently he had been hunting for food, and since all I had were cans and frozen meals, he just started ripping the house apart, looking for anything he could eat.

And then I saw it: *Travels With My Cats* lay in tatters, as if the raccoon had had a temper tantrum at the lack of food and had taken it out on the book, which I'd left on the kitchen table. Pages were ripped to shreds, the cover was in pieces, and he had even urinated on what was left.

I worked feverishly on it for hours, tears streaming down my face for the first time since I was a kid, but there was no salvaging it—and that meant there would be no Priscilla tonight, or any night until I found another copy of the book.

In a blind fury I grabbed my rifle and a powerful flashlight and killed the first six raccoons I could find. It didn't make me feel any better—especially when I calmed down enough to consider what she would have thought of my bloodlust.

I felt like morning would never come. When it did, I raced to the office, activated my computer, and tried to find a copy of Priscilla's book at www.abebooks.com and www.bookfinder.com, the two biggest computerized clusters of used book dealers. There wasn't a single copy for sale.

I contacted some of the other book dealers I'd used in the past. None of them had ever heard of it.

I called the copyright division at the Library of Congress, figuring they might be able to help me. No luck: *Travels With My Cats* was never officially copyrighted; there was no copy on file. I began to wonder if I hadn't dreamed the whole thing, the book as well as the woman.

Finally I called Charlie Grimmis, who advertises himself as The Book Detective. He does most of his work for anthologists seeking rights and permissions to obscure, long-out-of-print books and stories, but he didn't care who he worked for, as long as he got his money.

It took him nine days and cost me six hundred dollars, but finally I got a definitive answer:

Dear Ethan:

You led me a merry chase. I'd have bet halfway through it that the book didn't exist, but you were right: evidently you did own a copy of a limited, numbered edition.

Travels With My Cats was self-published by one Priscilla Wallace (d. 1926), in a limited, numbered edition of 200. The printer was the long-defunct Adelman Press of Bridgeport, Connecticut. The book was never copyrighted or registered with the Library of Congress.

Now we get into the conjecture part. As near as I can tell, this Wallace woman gave about 150 copies away to friends and relatives, and the final 50 were probably trashed after her death. I've checked back, and there hasn't been a copy for sale anywhere in the past dozen years. It's hard to get trustworthy records further back than that. Given that she was an unknown, that the book was a vanity press job, and that it went only to people who knew her, the likelihood is that no more than 15 or 20 copies still exist, if that many.

Best,
Charlie

☼

When it's finally time to start taking risks, you don't think about it—you just do it. I quit my job that afternoon, and for the past year I've been crisscrossing the country, hunting for a copy of *Travels With My Cats*. I haven't found one yet, but I'll keep looking, no matter how long it takes. I get lonely, but I don't get discouraged.

Was it a dream? Was she a hallucination? A couple of acquaintances I confided in think so. Hell, I'd think so too—except that I'm not traveling alone. I've got two feline companions, and they're as real and substantial as cats get to be.

So the man with no goal except to get through another day finally has a mission in life, an important one. The woman I love died half a century too soon. I'm the only one who can give her back those years, if not all at once then an evening and a weekend at a time—but one way or another she's going to get them. I've spent all my yesterdays and haven't got a thing to show for them; now I'm going to start stockpiling her tomorrows.

Anyway, that's the story. My job is gone, and so is most of my money. I haven't slept in the same bed twice in close to four hundred days. I've lost a lot of weight, and I've been living in these clothes for longer than I care to think. It doesn't matter. All that matters is that I find a copy of that book, and someday I know I will.

Do I have any regrets?

Just one.

I never touched her. Not even once.

Elaine Midcoh (a pseudonym) is a retired criminal justice/law professor. Her story, "The Battle of Donasi," was published in Writers of the Future, Volume 37 *and her story, "Man on the Moon," won the 2022 Jim Baen Memorial Short Story Award. She's thrilled to be published in* Galaxy's Edge *magazine!*

SIZED

by Elaine Midcoh

Arthur Enlight, Senior Advocate, crawled on the floor of his office, magnifying glass and ruler in hand, with newspaper comics spread about him. A tall slender man of thirty-two, well-groomed and professionally dressed, he moved gracefully in the confined space between his desk and the wall while taking measurements.

"Got you!" he said. The newspapers had definitely violated Good Government Rule #389945.783: Size of Comics Print to Avoid Eye Strain. At least five of the comic strips had the word print too small.

Arthur grinned. As a Senior Advocate he mostly worked Recommendation cases (who didn't?), but this was his fourth Rules case, quite an accomplishment for someone with just seven years of relevance.

Arthur was still on the floor when the old man banged his walker against the office door and pushed it open. He stopped when he spotted Arthur and gazed at him with watery eyes. "Are you the Advocate Arthur Enlight?" the old man asked.

Arthur stood up. "Yes."

The old man proceeded into the room, not noticing that he and his walker were treading over and ripping the newspaper comics scattered over the floor. He made it to the chair and sat down, wheezing.

He was wearing shorts and a plain white tee shirt. His legs were like swollen tree trunks, completely disproportionate to the slightness of his body. They were a bright feverish red and had multiple open sores. The man's arms had open sores too, and his fingers were gnarled and twisted in ways not normal. His face was weathered with deep wrinkles and dark spots as if he never followed Good Government Recommendation #172368.34: Care and Treatment for Maintaining Pleasing Facial Esthetics. Likewise,

his white hair had wild tufts jutting out randomly with other spots almost bald.

And then Arthur smelled it. It was an odd smell, a mix of medicine, bad breath, urine and something else—like something rotting, as if the man's body was decomposing before death. Arthur involuntarily took a step back, but then recovered by moving behind his desk and sitting in his own chair.

"How may I serve you?" Arthur asked, giving the traditional Advocate's greeting.

The old man rested his arms on Arthur's desk. Arthur eyed the open sores and mentally noted the areas of his desk to disinfect later. The old man said in a gravelly voice, "They've listed me for Elder Sizing and I don't want to be sized."

Arthur nodded. "Who recommended it? Family?"

"Only family I have is my granddaughter and she's out most of the time. No, it was the neighbors and the block captain. The bastards called for a welfare check and a stupid ass Care Specialist came out. Says I'm not relevant anymore, says I should be sized. Piss-ant."

Arthur noted the man's use of language as possible violation of Good Government Recommendation # 7775498.b: Appropriate Speech to Avoid Social Discord, but decided not to mention it. Per the Advocacy Code it was for Arthur to maintain a "welcoming environment congenial for open discussion."

"Sir, how shall I address you?" asked Arthur.

The old man grinned. "Call me Grandpa Jones," he said. "I'm Rebel Jones' grandfather. Remember her?"

"Of course," Arthur said, smiling. Rebel Jones was Arthur's star client two years earlier. She brought him his first major case: Good Government Recommendation 34765.89: Hub Cap Conformity for Vehicle Wheels. Who could forget Rebel Jones, the wild girl who fought for beauty? She was an artist and wanted to paint flowers on the recommended plain tin hub caps. Arthur argued for a Change in Recommendation, demonstrating that when cars were moving the hub cap paintings could not be distinguished and thus posed no distraction for drivers. The case attracted much attention and, after it was won, hundreds of people painted their hub caps too. Arthur and Rebel Jones were even invited to ride in an auto parade where every few feet the cars would stop and all the onlookers would cheer the decorated hub caps. Even now, two years later, Arthur occasionally saw flyers for Hub Cap art festivals.

Grandpa Jones said, "You represented her, now you can represent me. I don't want to be sized." Grandpa Jones leaned forward. A bit of drool emerged from the side of his mouth. "I'm still relevant."

Arthur leaned back in his chair and watched as the drool dripped down onto Grandpa Jones chin and then drop to the front of his shirt.

Arthur mentally reviewed what he knew about the Elder Sized. It was simple, really. When you became old and your body failed and your care became a burden and you were no longer relevant, you were sized. Your old, wasted wretched body was converted to toddler-like being and you became an Oldie Goldie. No longer ugly, you were cute, and being sized eliminated the aches and pains of old age. In time, when the diseases of the aged emerged again and overwhelmed the sized body, death came painlessly and fast.

In the days before Good Government, it sometimes it took two or three people to care for an aged person. They lifted the person to the toilet or to the bath and the aged would be in misery, experiencing pain and helplessness, lying in beds they were too weak to leave. Families unable to cope might leave the aged in places called "nursing homes," where the old simply waited to die.

Sizing changed everything. It was fun to care for Oldie Goldies. Families often took in their Oldie Goldie, for there was no difficulty in washing or diapering their grandpa or grandma or mother or father, and if you put food in front of them, they could typically feed themselves. And yes, Oldie Goldies couldn't walk, but they could still crawl. They could move about the home and be easily carried outside for excursions, perhaps to a picnic or food shopping or to Festival on Good Government Day. In residential designated areas it was common to see a family push a double stroller, with a Cutie Pie toddler in the front and an Oldie Goldie in the back.

Oldie Goldies without families went to a Good Government Care Center. These were fine places, with plenty of activities where the Oldie Goldies engaged in social interactions under the watchful eyes of a Care Specialist. Of course, the Oldie Goldies couldn't talk with each other, as sizing left them with just elder-voice babble, but they still played games and could point when they needed something.

"Grandpa Jones, why not be sized?" Arthur nodded toward the walker. "You won't need that any more. No more illness, no more pain." Arthur was too polite to mention Grandpa Jones' swollen legs and open sores, but those would be gone too.

A big spit hurled from Grandpa Jones' mouth, landing just to the side of Arthur's desk. Arthur hoped the glob landed on some newspaper and not on the hardwood floor. "Sure," said Grandpa Jones, "And no more being my own man. No more going where I want when I want. No more being able to speak." Grandpa Jones licked his lips like a wolf ready to down a fresh kill meal. He grinned and Arthur saw his yellowed and cracked teeth. "Besides, I'm still relevant."

Arthur shook his head. Grandpa Jones' body was failing. He was beyond contributing and no doubt was somewhat burdensome, all of which clearly indicated sizing. "But you said a Care Specialist deemed you irrelevant. In accordance with Rule 64883.761 once someone is deemed irrelevant then he or she will be Elder Sized."

"Right, Advocate-boy, but I don't deem me irrelevant."

"I don't understand," said Arthur.

"What does your Rule say about *who* decides whether someone's irrelevant?"

Arthur thought a moment. "It doesn't designate anyone."

"Right!"

Arthur said, "Still, clearly a Care Specialist someone with training and experience, is the appropriate person—"

"More appropriate than me?" Grandpa Jones licked his lips in a frenzy. "Don't you see, Advocate boy, we've got a loop-hole here."

"Loop-hole?" asked Arthur.

Grandpa Jones groaned. "A way to beat the system. Something the Good Government crew forgot to cover in their Rules and Recommendations and Laws. They don't say who decides when someone's no longer relevant, so why shouldn't it be me? Who knows me better than me? A loop-hole!"

"Loop-hole," said Arthur, trying out the word.

Grandpa Jones pounded Arthur's desk, laughing. "You see, I am still relevant. I just enriched you, Advocate-boy. I taught you a new word. Will you take my case?"

Arthur felt a sense of discord. He wasn't sure whether it was the interesting concept of loop-holes or the surprise of having another Rule case come his way, but he felt excited and confused. And then he remembered.

"Wait," Arthur said. "Did you submit your claim for Advocacy Review?"

Grandpa Jones stopped his laugh. "No."

"But every claim goes through Advoca—"

"That's Recommendation, boy, not Rule, not Law —just Recommendation."

Arthur's eyes widened. Every case was issued through the Advocacy. That was Recommendation # 334789.76 Proper Procedures for Good Government Functions. He never heard of a case not going through the Advocacy. "But—"

"Recommendation, boy! You don't have to follow Recommendations, that's why they're Recommendations."

Who didn't follow Recommendations? Following Recommendations was the key component of Good Government, preventing social discord and promoting positive social interactions. Everyone knew that.

Grandpa Jones leaned on Arthur's desk and slowly stood up. His arms shook with the burden of his weight. "Listen to me. Recommendations don't *have* to be followed. They're just Recommendations. It's another loop-hole. If you had to follow Recommendations, then they would be Rules, wouldn't they? Or Laws?"

"Loop-hole," echoed Arthur.

Grandpa Jones sat down again and wheezed with the effort. "That's right, Advocate-boy. Loop-hole." He nodded and some drool dripped from his mouth onto his shirt.

A few hours after Grandpa Jones left, Arthur received a phone call from Max Troot, a popular columnist in both of the district's major papers, *Good Government News* and *Social Harmony Times*. Max had publicized Arthur's case with Rebel Jones and the hub caps. Since then, he and Arthur had gotten to know each other, meeting occasionally for a lunch-designated all beef, low fat hot dog with whole grain bun. Twice they even met on a designated one beer Friday.

"Greetings Arthur! How's my favorite Advocate?"

Arthur was just finishing disinfecting his desk. "Doing well. You?"

"Tops. An interesting fellow came to see me today. An old one, pretty sickly."

"Grandpa Jones," said Arthur, dropping his cleaning rags on the desk.

"Arthur, he says you're taking his case about being sized—or should I say, *not* being sized. Is it true?"

Arthur had told Grandpa Jones that he would consider taking the case, but hadn't committed. That Grandpa Jones had approached Max was surprising.

"It's quite a case, isn't it?" Arthur asked.

"A stunner," Max replied.

Arthur thought a moment. "Yes, Max, I'm doing it."

When Arthur woke the next morning, he went to his front door to get the morning papers and saw that Max's story was the lead. There was a photograph of Grandpa Jones glaring as he leaned on his walker with the caption: "No Sizing for Me!" and there were two photographs of Arthur and Rebel Jones, one taken after they'd won the hub cap case and the other as they rode in the hub cap car parade. Max's story took three columns in *Good Government News* and two and a half columns in *Social Harmony Times*.

Arthur lived alone because he had been skipped during his First Opportunity for Social Pairing. At the time he was only a Junior Advocate, so wasn't surprised. His Second Opportunity was 18 months away and Arthur felt his chance at Social Pairing would be strong then. For now though he always ate breakfast by himself. He prepared that day's designated Good Government recommended one grain one fruit one juice breakfast and settled down to read the articles when his phone rang.

Before Arthur could even say "Greetings," a voice screamed at him.

"Good Government! What have you done to me?" It was Max.

"What's wrong?"

"Arthur, you didn't tell me that Grandpa Jones' claim wasn't reviewed through the Advocacy. Do you have any idea what trouble we're in?"

"What are you talking about?" asked Arthur, using his calm Advocate's voice.

Max took a deep breath and spoke slowly. "Grandpa Jones' case was not reviewed by the Advocacy." He paused again. "The-Advocacy-did-not-approve-his-case." Max was almost crying.

"I know."

"You know? Are you crazy, are you insane, are you—"

"Listen," Arthur said, "You don't have to bring a case through the Advocacy. That's just a Recommendation, not Rule or Law."

Max didn't say anything for a moment, then Arthur heard him murmur, "Christ Almighty."

"What?"

"I don't know. My grandfather used to say that sometimes. Arthur, can I record you? Record you about Recommendation not being Rule or Law?"

Arthur saw no reason to object. "Sure."

"Hang on," Max said.

A few seconds later Max, voice calm, asked, "Advocate Enright, could you explain why Grandpa Jones' claim was not reviewed by the Advocacy."

"Certainly," Arthur replied. "To bring a claim through the Advocacy is merely a Recommendation and Recommendations do not have to be followed. If they had to be followed, then they would be Rule or Law. Grandpa Jones came to me directly and I agreed to take his case." He was about to explain the concept of loop-holes, but Max interrupted him.

"And in our discussion yesterday, did you ever indicate to me that this case was not reviewed by the Advocacy?"

"No. But what difference does that make?"

There was no answer. Max had hung up.

Over the next few days Max did not return Arthur's phone calls. Still, Arthur knew Max was deep in the story. There were numerous articles in the papers, many authored by Max. Most talked about the medical benefits of sizing or had interviews with family members of sized people. And there were photos of the Elder Sized, all so cute and happy, some with families and some at Good Government Care Centers.

One story had interviews with Grandpa Jones' block captain and two neighbors, where they explained how in accordance with Good Government Recommendation 67993.54 Surveillance of Neighbors for Their Own Benefit, they had noticed Grandpa Jones' failing body and increasing lack of contribution.

Arthur worried that the opposing Advocate might call the neighbors to witness. Then Arthur realized that he had someone to witness too. Smiling, Arthur got his phone book and called Rebel Jones.

A few days later Rebel Jones and Grandpa Jones entered his office for their appointment.

Arthur stood up behind his desk, "My Good Government," he said, "Rebel Jones in the flesh." She hadn't changed much in two years; still slim and with the same flowing red hair across her shoulders. She was wearing a flowered dress, one that echoed her now famous hubcap paintings. Her face was a little older and her eyes were puffy, as if she woke up too early and needed to go back to sleep.

"Where's the pisser?" asked Grandpa Jones.

"The what?"

"Toilet," Rebel Jones said.

"Oh," said Arthur. "Down the hall to your left."

Rebel Jones held the door open for her grandfather. When he was gone she closed the door and turned to Arthur.

"Rebel Jones, you look—"

"Why did you take my grandfather's case?"

Recalling his phone conversation with Max, Arthur said, "I know your grandfather didn't file his claim through the Advocacy like you did, but—"

"Oh for Good Government's sake, I never went through the Advocacy."

"Yes you did," said Arthur. He'd seen the paperwork.

"No," she said. "The Advocacy came to me. I took painting in the Good Government Suggested Program of Organized Activities for the Relevant. It was for fun. One day they came to me, not me to them. They asked me to file the claim. Don't you get it?"

He did not. "Rebel Jones—"

"I'm not Rebel Jones," she said. "I'm Annie McClursky."

"What?" asked Arthur.

"The Advocacy gave me the name 'Rebel Jones,' the same way they created the case—the same way they determine all cases."

"Why would they change your name?" he asked.

"Why? Because Rebel Jones is a much better name for a hubcap artist than McClursky. Who cares about a rebellious artist named McClursky?"

This bit about names was strange and something he would think about, but later. The hearing was two days away and they had to focus. "Look, Rebel—I mean Annie—or Rebel—"

She sat down. "Just call me Rebel Jones."

He nodded. "I need you to witness. Will you witness on behalf of your grandfather? Will you speak in support of his claim?"

"Course she will," said Grandpa Jones, spittle flying from his mouth. His walker squeaked on the hardwood floor. "That's not just my granddaughter you're talking to. That's Rebel Jones!"

When Arthur and Grandpa Jones entered the courtroom, Arthur saw it was packed. Several reporters were in the first few rows, including Max. Arthur recognized court personnel hanging out near the back. The court crew always liked to sit in on good cases. The rest of the rows were filled with citizenry. Rebel Jones was at the end of the fifth row by the wall. Arthur wondered why she didn't sit behind the claimant's table, but maybe the reporters had grabbed those seats. Arthur walked in with Grandpa Jones, his walker making a slight banging sound against the marbled floor with each slow step. Arthur nodded to Max, but Max looked away.

When they reached their table, the bailiff walked over from his station in front of the Judge's bench. He slid the table aside so that Grandpa Jones could get to his seat using the walker. Then he held the chair steady as Grandpa Jones lowered himself. Once Grandpa Jones was seated the bailiff lifted the walker away and slid the table back in place.

"Thanks," said Arthur. The bailiff nodded and returned to his station.

"Thanks, my ass," said Grandpa Jones. "He did that to make me look weak. Watch out, Advocate-boy, the knives are out and they're pointing at you and me."

The side door opened and Gwen Gold walked in. Yes! They hadn't switched Advocates on him. Arthur still didn't understand how Gwen got the case. She was just a Junior Advocate. J.A.'s were never assigned Rule cases, and Gwen's reputation was nothing special.

Gwen came over to their table. She cupped her hands, "Greetings, Advocate Enlight. Greetings, Grandpa Jones. I am Advocate Gold. I welcome you to this courtroom and trust that the best outcome will result from our efforts today."

Arthur stood up and cupped his hands, "Greetings, Advocate Gold. On behalf of myself and Grandpa Jones, I thank you for your service and trust that the best outcome will result from our efforts today."

They shook hands. "Congratulations, Gwen," said Arthur. "I've never heard of a J.A. getting a Rules case. That's really something."

Gwen shrugged. "Maybe, maybe not."

"What do you mean?" he asked.

"If this really is a major case, why'd they give it to me?"

The bailiff cleared his throat and made his way to the side door. Gwen hurried to her table.

The bailiff opened the side door, calling, "All rise, all rise, for the Honorable Judge Jameson Dewrite. May Good Government reign in our land and in this Court."

Everyone stood except for Grandpa Jones. His chair was low for the height of the table and he had difficulty leveraging himself to get to his feet. He was still struggling when Judge Dewrite reached the bench. Judge Dewrite, looking impressive with his neatly trimmed grey hair and flowing black robe, scanned the courtroom. Instead of saying "Be seated," as judges usually did, he stood there watching Grandpa Jones struggle.

Arthur placed his arm under Grandpa Jones's arm trying to lift him, but they were side by side and the angle made it hard to help. After several seconds, Judge Dewrite said, "It's all right, Grandpa Jones, you don't have to stand. Everyone, be seated." They all sat down except for Grandpa Jones who had finally made it to a standing position and now had to work to lower himself down.

When Grandpa Jones at last settled in his seat, he whispered to Arthur, "Knives, boy, knives."

Judge Dewrite said, "Grandpa Jones, if you require a rest break, please inform the Court and we will accommodate you. Would you like some water now?"

Grandpa Jones was still winded, but hissed, "Piss-ant."

"Thank you, Judge. No accommodation is necessary." said Arthur.

Judge Dewrite nodded and the case began.

Gwen's case mostly echoed the newspapers. She called to witness a neighbor who described Grandpa Jones' unkempt lawn and home and his general lack of helpfulness regarding block affairs. The most damaging witness was the Care Specialist. She described Grandpa Jones' physical condition, stressing his lack of mobility, low endurance and limited ability to care for his home and himself. She noted that he could no longer contribute to Good Government or Social Harmony. He would only drain resources and efforts that could be better directed elsewhere. Quite simply, he was no longer relevant and should be sized.

With that Gwen rested her case. There was no surprise in her presentation and Arthur had come up with a fine plan to demonstrate Grandpa Jones' relevance.

"Advocate Enlight, present your case," said Judge Dewrite.

Arthur stood, "Thank you, Judge. Per Good Government Rule 64883.761 a person is sized when deemed irrelevant. We do not deny that Grandpa Jones' physical condition makes him somewhat burdensome in terms of care. However, we intend to prove that Grandpa Jones can still contribute."

Judge Dewright said, "But you acknowledge that Grandpa Jones' physical state makes him burdensome? If so, then he can't contribute. He takes, doesn't give. We can end this now." The judge reached for his gavel.

Arthur's heart jumped. Arthur said, "Judge, we can show Grandpa Jones' ability to contribute, but we need to present our case."

Judge Dewrite frowned. There was murmuring coming from the spectators and several reporters were writing in their notepads. "Proceed."

"Thank you. I call Grandpa Jones to witness."

With Arthur's help, Grandpa Jones once again struggled to his feet. The bailiff hurried over and slid the table out of the way and gave Grandpa Jones his walker. Grandpa Jones then slowly made his way to the witness chair. The bailiff eased Grandpa Jones into the witness chair and put the walker to one side.

Judge Dewrite asked, "Grandpa Jones, are you comfortable? We can take a break if you wish."

Grandpa Jones said, "No problem with me."

Arthur began, "Grandpa Jones, the issue before us is your relevance. You believe that you can still contribute. How?"

This was their moment. The one that Arthur and Grandpa Jones had worked out together.

Grandpa Jones grinned. "Well, I'll tell you. I know things from the old days before Good Government and I know things from now. I have experiences." He licked his lips. "And I can think," he said, glancing up at Judge Dewrite. "You want to know how I can contribute? I'll tell you. I can provide *enrichment.*"

The spectators' area exploded in whispers. Judge Dewrite pounded on his gavel and the bailiff took a step forward from his station which made everyone quiet down.

Gwen stood up. "Judge, this is ridiculous. There is no way that Grandpa Jones could ever be a Certified Enrichment Provider. For one thing, he could never keep up with the children."

Arthur said, "Your honor, Grandpa Jones did not say he wishes to become a Certified Enrichment Provider, he just said he could provide enrichment. And he didn't say to children."

"What are you talking about?" asked Gwen. "How else is enrichment provided?"

"I'll tell you, young lady," said Grandpa Jones. "I can provide enrichment to *you.*"

"To me? I'm already relevant. I finished enrichment three years ago."

"Even so, I know things you don't that I can share with you. That makes me relevant. I am relevant."

The murmuring rose louder and the judge again banged his gavel. "Quiet down," he said.

Arthur stepped forward. "Your honor, may we demonstrate?"

Judge Dewrite looked out at the spectators and at the reporters with their pens and pencils posed above their pads. He sighed. "Proceed."

Arthur turned to the witness chair. "Grandpa Jones, how might you provide enrichment to ... " He scanned the courtroom apparently randomly. Of course, all the experienced court room observers knew it wasn't random at all and they leaned forward in anticipation when Arthur's eyes finally settled on Gwen. "How would you provide enrichment to Advocate Gold?"

Gwen's face turned slightly red but, to her credit, she stood and faced Grandpa Jones.

Grandpa Jones said, "Well young miss, you say you're three years out of enrichment, right?" Gwen nodded. "So, it's almost your First Opportunity for Social Pairing, isn't it?" She nodded again. "Well then, I can tell you a thing or two—that is, I can enrich you—all about wooing and courtship."

Gwen smiled. "I don't need you to enrich me. Social Pairing, Courtship and Wooing are all covered by Good Government Rule 7777654.8 Behaviors Prohibited in Forming Social Pairs and by Good Government Recommendation 654987.23a Appropriate and Effective Interactions in Forming Social Pairs. Any information I or anyone else needs about wooing can easily be reviewed. I've been enriched on prescreen polite inquiry, intermediate common interests development, prescribed social activities to encourage—"

"What about going into the park at midnight?" asked Grandpa Jones.

"Sir?" she asked.

"Do you know that you should go to the park at midnight?"

"All parks close at dusk," Gwen said.

Grandpa Jones nodded. "Yes, but after your polite inquiry, as you are developing common interests, you and the young man should go to the park at midnight."

"But the parks are closed," she said again.

"That's right," said Grandpa Jones. "But you should go in anyway." With that there were many whispers among the spectators. Judge Dewrite banged his gavel.

The room hushed. "Continue," he said.

Grandpa Jones looked at the judge and then at the spectators and finally focused on Gwen. His gravelly voice echoed around the court room. "And after you go into the park, you follow the path to the lake and there, alone with your young man, you stand together under the moonlight. There's no noise except the calls of a few birds. The wind rustles through the leaves and messes your hair." Grandpa Jones closed his eyes. "Then you walk to the edge of the lake and together you kneel down to see your reflections.

They ripple in the water. You say his name and he says yours. And then he takes your hand." Grandpa Jones opened his eyes. "And that, young lady, is how you develop common interests. I just enriched you about wooing."

Gwen stood there, holding her two hands together against her chest.

"Advocate Enlight?" It was Judge Dewrite. "Advocate Enlight?" he repeated.

"Sir?" said Arthur, tearing his eyes away from Gwen.

"Are you finished with Grandpa Jones?"

"Yes, we're done."

"Fine. Grandpa Jones, you may return to the claimant's table. Advocate Gold, you can sit down too." Gwen flushed and took her chair.

Once Grandpa Jones made his way back to the claimant's table and was safely seated, Judge Dewrite asked Arthur, "Anyone else to witness?"

"Yes, we call Rebel Jones."

The spectators and reporters jostled each other for a better view. Rebel Jones wore a long dress with a muted flowery design, appropriate for an artist and the courtroom. To Arthur she seemed scared, very different from the brazen care-free girl he represented two years earlier.

After Rebel Jones affirmed the Statement of Accurate Telling, Arthur approached her.

"Sit down, Advocate Enlight. I will conduct this witnessing," Judge Dewrite said.

Arthur stopped. "But Judge, according to the Advocacy Code it is for the Advocates to conduct the witnessing and—"

"Approach," said the judge.

Both Arthur and Gwen approached the bench. Arthur glanced at Gwen. She shook her head and shrugged.

"Advocate Enlight," Judge Dewrite whispered, "I said I will conduct the witnessing and that is what I will do. I do not want any protest from you."

"Your honor, the Advocacy Code clearly states—"

"But that's only Recommendation, isn't it? And Recommendations don't have to be followed, do they?" Judge Dewrite's voice was ice. "Sit down."

This was not good. Arthur's plan to have Rebel Jones describe how Grandpa Jones enriched her was falling in ruin. He had no idea what Judge Dewrite might ask. "But, Judge."

"Sit down now," Judge Dewrite said. Arthur turned from the bench and saw Rebel Jones watching him, eyes wide. He nodded to her in reassurance, but felt only panic.

Once Arthur and Gwen were seated, Judge Dewrite swiveled his chair toward Rebel Jones.

"Now then, Rebel Jones," he began, "When your grandfather was listed for sizing, were you present?"

"No."

"Where were you?"

"I was at a hubcap art festival."

Judge Dewrite smiled. "Ah, yes. Your hubcap art has made quite the impression. You've brought much credit to our district."

The spectators nodded. District folk were always proud when one of their own made Significant Contribution.

Judge Dewrite said, "So when Grandpa Jones filed his claim through Advocate Enlight, were you part of that decision?"

She shook her head. "No. I found out about it when I read the newspaper."

Judge Dewrite leaned toward her. "Rebel Jones, is your grandfather burdensome to you?"

Rebel Jones said nothing. She glanced at Arthur, but Arthur could offer no help. Beside him Grandpa Jones nervously licked his lips over and over.

"I love my grandfather," she answered.

"Of course, you do," Judge Dewrite said, "But is he burdensome?"

"Well…"

"Is he?"

She stared up at the ceiling as if hoping an answer was spray painted there.

"Rebel Jones?"

"He sometimes requires care—as we all do sometimes."

"Yes, we all do sometimes," Judge Dewrite said. "But eventually sometime becomes all the time. Is it sometime or all the time?

She said, "I can't say, really. Is having to make breakfast for someone every day 'all the time' or is that 'sometime' because it's only breakfast? It's hard to say."

Judge Dewrite sighed. "Perhaps I can help. Rebel Jones, your hubcap art has brought you much attention, hasn't it?"

"Yes."

"Have you received any offers?"

"Offers?"

"Yes, offers," Judge Dewrite said. "Have you received any offers lately related to your hubcap art?"

Rebel Jones flicked her eyes at the claimant's table. Arthur knew something was going on but didn't know what. Grandpa Jones was still, frozen in his chair.

"Rebel Jones," Judge Dewrite said.

"Yes, I've received offers."

"And what is your most recent offer?"

"My most recent offer is to have a showing of my hubcap art and to host a series of hubcap art festivals."

"Where is this showing?"

She paused then said, "At the Good Government Art Museum."

That really got to the spectators and one even clapped. The GG was the nation's premiere art museum. Anyone who visited the Capital always went to the GG. For one of their own to have her work displayed there was amazing. Judge Dewrite did not bang his gavel. He too was enjoying this good news

Arthur turned to Grandpa Jones. "When did this happen?"

"Yesterday morning she got the call." Grandpa Jones pulled at his fingers. "It's knives, knives, knives," he whispered.

"Many congratulations," said Judge Dewrite "When do you go?"

Rebel Jones peered up at him and did not answer.

"Rebel Jones, when do you go?"

She still didn't answer.

Judge Dewrite leaned in again. "Rebel Jones, you accepted this offer, didn't you?"

She stared straight ahead, not at the judge, not at Arthur and not at her grandfather. "No."

"Why not?" Judge Dewrite asked.

She turned back to Judge Dewrite. "Because I can't go. I would be gone for at least a month. I have to stay here to take care of my grandfather."

The air seemed to leave the courtroom. The spectator who had clapped before now loudly groaned.

Judge Dewrite turned to Rebel Jones and spoke so softly that those in the back strained to hear him. "Rebel Jones, do you want your grandfather to be sized?"

Arthur felt Grandpa Jones grip his arm.

"I love my grandfather," she said again.

"I know," Judge Dewrite said. "But should he be sized?"

Everyone waited. Finally, she said, "I don't know." She looked up at Judge Dewrite. "I leave it to the judgment of this good court. I'm too close to this case to know what's right." She nodded her head and her voice grew stronger. "I leave it to this good court."

"You trust in the judgment of this court?" asked Judge Dewrite.

She nodded. "I do."

Grandpa Jones whispered, "Piss-ant."

"Rebel Jones, you may step down."

Judge Dewrite waited until she sat down. Then he turned to Arthur. "Anyone else?"

"No, Judge."

"Very well," Judge Dewrite said. "Advocates will rise. Grandpa Jones, you may remain seated."

Arthur and Gwen stood. Everyone in the courtroom seemed to freeze as they waited for the judge's decision. Judge Dewrite's voice rang out strong and loud. "The issue before us is whether Grandpa Jones is still relevant. His neighbors, his block captain and his Care Specialist say he is not. Grandpa Jones and his Advocate say that he is. And his granddaughter—his granddaughter loves him."

Judge Dewrite's voice deepened. "It is the decision of this court that Grandpa Jones shall be deemed relevant." The breaths being held explosively released. Judge Dewrite pounded his gavel. "I'm not finished." He waited for quiet. "However, this decision will be subject to review in three months, at which time an inquiry will be made regarding Grandpa Jones' relevance at that time. This Good Court is adjourned."

Arthur was unbelievably relieved. He thought for sure they had lost, but they'd won. And who cared about the review in three months? He would show that Grandpa Jones continued to make contribution. He thought about the words he could learn—loopholes. He could even call himself to witness as to how Grandpa Jones enriched him. No Advocate had done that before.

The spectators began leaving the courtroom, but Max stayed seated. Arthur waved. After a few seconds Max nodded back, his lips pressed together in a tight thin line. Then he too left. Rebel Jones pushed against the exodus to get to their table.

"I'm relevant, relevant, relevant," chanted Grandpa Jones as Rebel Jones joined them.

Arthur smiled at her. "You did fine. The judge was tough, but you handled it."

"Sure, I did great," she said. "Grandpa, let's go home." She moved the table, retrieved the walker and placed it in front of Grandpa Jones. Then she helped him get up.

Grandpa Jones turned to Arthur. "Three months review. You'll be there, won't you?"

"Of course. I'm your Advocate-boy."

Grandpa Jones smiled. "That you are." He turned and made his way out the courtroom. Rebel Jones began to follow, but Arthur touched her arm. She turned to him.

"And see you in three months, too, right?" he asked.

"Oh, Arthur," she said. Then she was gone.

The courtroom was empty except for Arthur, Gwen, Judge Dewrite and the bailiff.

"Are you ready to debrief?" asked Judge Dewrite.

"Sure, Judge," said Arthur.

"Yes, indeed," said Gwen.

Arthur loved debriefing. After a hearing the Advocates meet with the judge to comment on each other's performance. No matter how hot the case, during the debriefing both sides extend professional courtesy, offer compliments and there's usually laughter too. Debriefing ensured that no hard feelings or angry passions persisted beyond the courtroom. It maintained the prescribed civility of the Advocacy.

Arthur and Gwen approached the bench. Arthur loosened his tie and Gwen took off her jacket, slinging it on the back of the witness chair. Arthur expected Judge Dewrite to remove his robe as most judges do during debriefing, but Judge Dewrite kept his on.

"You brought an interesting case, Arthur," said Judge Dewrite.

"Yes, it was." Arthur hid his disappointment. Judges typically opened debriefing by saying, "You argued a good case," or "Excellent presentation." "Interesting" meant nothing. It was neutral. Arthur thought he did a terrific job. Having Grandpa Jones enrich Gwen on wooing and courtship worked brilliantly and certainly demonstrated his relevance. Maybe Judge Dewrite wasn't offering praise because the case would be under review in three months.

Judge Dewrite said, "Arthur, there's another interesting case coming up the docket."

Arthur glanced at Gwen. Per debriefing protocol, Judge Dewrite should now offer commentary on Gwen's performance, but Judge Dewrite didn't even look at her. Gwen shrugged her shoulders.

"What case would that be?" Arthur asked.

Judge Dewrite said, "It's a Law case."

Gwen sharply inhaled. Judge Dewrite acknowledged her. "You did fine, Gwen. Good job." Then he turned back to Arthur. Arthur didn't say anything but he certainly felt his heart beating faster. A Law case?

"This case involves Law 335987.421.a."

Judge Dewrite waited and Arthur realized what he was supposed to do. "Law 335987.421.a: Determination of Appropriate Tradecraft Based on Skills, Knowledge and Attitude."

Judge Dewrite nodded. "Right. The claimant is a young man of nineteen. During his formal assessment he was designated for a Beta tradecraft in the area of transportation. Per Law, formal assessment is done two months before the completion of the 13th year of enrichment. The young man claims that the entire 13th year of enrichment should be included in his formal assessment. Apparently, he showed marked improvement."

Arthur said, "So he's asking for Reasonable Exception based on marked improvement in his 13th year?"

"No." Judge Dewrite paused. "He's asking for Change in Law."

"Good Government," Gwen murmured.

"Exactly," said Judge Dewrite. "This will be quite a case. The young man is most determined. He says there shouldn't just be an exception for him, but that the law should change for all the young people."

No one said anything, each contemplating the significance of a Change in Law case. Finally, the judge spoke.

"Arthur, I've talked with other members of the Advocacy. We think you're ready for a Law case. That is, if you think you're ready."

"Thank you, Judge." He took a breath and said in formal Advocate language, "I shall be pleased to serve as Advocate and will represent the young

man with both zeal and compassion in full service to him and in keeping with the principles of Good Government."

Judge Dewrite grinned. "Excellent Arthur, I'm proud of you."

Gwen offered her hand. "Congratulations."

Judge Dewrite said, "One more thing. There is a schedule conflict. The young man's case is on the docket in three months. You'll have to resign from Grandpa Jones' case. There's no way you can do both."

Arthur stared at Judge Dewrite. Involuntarily, the word *knives* flashed through his brain.

Arthur asked, "Judge, can't I get a continuance for Grandpa Jones' review?"

"Grandpa Jones' case was questionable, but I still ruled in his favor. Requiring a review in three months seems both fair and appropriate." Judge Dewrite smiled pleasantly.

"Perhaps we can delay the young man's case. Or move it up?"

Judge Dewrite shook his head. "This is a Law case. You need proper time to prepare. As for delaying it, anything longer than three months would impact the students scheduled to enter their 13th year of enrichment. It's only fair that they know whether the full 13th year will count toward their assessment. No Arthur, three months is just right. It's just right." He smiled again.

"But if I were to take this case, what would happen to Grandpa Jones' case?"

"His case will be assigned to another Advocate. Of course, it will have to go through Advocacy Review first. I doubt that any other Advocate would take a case without it first going through Review. Isn't that right, Gwen?"

Gwen seemed surprised to be addressed. "Yes, of course. No Advocate may accept a case without it first going through Advocacy Review."

"That's not true," Arthur said. "Going through Review is Recommendation, not Rule and not Law and Recommendations don't have to be followed."

"Excuse me?" asked Gwen.

"It's a loop-hole," said Arthur.

"A what?" she asked.

"Quiet!" Judge Dewrite said. "Arthur, do you understand what would happen if people ignored Recommendations? Think back to the days before Good

Government; the social discord, the disharmony. You should read what people put on the Telenet before posting was forbidden. Hateful things. And the violence? Endless. Absolute social cannibalism. It only stopped because we—all of us—embraced the tenets of Good Government."

He took a deep breath. "And as for Grandpa Jones, sizing allows those no longer relevant to be cared for without being burdensome."

"But Grandpa Jones is relevant," said Arthur. "He enriches us."

Judge Dewrite held his hands to his face and rubbed his eyes. "Arthur, will you take the young man's Law case regarding formal assessment and serve as his Advocate?"

Arthur didn't answer. He stared at the floor for several seconds.

"Arthur?"

Arthur lifted his head. "I am Grandpa Jones' Advocate. I am committed to my citizen client and will remain his Advocate."

Judge Dewrite leaned back in his chair, picked up his gavel and twirled it in his hand, round one way then the other, all the while peering at Arthur. Then he stopped the twirling. "Very well, Advocate Enlight. As Judge of this Good Court, I find your decision making process flawed, so flawed that you are a burden to our Good Government. Thus, I decree you to be no longer relevant. I thereby order that you be sized." He banged the gavel with such force that the noise bounced off the wall and echoed back.

Arthur said, "I protest." At least, that is what he wanted to say. Later he worked out exactly what he would have said. "I protest this ruling. I have not been given a hearing, nor have I been allowed to call myself or anyone to witness. And finally, most important, I am still relevant." In his head he would say those words with such deep emotion that tears would form on Judge Dewrite's eyes and the judge would recant and beg forgiveness. But that was just imagination. For at the exact moment that Arthur began finally to utter, "I protest," he was sized.

He had a dizzying sensation of falling, not to the ground, but into himself. He watched as his left hand and arm contracted, though they felt no different. It was his insides that he could feel folding, his liver flip-flopping, kidneys vibrating, intestines aroused then settling, and all the while his heart maintained its steady beat. And then it was over. Arthur could not even see over the judge's bench.

When Arthur tried to say "I protest," this is what he really said: "Pwo, pwo. Pwo, pwo."

The bailiff untangled Arthur from his now too big clothing. Arthur was naked and the bailiff lifted him up high. "Well, well," said the bailiff. "Aren't you a handsome Oldie Goldie." He turned Arthur so that he was facing Judge Dewrite. Arthur flailed his tiny arms.

Judge Dewrite smiled. "He is a fine little fellow."

Arthur began to cry and the bailiff held Arthur to his shoulder, "There, there, little man—it's all right." He patted Arthur gently and, much to Arthur's distress, Arthur burped. The bailiff and Judge Dewrite laughed.

Judge Dewrite reached behind the bench and took out two Oldie Goldie outfits, one brown and one gray. He held them both up.

"Gwen, which do you think would look best on Arthur?"

Advocate for me, thought Arthur.

Gwen was staring at Arthur. She slowly turned to Judge Dewrite. "Ah," she said, then stopped. "Sir," she began again. Judge Dewrite swished the two outfits back and forth giving her a better look. Gwen took a firm step toward the bench. "Judge, I think—" She suddenly seemed out of air. Her face took on a startled expression as if the lack of oxygen surprised her. She breathed in deeply and closed her eyes. After a few moments she opened them. She said, "Judge, I think gray would be best."

Judge Dewrite handed her the gray outfit. She took it to the bailiff and held it up against Arthur. Arthur was still crying and couldn't see clearly. For a second he thought Gwen was crying too, but then she smiled, a big smile showing all her teeth. "Oh yes, this goes well with your eyes. Good Government, Arthur, you are one gorgeous Oldie Goldie!"

"Pwo, pwo," said Arthur. "Pwo, pwo."

Copyright © 2022 by Elaine Midcoh.

George R.R. Martin, also known as GRRM, is an American novelist, screenwriter, television producer and short story writer. He is the co-creator and series editor of the Wildcard series, and author of the fantasy novel series A Song of Ice and Fire, which was adapted into the Emmy Award-winning HBO series Game of Thrones. His new series, House of Dragons, set in the same universe, is airing now on HBO.

Howard Waldrop is a science fiction author who works primarily in short fiction, notably known for the pieces "The Ugly Chicken" and "Night of the Cooters" (which is currently being adapted into a movie by his sometime collaborator, George R.R. Martin). He's won World Fantasy and Nebula Awards, and received the World Fantasy Award for Life Achievement in 2021.

MEN OF GREYWATER STATION

by George R.R. Martin & Howard Waldrop

The men of Greywater Station watched the shooting star descend, and they knew it for an omen.

They watched it in silence from the laser turret atop the central tower. The streak grew bright in the northeast sky, divided the night though the thin haze of the spore dust. It went through the zenith, sank, fell below the western horizon.

Sheridan, the bullet-headed zoologist, was the first to speak. "There they went," he said, unnecessarily.

Delvecchio shook his head. "There they are," he said, turning toward the others. There were only five there, of the seven who were left. Sanderpay and Miterz were still outside collecting samples.

"They'll make it," Delvecchio said firmly. "Took too long crossing the sky to burn up like a meteor. I hope we got a triangulation on them with the radar. They came in slow enough to maybe make it through the crash."

Reyn, the youngest of the men at Greywater, looked up from the radar console and nodded. "I got them, all right. Though it's a wonder they slowed enough before hitting the atmosphere. From the little that got through jamming, they must have hit pretty hard out there."

"If they live, it puts us in a difficult position," said Delvecchio. "I'm not quite sure what comes next."

"I am," said Sheridan. "We get ready to fight. If anybody lives through the landing, we've got to get ready to take them on. They'll be crawling with fungus before they get here. And you know they'll come. We'll have to kill them."

Delvecchio eyed Sheridan with new distaste. The zoologist was always very vocal with his ideas. That didn't make it any easier for Delvecchio, who then had to end the arguments that Sheridan's ideas usually started. "Any other suggestions?" he asked, looking to the others.

Reyn looked hopeful. "We might try rescuing them before the fungus takes over." He gestured toward the window, and the swampy, fungus-clotted landscape beyond. "We could maybe take one of the flyers to them, shuttle them back to the station, put them in the sterilization ward…" Then his words trailed off, and he ran a hand nervously through his thick black hair. "No. There'd be too many of them. We'd have to make so many trips. And the swampbats…I don't know."

"The vaccine," suggested Granowicz, the wiry extee psychologist. "Bring them some vaccine in a flyer. Then they might be able to walk it."

"The vaccine doesn't work right," Sheridan said. "People build up an immunity, the protection wears off. Besides, who's going to take it to them? You? Remember the last time we took a flyer out? The damn swampbats knocked it to bits. We lost Blatt and Ryerson. The fungus has kept us out of the air for nearly eight months now. So what makes you think it's all of a sudden going to give us a free pass to fly away into the sunset?"

"We've got to try," Reyn said hotly. From his tone Delvecchio could see there was going to be a hell of an argument. Put Sheridan on one side of a fight and immediately Reyn was on the other.

"Those are men out there, you know," Reyn continued. "I think Ike's right. We can get them some vaccine. At least there's a chance. We can fight the swampbats. But those poor bastards out there don't have a chance against the fungus."

"They don't have a chance whatever we do," Sheridan said. "It's us we should worry about. They're finished. By now the fungus knows they're there. It's probably already attacking them. If any survived."

"That seems to be the problem," said Delvecchio quickly, before Reyn could jump in again. "We have to assume some will survive. We also have to assume the fungus won't miss a chance to take them over. And that it will send them against us."

"Right!" said Sheridan, shaking his head vigorously. "And don't forget, these aren't ordinary people we're dealing with. That was a troop transport up there. The survivors will be armed to the teeth. What do we have besides the turret laser? Hunting rifles and specimen guns. And knives. Against screechers and seventy-five mikemikes and God knows what else. We're finished if we're not ready. Finished."

"Well, Jim?" Granowicz asked. "Is he right? What do you think our chances are?"

Delvecchio signed. Being the leader wasn't always a very comfortable position. "I know how you feel, Bill," he said with a nod to Reyn. "But I'm afraid I have to agree with Sheridan. Your scheme doesn't have much of a chance. And there are bigger stakes. If the survivors have screechers and heavy armament, they'll be able to breach the station walls. You all know what that would mean. Our supply ship is due in a month. If the fungus gets into Greywater, then Earth won't have to worry about the Fyndii anymore. The fungus would put a permanent stop to the war—it doesn't like its hosts to fight each other."

Sheridan was nodding again. "Yes. So we have to destroy the survivors. It's the only way."

Andrews, the quiet little mycologist, spoke up for the first time. "We might try to capture them," he suggested. "I've been experimenting with methods of killing the fungus without damaging the hosts. We could keep them under sedation until I got somewhere."

"How many years would that take?" Sheridan snapped.

Delvecchio cut in. "No. We've got no reason to think we'll even be able to fight them, successfully. All the odds are with them. Capture would be clearly impossible."

"But rescue isn't." Reyn was still insistent. "We should gamble," he said, pounding the radar console with his fist. "It's worth it."

"We settled that, Bill," Delvecchio said. "No rescue. We've got only seven men to fight off maybe hundreds—I can't afford to throw any away on a useless dramatic gesture."

"Seven men trying to fight off hundreds sounds like a useless dramatic gesture to me," Reyn said. "Especially since there may be only a few survivors who could be rescued."

"But what if all of them are left?" said Sheridan. "And all of them have already been taken over by the fungus? Be serious, Reyn. The spore dust is everywhere. As soon as they breathe unfiltered air, they'll take it in. And seventy-two hours they'll be like the rest of the animal life on this planet. Then the fungus will send them against us."

"Goddammit, Sheridan!" yelled Reyn. "They could still be in their pods. Maybe they don't even know what happened. Maybe they're still asleep. How the hell do I know? If we get there before they come out, we can save them. Or something. We've got to try!"

"No. Look. The crash is sure to have shut the ship down. They'll be awake. First thing they'll do is check their charts. Only the fungus is classified, so they won't know what a hell of a place they've landed on. All they *will* know is that Greywater is the only human settlement here. They'll head toward us. And they'll get infected and possessed."

"That's why we should work fast," Reyn said. "We should arm three or four flyers and leave at once. Now."

Delvecchio decided to put an end to the argument. The last one like this had gone all night. "This is getting us nowhere," he said sharply, fixing both Sheridan and Reyn with hard stares. "It's useless to discuss any longer. All we're doing is getting mad at each other. Besides, it's late." He looked at his watch. "Let's break for six hours or so and resume at dawn when we're cooler and less tired. We'll be able to think more clearly. And Sanderpay and Miterz will be back then, too. They deserve a voice in this."

There were three rumbles of agreement. And one sharp note of dissent.

"No," said Reyn. Loudly. He stood up, towering over the others in their seats.

"That's too late. There's no time to lose."

"Bill, you—" Delvecchio started.

"Those men might be grabbed while we sleep," Reyn went on, plowing right over his superior. "We've got to *do* something."

"No," said Delvecchio. "And that's an order. We'll talk about it in the morning. Get some sleep, Bill."

Reyn looked around for support. He got none. He glared at Delvecchio briefly. Then he turned and left the tower.

Delvecchio had trouble sleeping. He woke up at least twice, between the sheets that were cold and sticky with sweat. In his nightmare, he was out beyond Greywater, knee deep in the grey green slime, collecting samples for analysis. While he worked, he watched a big amphibious mud tractor in the distance, wallowing toward him. On top was another human, his features invisible behind filter mask and skinthins. In the dream Delvecchio waved to the tractor as it neared, and the driver waved back. Then he pulled up nearby, climbing down from the cab, and grasped Delvecchio in a firm handshake.

Only by that time, Delvecchio could see through the transparent filter mask. It was Ryerson, the dead geologist, his friend Ryerson. But his head was swollen grossly and there were trails of fungus hanging from each ear.

After the second nightmare he gave it up as a bad show. They never found Ryerson or Blatt after the crash. Though they knew from the impact that there wouldn't be much to find. But Delvecchio dreamed of them often, and he suspected that some of the others did, too.

He dressed in darkness, and made his way to the central tower. Sanderpay, the telecom man, was on watch. He was asleep in the small ready bunk near the laser turret, where the station monitors could awaken him quickly if anything big approached the walls. Reinforced duralloy was tough stuff, but the fungus had some pretty wicked creatures at its call. And there were the airlocks to consider.

Delvecchio decided to let Sanderpay sleep, and went to the window. The big spotlights mounted on the wall flooded the perimeter around Greywater with night white lights that made the mud glisten sickly. He could see drifting spores reflected briefly in the beams. They seemed unusually thin, especially toward the west, but that was probably his imagination.

Then again, it might be a sign that the fungus was uneasy. The spores had always been ten times thicker around Greywater as elsewhere on the planet's surface. That had been one of the first pieces of evidence that the damned fungus was intelligent. And hostile.

They still weren't sure just how intelligent. But of the hostility there was no more doubt. The parasitic fungus infected every animal on the planet. And had used most of them to attack the station at one point or another. It wanted them. So the blizzard of spores that rained on Greywater for more than a year now. The overhead force screens kept them out, though, and the sterilization chambers killed any that clung to the mud tractor or skinthins or drifted into the airlocks. The fungus kept trying.

Across the room, Sanderpay yawned and sat up in his bunk. Delvecchio turned toward him. "Morning, Otis."

Sanderpay yawned again, and stifled it with a big red hand. "Morning," he replied, untangling himself from the bunk in a tangle of long arms and legs. "What's going on? You taking Bill's shift?"

Delvecchio stiffened. "What? Was Reyn supposed to relieve you?"

"Uh-huh," said Sanderpay, looking at the clock. "Hour ago. The bastard. I get cramps sleeping in this thing. Why can't we make it a little more comfortable, I ask you?"

Delvecchio was hardly listening. He ignored Sanderpay and moved swiftly to the intercom panel against one wall. Granowicz was closest to the motor pool. He rang him.

A sleepy voice answered. "Ike," Delvecchio said. "This is Jim. Check the motor pool, quick. Count the flyers."

Granowicz acknowledged the order. He was back in less than two minutes, but it seemed longer. "Flyer five is missing," he said. He sounded awake all of a sudden.

"Shit," said Delvecchio. He slammed down the intercom and whirled toward Sanderpay. "Get on the radio, fast. There's a flyer missing. Raise it."

Sanderpay looked baffled, but complied. Delvecchio stood over him, muttering obscenities and thinking worse ones, while he searched through the static.

Finally an answer. "I read you, Otis." Reyn's voice of course.

Delvecchio leaned toward the transmitter. "I told you no rescue."

The reply was equal parts laughter and static. "Did you? Hell! I guess I wasn't paying attention, Jim. You know how long conferences always bored me."

"I don't want a dead hero on my hands. Turn back."

"I intend to. After I deliver the vaccine. I'll bring as many of the soldiers with me as I can. The rest can walk. The immunity wears off, but it should last long enough if they landed where we predict."

Delvecchio swore. "Dammit, Bill. Turn back. Remember Ryerson."

"Sure I do. He was a geologist. Little guy with a pot belly, wasn't he?"

"Reyn!" There was an edge to Delvecchio's voice.

Laughter. "Oh, take it easy, Jim. I'll make it. Ryerson was careless, and it killed him. And Blatt too. I won't be. I've rigged some lasers up. Already got two big swampbats that came at me. Huge fuckers, easy to burn down."

"Two! The fungus can send hundreds if it gets an itch. Damnit, listen to me. Come back."

"Will do," said Reyn. "With my guests." Then he signed off with a laugh.

Delvecchio straightened, and frowned. Sanderpay seemed to think a comment was called for, and managed a limp, "Well…" Delvecchio never heard him.

"Keep on the frequency, Otis," he said. "There's a chance the damn fool might make it. I want to know the minute he comes back on." He started across the room.

"Look. Try to raise him every five minutes or so. He probably won't answer. He's in for a world of shit if that jury-rigged laser fails him."

Delvecchio was at the intercom. He punched Granowicz' station. "Jim again, Ike. What kind of laser's missing from the shop? I'll hold on."

"No need to," came the reply. "Saw it just after I found the flyer gone. I think one of the standard tabletop cutters, low power job. He's done some spot-welding, left the stat on the power box. Ned found that, and places where he'd done some bracketing. Also, one of the vacutainers is gone."

"Okay, Thanks, Ike. I want everybody up here in ten minutes. War council."

"Oh, Sheridan will be so glad."

"No. Yes. Maybe he will." He clicked off, punched for Andrews.

The mycologist took a while to answer. "Arnold?" Delvecchio snapped when the acknowledgment finally came.

"Can you tell me what's gone from the stores?"

There were a few minutes of silence. Then Andrews was back. "Yeah, Jim. A lot of medical supplies. Syringes, bandages, vaccine, plastic splints, even some body bags. What's going on?"

"Reyn. And from what you say, it sounds like he's on a real mercy mission there. How much did he take?"

"Enough, I guess. Nothing we can't replace, however."

"Okay. Meeting up here in ten…five minutes."

"Well, all right." Andrews clicked off.

Delvecchio hit the master control, opening all the bitch boxes. For the first time in four months, since the slinkers had massed near the station walls. That had been a false alarm. This, he knew, wasn't.

"Meeting in five minutes in the turret," he said.

The words rang through the station, echoing off the cool humming walls.

"…that if we don't make plans now, it'll be way too late." Delvecchio paused and looked at four men lounging on the chairs. Sanderpay was still at the radio, his long legs spilling into the center of the room. But the other four were clustered around the table, clutching coffee cups.

None of them seemed to be paying close attention. Granowicz was staring absently out the window, as usual, his eyes and forebrain mulling the fungus that grew on the trees around Greywater. Andrews was scribbling in a notepad, very slowly. Doodling. Ned Miterz, big and blond and blocky, was a bundle of nervous tension; Bill Reyn was his closest friend. He alternated between drumming his fingers on the tabletop, swilling his coffee, and tugging nervously at his drooping blond mustache. Sheridan's bullet-shaped head stared at the floor.

But they were all listening, in their way. Even Sanderpay, at the radio. When Delvecchio paused, he pulled his long legs back under him, and began to speak. "I'm sorry it's come to this, Jim," he said, rubbing his ear to restore circulation. "It's bad enough those soldiers are out there. Now Bill has gone after them, and he's in the same spot. I think, well, we have to forget him. And worry about attacks."

Delvecchio sighed. "It's hard to take, I know. If he makes it, he makes it. If he finds them, he finds them. If they've been exposed, in three days they'll be part of the fungus. Whether they take the vaccine or not. If he brings them back, we watch them three days to see if symptoms develop. If they do, we have to kill them. If not, then nobody's hurt, and when the rest walk in we watch for symptoms in them. But those are iffy things. If he doesn't make it, he's dead. Chances are, the troopers are dead. Or exposed. Either way, we prepare for the worst and forget Reyn until we see him. So what I'm asking for now are practical suggestions as to how we defend ourselves against well-armed soldiers. Controlled by some intelligence we do not understand."

He looked at the men again.

Sanderpay whooped. He grabbed the console mike as they jumped and looked at him.

"Go ahead, Bill," he said, twisting the volume knob over to the wall speaker. The others winced as the roar of frequency noise swept the room.

"…right. The damn thing's sending insects into the ship. Smear…ing…smear windscreen…on instruments." Reyn's voice. There was a sound in the background like heavy rain.

"…swampbats just before they came…probably coming at me now. Goddamn laser mount loosened…" There was a dull thud in the background. "No lateral control…got that bastard…ohmigod…" Two more dull thuds. A sound like metal eating itself.

"…in the trees. Altitude…going down…swampbats…something just got sucked in the engine… Damn, no power…nothing…if…"

Followed by frequency noise.

Sanderpay, his thin face blank and white, waited a few seconds to see if more transmission came through, then tried to raise Reyn on the frequency. He turned the volume down again after a while.

"I think that's about what we can expect will happen to us in a couple of days," said Delvecchio. "That fungus will stop at nothing to get intelligent life. Once it has the soldiers who survive, they'll come after the station. With their weapons."

"Well," snapped Sheridan. "He knew not to go out there in that flyer."

Miterz slammed down his coffee cup, and rose. "Goddamn you, Sheridan. Can't you hold it even a minute? Bill's probably dead out there. And all you want to do is say I-told-you-so."

Sheridan jumped to his feet too. "You think I like listening to someone get killed on the radio? Just because I didn't like him? You think it's fun? Huh? You think I want to fight somebody who's been trained to do it? Huh?" He looked at them, all of them, and wiped sweat from his brow with the back of his hand. "I don't. I'm scared. I don't like making plans for war when men could be out there wounded and dying with no help coming."

He paused. His voice, stretched thin, began to waver. "Reyn was a fool to go out there. But maybe he was the only one who let his humanity come through. I made myself ignore them. I tried to get you all to plan for war in case any of the soldiers made it. Damn you. I'm afraid to go out there. I'm afraid to go near the stuff, even inside the station I'm a zoologist, but I can't even work. Every animal on this planet has that—that stuff on it. I can't bear to touch it. I don't want to fight either. But we're going to have to. Sooner or later."

He wiped his head again, looked at Delvecchio. "I—I'm sorry, Jim. Ned, too. The rest of you. I'm—I have—I just don't like it any more than you. But we have to."

He sat down, very tiredly.

Delvecchio rubbed his nose, and reflected again that being the nominal leader was more trouble than it was worth. Sheridan had never opened up like this before. He wasn't quite sure how to deal with it.

"Look," he finally said. "It's okay, Eldon" It was the first time he could remember that he—or any of them—had used Sheridan's first name. "This isn't going to be easy on any of us. You may be right about our humanity.

Sometimes you have to put humanity aside to think about…well, I don't know.

"The fungus has finally found a way to get to us. It will attack us with the soldiers, like it has with the slinkers and the swampbats and the rest. Like it's trying to do now, while we're talking, with the burrowing worms and the insects and the arthropoda. The station's defenses will take care of those. All we have to worry about are the soldiers."

"All?" said Granowicz, sharply.

"That, and what we'll do if they breach the wall of the field. The field wasn't built to take screechers or laser explosives. Just to keep out insects and flying animals. I think one of the first things we've got to do is find a way to beef up the field. Like running in the mains from the other power sources. But that still leaves the wall. And the entry chambers. Our weakest links. Ten or twenty good rounds of high explosives will bring it right down. How do we fight back?"

"Maybe we don't," said Miterz. His face was still hard and angry. But now the anger was turned against the fungus, instead of Sheridan. "Maybe we take the fight to them."

The suggestions flew thick and fast from there on. Half of them were impossible, a quarter improbable, the most of what were left were crazy. At the end of an hour, they had gotten past the points of mining, pitfalls, electrocution.

To Delvecchio's ears, it was the strangest conversation he had ever heard. It was full of the madness of men planning against each other, made stranger by the nature of the men themselves. They were all scientists and technicians, not soldiers, not killers. They talked and planned without enthusiasm, with the quiet talk of men who must talk before being pallbearers at a friend's funeral, or the pace of men who must take their turns as members of a firing squad the next morning.

In a way, they were.

An hour later, Delvecchio was standing up to his ankles in grey-green mud, wrestling with a power-saw and sweating freely under his skinthins. The saw was hooked up to the power supply on his mud-tractor. And Miterz was sitting atop the tractor, with a hunting laser resting across his knee, occasionally lifting it to burn down one of the slinkers slithering through the underbrush.

Delvecchio had already cut through the bases of four of the biggest trees around the Greywater perimeter—about three quarters of the way through, anyway. Just enough to weaken them, so the turret laser could finish the job quickly when the need arose. It was a desperate idea. But they were desperate men.

The fifth tree was giving him trouble. It was a different species from the others, gnarled and over-hung with creepers and rock-hard. He was only halfway through, and already he'd had to change the blade twice. That made him edgy. One slip with the blade, one slash in the skinthins, and the spores could get at him.

"Damn thing," he said, when the teeth began to snap off for the third time. "It cuts like it's half petrified. Damn."

"Look at the bright side," suggested Miterz. "It'll make a mighty big splat when it falls. And even duralloy armor should crumple pretty good."

Delvecchio missed the humor. He changed the blade without comment, and resumed cutting.

"That should do it," he said after a while. "Looks deep enough. But maybe we should use the lasers on this kind, if we hit any more of them."

"That's a lot of power," said Miterz. "Can we afford it?" He raised his laser suddenly, and fired at something behind Delvecchio. The slinker, a four-foot-long mass of scales and claws, reared briefly from its stomach and then fell again, splattering mud in their direction. Its dying scream was a brief punctuation mark. "Those things are thick today," Miterz commented.

Delvecchio climbed up into the tractor. "You're imagining things," he said.

"No, I'm not." Miterz sounded serious. "I'm the ecologist, remember? I know we don't have a natural ecology around here. The fungus sends us its nasties, and keeps the harmless life forms away. But now there's even more than usual." He gestured with the laser. Off through the underbrush, two big slinkers could be seen chewing at the creepers around a tree, the fungus hanging like a shroud over the back of their skulls. "Look there. What do you think they're doing?"

"Eating," said Delvecchio. "That's normal enough." He started the tractor, and moved it forward jerkily. Mud, turned into a watery slime, spouted out behind the vehicle in great gushes.

"Slinkers are omnivores," Miterz said. "But they prefer meat. Only ear creepers when there's no prey. But there's plenty around here." He stopped, stared at the scene, banged the butt of the laser rifle on the cab flood in a fit of sudden nervous tension.

Then he resumed in a burst of words. "Damn it, damn it. They're clearing a path!" His voice was an accusation. "A path for the soldiers to march on. Starting at our end and working toward them. They'll get here faster if they don't have to cut through the undergrowth."

Delvecchio, at the wheel, snorted. "Don't be absurd."

"What makes you think it's absurd? Who know what the fungus is up to? A living ecology. It can turn every living thing on this planet against us if it wants to. Eating a path through a swamp is nothing to something like that." Miterz' voice was distant and brooding.

Delvecchio didn't like the way the conversation was going. He kept silent. They went on to the next tree, and then the next. But Miterz, his mind racing, was getting more and more edgy. He kept fidgeting in the tractor, and playing with the rifle, and more than once he absently tried to yank at his mustache, only to be stopped by the filtermask. Finally, Delvecchio decided it was time to head in.

Decontamination took the usual two hours. They waited patiently in the entry chamber and sterilization rooms while the pump sprays, heatlamps, and ultraviolet systems did their work on them and the tractor.

They shed their sterilized skinthins as they came through the final airlock.

"Goddamn," said Delvecchio. "I hope we don't have to go out again. Decon takes more time than getting the work done."

Sanderpay met them, smiling. "I think I found something we could use. Nearly forgot about them."

"Yeah? What?" Miterz asked as he unloaded the laser charge and placed it back in the recharge rack. He punched several buttons absently.

"The sounding rockets."

Delvecchio slapped his head. "Of course. Damn. Didn't even consider them." His mind went back. Blatt, the dead meteorologist, had fired off the six-foot-sounding rockets regularly for the first few weeks, gaining data on the fungus. They had discovered that spores were frequently found up to 50,000 feet, and a few even reached as high as 80,000. After Blatt covered that he still made a twice-daily ritual of firing the sounding rockets, to collect information on the planet's shifting wind patterns. They had weather balloons, but those were next to useless; the swampbats usually vectored in on them soon after they were released. After Blatt's death, however, the

readings hadn't meant as much, so the firings were discontinued. But the launching tubes were still functional, as far as he knew.

"You think you can rig them up as small guided missiles?" Delvecchio asked.

"Yep," Sanderpay said with a grin. "I already started. But they won't be very accurate. For one thing they'll reach about a mile in altitude before we can begin to control them. Then, we'll be forcing the trajectory. They'll want to continue in a long arc. We'll want them back down almost to the launching point. It'll be like wrestling a two-headed alligator. I'm thinking of filling half of them with that explosive Andrews is trying to make, and the rest with white phosphorus. But that might be tricky."

"Well, do whatever you can, Otis," said Delvecchio. "This is good news. We needed this kind of punch. Maybe it isn't as hopeless as I thought."

Miterz had been listening carefully, but he still looked glum. "Anything over the commo?" he put in. "From Bill?"

Sanderpay shook his head. "Just the usual solar shit, and some mighty nice whistlers. Must be a helluva thunderstorm somewhere within a thousand miles of here. I'll let you know if anything comes in, though."

Miterz didn't answer. He was looking at the armory and shaking his head.

Delvecchio followed his eyes. Eight lasers were on the racks. Eight lasers and sixteen charges, standard station allotment. Each charge good for maybe fifty fifth-second bursts. Five tranquilizer rifles, an assortment of syringes, darts, and projectiles. All of which would be useless against armored infantry. Maybe if they could adapt some of the heavier projectiles to H.E....but such a small amount wouldn't dent duralloy. Hell.

"You know," said Miterz. "If they get inside, we might as well hang it up."

"If," said Delvecchio.

Night at Greywater Station. They had started watch-and-watch. Andrews was topside at the laser turret and sensor board. Delvecchio, Granowicz and Sanderpay lingered over dinner in the cafeteria below. Miterz and Sheridan had already turned in.

Sanderpay was talking of the day's accomplishments. He figured he had gotten somewhere with the rockets. And Andrews had managed to put together some explosive from the ingredients in Reyn's lab.

"Arnold doesn't like it much, though," Sanderpay was saying. "He wants to get back to his fungus samples. Says he's out of his field, and not too sure he knows what he's doing. He's right, too. Bill was your chemist."

"Bill isn't here," Delvecchio snapped. He was in no mood for criticism. "Someone has to do it. At least Arnold has some background in organic chemistry, no matter how long ago it was. That's more than the rest of us have." He shook his head. "Am I supposed to do it? I'm an entomologist. What good is that? I feel useless."

"Yep, I know," said Sanderpay. "Still. It's not easy for me with the rockets, either. I had to take half the propellant from each one. Worked nine hours, finished three. We're gonna be fighting all the known laws of aerodynamics trying to force those things down near their starting point. And everybody else is having problems, too. We tinker and curse and it's all a blind alley. If we do this, we gotta do that. But if we do that, it won't work. This is a research station. So maybe it looks like a fort. That doesn't make it one. And we're still scientists, not demolition experts."

Granowicz gave a thin chuckle. "I'm reminded of that time, back on Earth, in the twentieth century, when that German scientist…von Brau? von…. Von Braun and his men were advised that the enemy forces would soon be there. The military began giving them close-order drill and marksmanship courses. They wanted them to meet the enemy on the very edge of their missile complex and fight them hand to hand."

"What happened?" said Sanderpay.

"Oh, they ran 300 miles, and surrendered," Granowicz replied dryly.

Delvecchio downed his two hundredth cup of coffee, and put his feet up on the table. "Great," he said. "Only we've got no place to run to. So we're going to *have* to meet them on the edge of *our* little missile complex, or whatever. And soon."

Granowicz nodded. "Three days from now. I figure."

"That's if the fungus doesn't help them," said Delvecchio.

The other two looked at him. "What do you mean?" asked Granowicz.

"When Ned and I were out this morning, we saw slinkers. Lots of them. Eating away at the creepers to the west of the station."

Granowicz had a light in his eyes. But Sanderpay, still baffled, said, "So?"

"Miterz thinks they're clearing a path."

"Uh-oh," said Granowicz. He stroked his chin with a thin hand. "That's very interesting, and very bad news. Clearing away at both ends, and all along, as I'd think it would do. Hmmm."

Sanderpay looked from Delvecchio to Granowicz and back, grimaced, uncoiled his legs and then coiled them around his chair again in a different position. He said nothing.

"Ah, yes, yes," Granowicz was saying. "It all fits, all ties in. We should have anticipated this. A total assault, with the life of a planet working for our destruction. It's the fungus…a total ecology, as Ned likes to call it. A classic case of the parasitic collective mind. But we can't understand it. We don't know what its basic precepts are, its formative experiences. We don't know. No research has been carried out on anything like it. Except maybe the water jellies of Noborn. But that was a collective organism formed of separate colonies for mutual benefit. A benign form, as it were. As far as I can tell, Greywater, the fungus, is a single all-encompassing mass which took over this planet starting from some single central point."

He rubbed his hands together and nodded. "Yes. Based on that, we can make guesses as to what it thinks. And how it will act. And this fits, this total hostility."

"How so?" asked Sanderpay.

"Well, it's never run up against any other intelligence, you see. Only lower forms. That's important. So it judges us by itself, the only mind it has known. It is driven to dominate, to take over all life with which it comes in contact. So it thinks we are the same, fears that we are trying to take over this planet as it once did.

"Only, like I've been saying all along, it doesn't see us as the intelligence. We're animals, small, mobile. It's known life like that before and all lower form. But the station itself is something new, something outside its experience. It sees the station as the intelligence, I'll bet. An intelligence like itself. Land, establishing itself, sending out extensions, poking at it and its hosts. And us, us poor animals, the fungus sees as unimportant tools."

Delvecchio signed. "Yeah, Ike. We've heard this before. I agree that it's a persuasive theory. But how do you prove it?"

"Proof is all around us," said Granowicz. "The station is under a constant around-the-clock attack. But we can go outside for samples, and the odds are fifty-fifty whether we'll be attacked or not. Why? We don't kill every slinker we see, do we? Of course not. And the fungus doesn't try to kill us, except if we get annoying. Because we're not important, it thinks. But something like the flyers—mobile but not animal, strange—it tries to eradicate. Because it perceives them as major extensions of Greywater."

"Then why the spores?" Delvecchio said.

Granowicz dismissed that with an airy wave. "Oh, the fungus would like to take us over, sure. To deprive the station of hosts. But it's the station it wants to eradicate. It can't conceive of cooperating with another intelligence—maybe, who knows, it had to destroy rival fungus colonies of its own species before it came to dominate this planet. Once it perceives intelligence, it is threatened. And it perceives intelligence in the station."

He was going to go on. But Delvecchio suddenly took his feet from the table, sat up, and said, "Uh oh."

Granowicz frowned. "What?"

Delvecchio stabbed at him with a finger. "Ike, think about this theory of yours. What if you're right? Then how is the fungus going to perceive the spaceship?"

Granowicz thought a moment, nodded to himself, and gave a slow, low whistle.

"So? How?" said Sanderpay. "Whattaya talking about?"

Granowicz turned on him. "The spaceship was mobile, but not animal. Like the station. It came out of the sky, landed, destroyed a large area of the fungus and host forms. And hasn't moved since. Like the station. The fungus probably sees it as another station, another threat. Or an extension of our station."

"Yes," said Delvecchio. "But it gets worse. If you're right, then maybe the fungus is launching an all-out attack right at this moment on the spaceship hull. While it lets the men march away unharmed."

There was a moment of dead silence. Sanderpay finally broke it, looking at each of the others in turn and saying in a low voice, "Oh. Wow. I see."

Granowicz had a thoughtful expression on his face, and he was rubbing his chin again. "No," he said at last. "You'd think that, but I don't think that's what is happening."

"Why not?" asked Delvecchio.

"Well, the fungus may not see the soldiers as the major threat. But it would at least try to take them over, as it does with us. And once it had them, and their weapons, it would have the tools to obliterate the station and the spaceship. That's almost sure to happen, too. Those soldiers will be easy prey for the spores. They'll fall to the fungus like ripe fruit."

Delvecchio clearly looked troubled. "Yeah, probably. But this bothers me. If there's even a slight chance that the soldiers might get here without being taken over, we'll have to change out plans."

"But there's no chance of that," Granowicz said shaking his head. "The fungus already has those men. Why else would it be clearing a path?"

Sanderpay nodded in agreement. But Delvecchio wasn't that sure.

"We don't know that it's clearing a path," he insisted. "That's just what Miterz thinks is happening. Based on very scant evidence. We shouldn't accept it as an accomplished fact."

"It makes sense, though," Granowicz came back "It would speed up the soldiers getting here, speed up the…"

The alarm from the turret began to hoot and clang

"Slinkers," said Andrews. "I think out by those trees you were working on."

He drew on a pair of infrared goggles and depressed a stud on the console. There was a hum.

Delvecchio peered through the binoculars. "Think maybe it's sending them to see what we were up to?"

"Definitely," said Granowicz, standing just behind him and looking out the window over his shoulder.

"I don't think it'll do anything," said Delvecchio hopefully. "Mines or anything foreign it would destroy, of course. We've proved that. But all we did is slash a few trees. I doubt that it will be able to figure out why."

"Do you think I should fire a few times?" Andrews asked from the laser console.

"I don't know," said Delvecchio. "Wait a bit. See what they do."

The long, thick lizards were moving around the tree trunks. Some slithered through the fungus and the mud, others scratched and clawed at the notched trees.

"Switch on some of the directional sensors," said Delvecchio. Sanderpay, at the sensor bank, nodded and began flicking on the directional mikes. First to come in was the constant tick of the continual spore bombardment on the receiver head. Then, as the mike rotated, came the hissing screams of the slinkers.

And then the rending sound of a falling tree.

Delvecchio, watching through the binoculars, suddenly felt very cold. The tree came down into the mud with a crashing thud. Slime flew from all sides, and several slinkers hissed out their lives beneath the trunk.

"Shit," said Delvecchio. And then, "Fire, Arnold."

Andrews pushed buttons, sighted in the nightscope, lined the crossnotches up on a slinker near the fallen tree, and fired.

To those not watching through goggles or binoculars, a tiny red-white light appeared in the air between the turret laser and the group of lizards. A gargling sound mixed with the slinker hissing. One of the animals thrashed suddenly, and then lay still. The others began slithering away into the undergrowth. There was stillness for a second.

And on another part of the perimeter, a second tree began to fall.

Andrews hit more buttons, and the big turret laser moved and fired again. Another slinker died. Then, without waiting for another crash, the laser began to swivel to hit the slinkers around the other trees.

Delvecchio lowered the binoculars very slowly. "I think we just wasted a day's work out there," he said. "Somehow the fungus guessed what we were up to. It's smarter than we gave it credit for."

"Reyn," said Granowicz.

"Reyn?" said Delvecchio. With a questioning look.

"He knew we'd try to defend the station. Given that knowledge, it's logical for the fungus to destroy anything we do out there. Maybe Reyn survived the crash of his flyer. Maybe the fungus finally got a human."

"Oh, *shit*," said Delvecchio with expression. "Yes, sure, you might be right. Or maybe it's all a big coincidence. A bunch of accidents. How do we know? How do we know anything about what the damned thing is thinking or doing or planning?" He shook his head. "Damn. We're fighting blind. Every time something happens, there are a dozen reasons that might have been behind it. And every plan we make has to have a dozen alternatives."

"It's not that bad," said Granowicz. "We're not entirely in the dark. We've proved that the fungus can take over Earth forms. We've proved that it gets at least some knowledge from them; that it absorbs at least part of what they knew. We don't know how big a part, true, however—"

"However, if, but, maybe," Delvecchio swore, looking very disgusted. "Dammit, Ike, how big a part is the crucial question. *If* it has Reyn, and *if* it knows everything he knew, then it knows everything there is to know about Greywater and its defenses. In that case, what kind of chance will we have?"

"Well," said Granowicz. He paused, frowned, stroked his chin. "I—hmmmmm. Wait, there are other aspects to this that should be thought out. Let me work on this a while."

"Fine," said Delvecchio. "You do that." He turned to Andrews. "Arnold, keep them off the trees as best you can. I'll be back up to relieve you in four hours."

Andrews nodded. "Okay, I think," he said, his eyes locked firmly on the nightscope.

Delvecchio gave brief instructions to Sanderpay, then turned and left the turret. He went straight to his bunk. It took him the better part of an hour to drift to sleep.

✿

Delvecchio's dream:

He was old, and cool. He saw the station from all sides in a shifting montage of images; some near the ground, some from above, wheeling on silent wings. In one image, he saw, or felt as a worm must feel, the presence of the heavy weight of sunlight.

He saw the station twisted, old, wrecked. He saw the station in a series of images from inside. He saw a skeleton in the corner of an indefinite lab, and saw through the eyes of the skull out into the broken station. Outside, he saw heaped duralloy bodies with grey-green growths sprouting from the cracked faceplates. And he saw out of the faceplates, out into the swamp. Everywhere was grey-green, and damp and old and cold. Everywhere.

Delvecchio awoke sweating.

☼

His watch was uneventful. The slinkers had vanished as suddenly as they had assembled, and he only fired the laser once, at a careless swampbat that flew near the perimeter. Miterz relieved him. Delvecchio caught several more hours of sleep. Or at least of bunk time. He spent a large chunk of time lying awake, thinking.

When he walked into the cafeteria the next morning, an argument was raging.

Granowicz turned to him immediately. "Jim, listen," he began, gesturing with his hands. "I've thought about this all night. We've been missing something obvious. If this thing has Reyn, or the soldiers, or *any* human, this is the chance we've been waiting for. The chance to communicate, to begin a mutual understanding. With their knowledge, it will have a common tongue with us. We shouldn't fight it at all. We should try to talk to it, try to make it understand how different we are."

"You're crazy, Granowicz," Sheridan said loudly. "Stark, raving mad. *You* go talk to that stuff. Not me. It's after us. It's been after us all along, and now it's sending those soldiers to kill us all. We have to kill them first."

"But this is our *chance*," Granowicz said. "To begin to understand, to reach that mind, to—"

"That was your job all along," Sheridan snapped. "You're the extee psych. Just because you didn't do your job is no reason to ask us to risk our lives to do it for you."

Granowicz glowered. Sanderpay, sitting next to him, was more vocal. "Sheridan," he said, "sometimes I wish we could throw you out to the fungus. You'd look good with grey-green growths coming out of your ears. Yep."

Delvecchio gave hard glances to all of them. "Shut up, all of you," he said simply. "I've had enough of this nonsense. I've been doing some thinking too."

He pulled up a chair and sat down. Andrews was at another table, quietly finishing his breakfast. Delvecchio motioned him over, and he joined them.

"I've got some things I want to announce," Delvecchio said. "Number one, no more arguments. We waste an incredible amount of time hashing out every detail and yelling at each other. And we don't have time to waste. So, no more. I make the decisions, and I don't want any screaming and kicking. If you don't like it, you're free to elect another leader. Understand?" He looked at each of them in turn. Sheridan squirmed a little under the gaze, but none of them objected.

"Okay," Delvecchio said finally. "If that's settled, then we'll move on." He looked at Granowicz. "First thing is this idea of yours, Ike. Now you want us to talk. Sorry, I don't buy it. Just last night you were telling us how the fungus, because of its childhood traumas, was bound to be hostile."

"Yes," began Granowicz, "but with the additional knowledge it will get from—"

"No arguments," Delvecchio said sharply. Granowicz subsided. Delvecchio continued. "What do you think it will be doing while we're talking? Hitting us with everything it's got, if your theory was correct. And it sounded good to me. We're dead men if we're not ready, so we'll be ready. To fight, not talk."

Sheridan was smirking. Delvecchio turned on him next. "But we're not going to hit them with everything we've got as soon as we see them, like you want, Sheridan," he said. "Ike brought up a point last night that's been bothering me ever since. Nagging at me. There's an outside chance the fungus might not even try to take over the soldiers. It might not be smart enough to realize they're important. It might concentrate on the spaceship."

Sheridan sat up straight. "We *have* to hit them," he said. "They'll kill us, Delvecchio. You don't—"

Sanderpay, surprisingly, joined in. "It's eating a path," he said. "And the trees. And this morning, Jim, look out there. Slinkers and swampbats all around. It's got them, I know it. It wouldn't be building up this way otherwise."

Delvecchio waved them both silent. "I know, Otis, I know. You're right. All signs say that it has them. But we have to be sure. We wait until we see them, until we *know*. Then, if they're taken, hit them with everything, at once. It has to be hard. If it becomes a struggle, we've lost. They outnumber and outgun us, and in a fight, they'd breach the station easy. Only the fungus might just march 'em up. Maybe we can kill them all before they know what hit them."

Granowicz looked doubtful. Sheridan looked more than doubtful. "Delvecchio, that's ridiculous. Every moment we hesitate increases our risk. And for such a ridiculous chance. Of *course* it will take them."

"Sheridan, I've had about enough out of you," Delvecchio said quietly. "Listen for a change. There're two chances. One that the fungus might be too dumb to take them over. And one that it might be too smart."

Granowicz raised his eyebrows. Andrews cleared his throat. Sheridan just looked insulted.

"If it has Reyn," Delvecchio said. "Maybe it knows all about us. Maybe it won't take the soldiers over on purpose. It knows from Reyn that we plan to destroy them. Maybe it will just wait."

"But why would it have slinkers clearing a…" Sanderpay began, then shut up. "Oh. Oh, no. Jim, it couldn't…"

"You're not merely assuming the fungus is very intelligent, Jim," Granowicz said.

"You're assuming it's very devious as well."

"No," said Delvecchio. "I'm not assuming *anything*. I'm merely pointing out a possibility. A terrible possibility, but one we should be ready for. For over a year now, we've been constantly underestimating the fungus. At every test, it has proven just a bit more intelligent than we figured. We can't make another mistake like that. No margin for error this time."

Granowicz gave a reluctant nod.

"There's more," said Delvecchio. "I want those missiles finished *today*, Otis. In case they get here sooner than we've anticipated. And the explosive too, Arnold. And I don't want any more griping. You two are relieved of your watches until you finish those projects. The rest of us will double up."

"Also, from now on we all wear skinthins inside the station. In case the attack comes suddenly and the screens are breached."

Everyone was nodding.

"Finally, we throw out all the experiments. I want every bit of fungus and every Greywater life form within this station eradicated." Delvecchio thought of his dream again, and shuddered mentally.

Sheridan slapped the table and smiled. "Now that's the kind of thing I like to hear! I've wanted to get rid of those things for weeks."

Granowicz looked unhappy, though. And Andrews looked very unhappy. Delvecchio looked at each in turn.

"All I have is a few small animals, Jim," Granowicz said. "Root-snuffs and such. They're harmless enough, and safely enclosed. I've been trying to reach the fungus, establish some sort of communications—"

"No," said Delvecchio. "Sorry, Ike, but we can't take the chances. If the walls are breached or the station damaged, we might lose power. Then we'd have contamination inside and out. It's too risky. You can get new animals."

Andrews cleared his throat. "But, well, my cultures," he said. "I'm just getting them broken down, isolating properties of the fungus strains. Six months of research, Jim, and, well, I think—" He shook his head.

"You've got your research. You can duplicate it. If we live through this."

"Yes, well—" Andrews was hesitant. "But the cultures will have to be started over. So much time. And Jim—" He hesitated again and looked at the others.

Delvecchio smiled grimly. "Go ahead, Arnold. They might die soon. Maybe they should know."

Andrews nodded. "I'm getting somewhere, Jim. With *my* work, the real work, the whole reason for Greywater. I've bred a mutation of the fungus, a non-intelligence variety, very virulent, very destructive of its hosts.

I'm in the final stages now. It's only a matter of getting the mutant to breed in the Fyndii atmosphere. And I'm near. I'm so near." He looked at each of them in turn, eyes imploring. "If you let me continue, I'll have it soon. And they could dump in on the Fyndii homeworlds, and well, it would end the war. All those lives saved. Think about all the men who will die if I'm delayed."

He stopped suddenly, awkwardly. There was a long silence around the table.

Granowicz broke it. He stroked his chin and gave a funny little chuckle. "And I thought this was such a bold, clean venture," he said, his voice bitter. "To grope toward new intelligence, unlike any we had known, to try to find and talk to a mind perhaps unique in this universe. And now you tell me all my work was a decoy for biological warfare. Even here I can't get away from that damned war." He shook his head. "Greywater Station. What a lie."

"It had to be this way, Ike," Delvecchio said. "The potential for military application was too great to pass up, but the Fyndii would have easily found out about a big, full-scale biowar research project. But teams like Greywater's—routine planetary investigation teams—are common. The Fyndii can't bother to check on every one. And they don't."

Granowicz was staring at the table. "I don't suppose it matters," he said glumly. "We all may die in a few days anyway. This doesn't change that. But— but—" He stopped.

Delvecchio shrugged. "I'm sorry, Ike." He looked at Andrews. "And I'm sorry about the experiments, too, Arnold. But your cultures have to go. They're a danger to us inside the station."

"But, well, the war—all those people." Andrews looked anguished.

"If we don't make it through this, we lose it all anyway, Arnold," Delvecchio said.

Sanderpay put a hand on Andrews's shoulder. "He's right. It's not worth it."

Andrews nodded.

Delvecchio rose. "Alright," he said. "We've got that settled. Now we get to work. Arnold—the explosives. Otis—the rockets. Ike and I will take care of dumping the experiments. But first, I'm going to go brief Miterz. Okay?"

The answer was a weak chorus of agreement.

✿

It took them only a few hours to destroy the work of a year. The rockets, the explosives and the other defenses took longer, but in time, they too were ready. And then they waited, sweaty and nervous and uncomfortable in their skinthins.

Sanderpay monitored the commo system constantly. One day. Two. Three, a day of incredible tension. Four, and the strain began to tell. Five, and they relaxed a bit.

The enemy was late.

"You think they'll try and contact us first?" Andrews asked at one point.

"I don't know," said Sanderpay. "Have you thought about it?"

"I have," Granowicz put in. "But it doesn't matter. They'll try either way. If it's them, they'll want to reach us, of course. If it's the fungus, it'll want to throw us off our guard. Assuming it has absorbed enough knowledge from its hosts to handle a transmission, which isn't established. Still, it will probably try, so we can't trust a transmission."

"Yeah," said Delvecchio. "But, that's the problem. We can't trust anything. We have to suppose every thing we're working on. We don't have any concrete information to speak of."

"I know, Jim, I know."

✿

On the sixth day, the storms screamed over the horizon. Spore clouds flowed by in the wind whipped into random gaps. Overhead the sky darkened. Lightning sheeted in the west.

The radio screeched its agony and crackled. Whistlers moved up and down the scale. Thunder rolled. In the tower, the men of Greywater Station waited out the last few hours.

The voice had come in early that morning, had faded. Nothing intelligible had come through. Static had crackled most of the day. The soldiers were moving on the edge of the storm, Delvecchio calculated.

Accident? Or planning? He wondered. And deployed his men. Andrews to the turret laser. Sanderpay at the rocket station. Sheridan and himself inside the station with laser rifles. Granowicz to the flyer port, where the remaining flyers had been stocked with crude bombs. Miterz on the walls.

They waited in their skinthins, filtermasks locked on but not in place. The sky, darkened by the coming storm, was blackening toward twilight anyway. Soon night and the storm would reach Greywater Station hand in hand.

Delvecchio stalked through the halls impatiently. Finally, he returned to the tower to see what was happening. Andrews, at the laser console, was watching the window. A can of beer sat next to him on the nightscope. Delvecchio had never seen the quiet little mycologist drink before.

"They're out there," Andrews said. "Somewhere." He sipped at his beer, put it down again. "I wish that, well, they'd hurry up or something." He looked at Delvecchio. "We're all probably going to die, you know. The odds are so against us."

Delvecchio didn't have the stomach to tell him he was wrong. He just nodded, and watched the window. All the lights in the station were out. Everything was down but the generators, the turret controls, and the forcefield. The field, fed with the extra power, was stronger than ever. But strong enough? Delvecchio didn't know.

Near the field perimeter, seven or eight ghosting shapes wheeled against the storm. They were all wings and claw, and a long, razor-barbed tail. Swampbats. Big ones, with six-foot wingspans.

They weren't alone. The underbrush was alive with slinkers. And the big leeches could be seen in the water near the south wall. All sorts of life were being picked up by the sensors.

Driven before the storm? Or massing for the attack? Delvecchio didn't know that, either.

The tower door opened, and Sheridan entered. He threw his laser rifle on the table near the door. "These things are useless," he said. "We can't use them unless they get inside. Or unless we go out to meet them, and I'm not going to do that. Besides, what good will they do against all the stuff they've got?"

Delvecchio started to answer, but Andrews spoke first. "Look out there," he said softly. "More swampbats. And that other thing. What is it?"

Delvecchio looked. Something else was moving through the sky on slowly moving leathery wings. It was black and *big*. Twice the size of a swampbat.

"The first expedition named them hellions," Delvecchio said after a long pause.

"They're native to the mountains, a thousand miles from here." Another pause.

"That clinches it."

There was general movement on the ground and in the water to the west of Greywater Station. Echoes of thunder rolled and then piercing the thunder came a shrill whooping shriek.

"What was *that*?" Sheridan asked.

Andrews was white. "That one I know," he said. "It's called a screecher. A sonic rifle breaks down cell walls with concentrated sound. I saw them used once. I-it almost makes flesh liquefy."

"God," said Sheridan.

Delvecchio moved to the intercom. Every box in the station was on full volume. "Battle stations, gentlemen," he said, flipping down his filter mask. "And good luck."

Delvecchio moved out into the hall and down the stairs. Sheridan picked up his laser and followed. At the base of the stairs, Delvecchio motioned for him to stop.

"You stay here, Eldon. I'll take the main entry port."

Rain had begun to spatter the swamps around Greywater, although the field kept it off the station. A great sheet of wind roared from the west and suddenly the storm was no longer approaching. It was here. A blurred outline of the force bubble could be seen against the churning sky.

Delvecchio strode across the yards through the halls and cycled through decon quickly to the main entry port. The large viewplate gave the illusion of a window. Delvecchio watched it sitting on the hood of a mud-tractor. The intercom box was on the wall next to him.

"Burrowing animals are moving against the under-field, Jim," Andrews reported from the turret. "We're getting, oh, five or six shock inputs a minute. Nothing we can't handle however."

He fell silent again and the only noise was the thunder. Sanderpay began to talk, gabbing about the rockets. Delvecchio was hardly listening. The perimeter beyond the walls was a morass of rain-whipped mud. Delvecchio could see little. He switched from the monitor he was tuned to and picked up the turret cameras. He and Andrews watched with the same eyes.

"Under-field contacts are up," Andrews said suddenly. "A couple of dozen a minute now."

The swampbats were wheeling closer to the perimeter. First one, then another, skirting the very edge of the field, riding terribly and silently on the wet winds. The turret laser rotated to follow each, but they were gone before it could fire.

Then, there was motion on the ground. A wave of slinkers began to cross the perimeter. The laser wheeled, depressed. A spurt of light appeared, leaving a quick vanishing roil of steam. One slinker died, then another.

On the south, a leech rose from the grey waters near the base wall of the station. The turret turned. Two quick spurts of red burned. Steam rose once. The leech twisted at the second burst.

Delvecchio nodded silently, clutched his rifle tighter.

And Andrews's voice came over the intercom. "There's a man out there," he said. "Near you, Jim."

Delvecchio slipped on his infrared goggles and flicked back to the camera just outside the entry port. There was a dim shape in the undergrowth.

"Just one?" asked Delvecchio.

"All I read," Andrews said.

Delvecchio nodded and thought. Then, "I'm going out." Many voices at once on the intercom. "That's not wise. I don't think," said one, Granowicz? Another said, "Watch it, Jim. Be careful." Sanderpay, maybe. And Sheridan, unmistakable, "*Don't*, you'll let *them* in!"

Delvecchio ignored them all. He hit the switch to open the outer port doors and slid down into the driver's seat in the mud-tractor. The doors parted. Rain washed into the chamber.

The tractor moved forward, rattling over the entry ramp and sliding smoothly into the slime. Now he was out in the storm and the rain tingled through his skinthins. He drove with one hand and held the laser with the other.

He stopped the tractor just outside the port and stood up. "Come out!" he screamed as loud as he could, out shouting the thunder. "Let us see you! If you can understand me— If the fungus doesn't have you— Come out now."

He paused and hoped and waited a long minute. He was about to shout again when a man came running from the undergrowth.

Delvecchio had a fleeting glimpse of tattered torn clothes. Bare feet stumbling in the mud. Rain drenched dark hair. But he wasn't looking at those. He was looking at the fungus that all but covered the man's face and trailed across his chest and back.

The man—the thing—raised a fist and released a rock. It missed. He kept running and screaming. Delvecchio, numb, raised his rifle and fired. The fungus thing fell a few feet beyond the trees.

Delvecchio left the tractor where it was and walked back to the entry port on foot. The doors were still open. He went to the intercom. "It has them," he said. Then, again, "It has them. And it's hostile. So now we kill them."

There were no answers. Just a long silence, and a stifled sob, and then Andrews's slow, detached voice.

"A new reading. A body of men—thirty, forty, maybe—moving from the west. In formation. A lot of metal—duralloy, I think."

"The main force," Delvecchio said. "They won't be so easy to kill. Get ready. Remember, every thing at once."

He turned back into the rain, cradled his rifle, walked to the ramp. Through his goggles, Delvecchio saw the shapes of men. Only a few at first. Fanned out.

He went outside the station to the tractor, knelt behind it. As he watched, the turret turned. A red line reached out, touched the first dim shape. It staggered.

New sheets of rain washed in, obliterating the landscape. The laser licked out again. Delvecchio very slowly, lifted his rifle to his shoulder and joined it, firing at the dim outlines seen through the goggles.

Behind him, he felt the first sounding rocket leave up the launch tube, and he briefly saw the fire of its propellant as it cleared the dome. It disappeared into the rain. Another followed it, then another, then the firings became regular.

The dim shapes were all running together; there was a large mass of men just a few yards deep in the undergrowth. Delvecchio fired into the mass and noted where they were, and hoped Arnold remembered.

Arnold remembered. The turret laser depressed, sliced at the trunk of a nearby tree. There was the sound of wood tearing. Then the tree began to lean. Then it fell.

From what Delvecchio could see, it missed. Another idea that didn't quite work, he reflected bitterly. But he continued to fire into the forest.

Suddenly, near the edge of the perimeter, water gouted up out of the swamp in a terrific explosion. Dwarfing all else. A slinker flew through the air, surprised at itself. It rained leech parts.

The first rocket.

A second later, another explosion, among the trees this time. Then more, one after another. Several very close to the enemy. Two among the enemy. Trees began to fall. And Delvecchio thought he could hear screaming.

He began to hope. He continued to fire.

There was a whine in the sky above. Granowicz in the flier. Delvecchio took time to glance up briefly and watch it flit overhead toward the trees. Other shapes were mov ing up there too however, diving on the flier, but they were slower. Granowicz made a quick pass over the perimeter dumping bombs. The swamp shook and the mud and water from the explosions mixed with the rain.

Now, definitely, he *could* hear screaming.

And then the answer began to come.

Red tongues and a pencil of light flicked out of the dark, played against the walls causing steam whirlpools which washed away in the rain. Then projectiles. Explosions. A dull thud rocked the station. A second. And somewhere in the storm, someone opened up with a screecher.

The wall him behind rang with a humming glow. And there was another explosion much bigger overhead against the forcefield dome. The rain vanished for an instant in a vortex of exploding gases. Wind whipped the smoke away and the station rocked. Then the rains touched the dome again in sheets.

More explosions. Lasers spat and hissed in the rain. Back and forth the grizzly light show. Miterz was firing from the walls. Granowicz was making another pass. The rockets had stopped falling. Gone already?

The turret fired, moved, fired, moved, fired. Several explosions rocked the tower. The world was a madness of rain. Of noise. Of lightning. Of night.

Then, the rockets began again. The swamp and nearer forest shook to the hits. The eastern corner of the station *moved* as a sounding missile landed uncomfortably close.

The turret began to fire again. Short bursts lost in rain. Answering fire was thick. At least one screecher was shrieking regularly.

Delvecchio saw the swampbats appear suddenly around the flier. They converged from all sides, howling, bent on death. One climbed right up into the engine, folding its wings neatly. There was a terrible explosion that lit the night to ghosts of trailing rain.

More explosions around the force dome. Lasers screened off the dome and turret. The turret glowed red, steamed. On the south, a section of wall vanished in a tremendous explosion.

Delvecchio was still firing regularly, automatically. But, suddenly, the laser went dead, uncharged. He hesitated, rose. He turned just in time to see the hellion dive on the turret. Nothing stopped it. With a sudden chill, Delvecchio realized that the forcefield was out.

Laser rifles reached out and touched the hellion, but not the turret laser. The turret was still silent. The hellion hit the windows with a crash, smashing through, shattering glass and plastic and duralloy struts.

Delvecchio began to move back toward the ramp and the entry port. A slinker rose as he darted by, snapped at his leg. There was a red blur of pain, fading quickly. He stumbled, rose again, moved. The leg was numb and bleeding. He used the useless laser as a crutch.

Inside, he hit the switch to shut the outer doors. Nothing happened. He laughed suddenly. It didn't matter. Nothing mattered. The station was breeched. The fields were down.

The inner doors still work. He moved through, limped through the halls out to the yard. Around him he could hear the generators dying.

The turret was hit again and again. It exploded and lifted moaning. Three separate impacts hit the tower at once. The top half rained metal.

Delvecchio stopped in the yard, looked at the tower suddenly unsure of where he was going. The word "Arnold" formed on his lips, but stayed there.

The generators quit completely. Lasers and missiles and swampbats steamed overhead. All was night lit by lightning. By explosions. By lasers.

Delvecchio retreated to a wall and propped himself against it. The barrage continued. The ground inside the station was torn, turned, shook. Once there was a scream somewhere as though someone was calling him in their moment of death.

He lowered himself to the ground and lay still, clutching the rifle while more shells pounded the station. Then all was silent.

Propped up against a rubble pile, he watched helplessly as a big slinker moved toward him across the yard. It loomed large in the rain, but before it reached him, it fell screaming.

There was movement behind him. He turned. A figure in skinthins waved, took up a position near one of the ruined laboratories.

Delvecchio saw shapes moving on what was left of the walls, scrambling over. He wished he had a charge for his laser. A red pencil of light flashed by him in the rain. One of the shapes crumbled. The man behind him had fired too soon, though, and too obviously. The other figured leveled on him. Stabs of laser fire went searing over Delvecchio's head. Answering fire came briefly, then stopped.

Slowly, slowly, Delvecchio dragged himself through the med, toward the labs. They didn't seem to see him. After an exhausting effort, he reached the fallen figure in skinthins. Sanderpay, dead.

Delvecchio took the laser. There were five men ahead of him, more in the darkness beyond. Lying on his stomach, Delvecchio fired at one man, then another and another. Steam geysers rose around him as the shapes in duralloy fired back. He fired and fired and fired until all those around him were down. Then he plucked himself up, and tried to run.

The heel was shot off his boot, and warmth flooded his foot. He turned and fired, moved on, past the wrecked tower and the labs.

Laser stabs peeled overhead. Four, five, maybe six of them. Delvecchio dropped what had been a lab wall. He fired around the wall, saw one shape fall. He fired again. Then the rifle died on him.

Lasers tore into the wall, burning in, almost through. The men fanned. There was no hope.

Then the night exploded into fire and noise. A body, twisted flat, spun by. A stab of laser fire came on the teeth of the explosion, from behind Delvecchio.

Sheridan stood over him, firing into the men caught in the open, burning them down one by one. He quit firing for an instant, lobbed a vial of explosive, then went back to the laser. He was hit by a chunk of flying rubble, went down.

Delvecchio came back up as he did. They stood unsteadily. Sheridan wheeling and looking for the targets. But there were no more targets. Sheridan was coughing from exertion inside his skinthins.

The rain lessened. The pain increased.

They picked their way through the rubble. They passed many twisted bodies in duralloy, a few skinthins. Sheridan paused at one of the armored bodies, turned it over. The faceplate had been burned away with part of the face. He kicked it back over.

Delvecchio tried another. He lifted the helmet off, searched the nostrils, the forehead, the eyes, the ears. Nothing.

Sheridan had moved away, and was standing over a body in skinthins half covered by rubble. He stood there for a long time. "Delvecchio!" he called finally. "*Delvecchio!*"

Delvecchio walked to him, bent, pulled off the fil termask. The man was still alive. He opened his eyes "Oh, God, Jim," he said. "Why? Oh, *why?*"

Delvecchio didn't say anything. He stood stock still and stared down.

Bill Reyn stared back up.

"I got through, Jim," said Reyn, coughing blood "Once the flier was down...no trouble. Close...I walked it. They...they were still inside mostly with the heat. Only a few...had gone out."

Delvecchio coughed once, quietly.

"I got through...the vaccine...most, anyway. A few had gone out, infected...no hope. But...but, we took away their armor and their weapons. No harm that way...we...had to fight our way through. Me it...left alone, but, God, those guys in duralloy lost some men...leeches...slinkers."

Sheridan turned and dropped his rifle. He began to run toward the labs.

"We tried the suit radios, Jim... but the storm. should have waited, but the vaccine...short term... wearing off...we tried not...to hurt you...started killing us..."

He began to choke on his own blood. Delvecchio helpless, looked down. "Again," he said in a voice that was dead and broken. "We underestimated it again. We—no, I—I—"

Reyn did not die for another three or four hours Delvecchio never found Sheridan again. He tried to restart the generators alone, but to no avail.

Just before dawn the skies cleared. The stars came through bright and white against the night sky. The fungus had not yet released new spores. It was almost like a moonless night on Earth.

Delvecchio sat atop a mound of rubble. A dead soldier's laser rifle in his hands. Ten or eleven charges on his belt. He did not look off to where Reyn lay. He was trying to figure out how to get the radio working. There was a supply ship coming.

The sky to the east began to lighten. A swamp bat, then another, began to circle the ruins of Grey water Station.

And the spores began to fall.

Antony Paschos is a Greek author with short stories in Metaphorosis, Channel, Hyphenpunk *and other magazines. He has also published two books and several short stories in Greek. He is a member of the Athens Club of Science Fiction, and lives in Athens.*

A FLYING ARK FOR THE GHOST DOLPHINS

by Antony Paschos

I pass the lammeter across the dolphin skull and the gauge flutters. There are at least a few life-amperes left in it; radiation hasn't nullified its ghost yet. I eye it through the turbidness of my mask's lens. Smudged, dried up bone—it reminds me of a pelican with teeth. I throw it in my rucksack with the rest of the skulls.

My soles sink in the layer of muck that covers a floor littered with plastic parts, clay-crusted buckets, crumpled boxes. Careful steps, avoiding anything sharp. Frayed vinyl walls surround me. At a corner of the pool, hooked on a deckchair's frame, a shred of fabric flits with the feebleness of a dying sparrow; and that's probably the closest thing to a living creature I've seen today.

I climb the ladder out of the abandoned pool. A light wind stirs the dust and a film of dirt clouds my lens. It dims the rays of the sun dipping behind the zoo's walls. The plaster on them, once molded to imitate amber masonry is now blanched to a ghastly sepia.

A *clang* from the aquarium's entrance. I've grown a deaf ear to creaks and screeches but I've parked my pickup truck outside, so I hurry up anyway.

I take a look around the Toyota Hilux that I've been using lately. Nothing. What did I expect? I climb on its truck bed and empty my rucksack in an open crate. A dolphin, a shark, a seal and the rest of the sea creatures' skulls that I couldn't find at the fishmonger stalls. Elpida would have saved all the Earth's species if she could. Not me; I'm content with gathering the ones I promised her.

A *clang*, again. This time I'm certain, it came from the aquarium's reception building. I sigh—my lens fogs momentarily, my breath stinks of starvation.

I jump down and, feeling like an idiot, I go and check. Four walls, a window, a broken table and a lonely rock sitting on top of the dust blanket as if someone just threw it. I shudder; that's impossible. No one's here and I could probably loiter around safely forever, as I used to in the first days after I lost Elpida. No, I'm just wasting time, while my bra digs into my flesh and the radiation suit's tight fit has chafed my armpits.

I rush back to my Hilux and clamber on its truck bed. I take great care as I hammer a couple of nails through each crate cover—now that I'm finished, it would be a misfortune to pierce a glove.

Next comes driving; the easy part. Tomorrow I'll have to fly a fifty-ton jet aircraft with no experience other than a flight simulator.

A few minutes later, I pass through the ruined cargo gate of Eleftherios Venizelos airport. The truncated tower sprouts from the heap of piled debris, its top floors now collapsed. A Boeing 737 careens on one wing, its nose rammed between two gaping boarding bridges. More jets are left to rot here and there, one lacks an engine.

I get to the only aircraft that still works: an Airbus 320. There's no free space left in its cargo compartment, so I grab a box from my Hilux and climb the stairs to its front door. I jam it amidst two seats and carry on with unloading the rest. I leave the last one with the dolphin skull at the front row. When I'm finished, my suit's inner lining is sticky with sweat.

I stand on the front galley and take a look at the cabin. Crates everywhere; mounted on seats, brimming the aisle.

"I told you that I'd keep my promise, didn't I?"

My voice sounds loud inside my mask. There's nobody to answer in thousands of miles and ghosts don't speak.

Though everyone seemed to adopt the use of this word after the discovery of life currents, Elpida never approved of it. She recited the scientists' words who said that the life currents that the bones emit—especially their skulls—are just another type of molecular activity, that happens to be only good for cloning and diminishes with radiation. They've nothing to do with ghosts; they're not reflections of the dead, just remnants. Even less, memories. I didn't mind agreeing with her, until I lost her.

I scale down the stairs. I open my Hilux's door and take a moment to stare at the white giant behind me. "How the hell am I going to fly this thing?"

The shower's coolness dries on my skin as I rush to the kitchen table. There's a lammeter and a small aluminum box; I open it with soggy fingers and fish out the silky pouch that's inside. I scan it and the gauge springs. I breathe out.

Back when I first put the pouch in here, I used to talk to it regularly. Talking dwindled to murmuring goodmornings and whispering goodnights.

My clothes are warm and smell of shampoo. I use whatever is left in the fallout shelter's storage, I've quit raiding marts since Elpida and the rest of the crew perished at that landslide, whilst searching for rare animal skulls. As if the ones in the zoo weren't enough.

I've logged enough hours of flight simulation, so tonight I won't turn on the computer. The transceiver's static noise, the ventilator fan's buzz and the generator's rumble will escort my dinner. Does it sound like this in the cockpit when you actually fly a jet? I guess, come tomorrow, I'll know.

The sun lurks behind Hymettos mountain, excreting a sore purple at the sky's roots. The runway extends like a lengthy carpet, blurry lines delimiting its edges of soil-primed tarmac from the ditches left and right, as they fade faraway into the haze.

I breathe the moment in—a smell of plastic and sweat inside my mask. The cockpit's gray panels, labyrinths of pushbuttons and six displays with the aircraft's instruments and indications. I fondle the aluminum box that I've placed on the pedestal, between the thrust lever and the parking brake.

The mere fact that your dear ones leave something behind—even if it's some kind of current lingering in bones that people erroneously called ghosts—ties another thread of connection to the dead. Most people in the shelter kept their beloved ones' skull. Now, their own skulls are inside my cargo.

But not Elpida's. She had promised to sit by my side, and she will, one way or another.

Burying these bones in a vault, so that the earth's animal heritage can be cloned in the distant future, was her dream. Flying them, was mine. I've memo-

rized the Airbus procedures and I've been through its manuals. I used to rush to Elpida, with bits of information—damn, this clunker uses a fucking 086 processor!—the same way she used to come up to me after an excited find: "look, Nina, this mammoth's skull has still 0.01 life-amperes left; perhaps it could be cloned in the future!"

I'd reply that perhaps, when aliens come around they'll clone creatures from bones with depleted currents—I wouldn't dare call them ghostless in front of her. The lack in humor, I made up with sour comments.

I sigh. "Yes, baby." My fingers, all sweaty inside my gloves, stop drumming on the thrust levers. "This must be the stupidest of ideas. But now, we're clear for takeoff."

I move the levers up a notch. The jet engines lag then their blowing rustle turns into a whirring noise—quite different than the shelter's ventilator fan.

What was that knock? Did it come from the turbines? Probably no, the left engine's temperature is slightly higher but all indications are within limits. Maybe a box dropped from a seat, back in the cabin. The aircraft starts to build up speed.

Takeoff power. The aircraft yaws slightly; I press on the rudder pedals with trembling feet, struggling to keep the center line. No warning chimes, the aircraft is light and accelerates quickly to one hundred and forty knots, shaking and bouncing, like my Hilux on its crippled shock absorbers. I pull the stick aft gently, the nose lifts up and the miracle that I've been waiting for the past years becomes reality, the bumps cease, the aircraft's attitude rises so high that the instrument panel blocks my front view, the stumped tower on my window shrinks and, for the first time in my lifetime, I fly.

Everything happens faster than in the flight simulator and I forget things; I delay to raise the gear, to retract the flaps. I turn the autopilot on, but nonetheless I remain busy scanning instruments and indications. When I let myself pee in my diapers for the first time, I've already climbed at thirty-six thousand feet and haven't gazed out of the windshield yet.

Two different seas stretch below me; the inky waters of the Aegean and the tawny haze polluting the earth; the jaundiced dazzle of the rising sun coalescing their limit. The mountains of the Peloponnese jut out of the blurry morass; dismembered wind turbines are perked on their ashen crests, one still rotating its blades languidly. Clusters of gaunt houses cling to the wounded slopes like hollow limpets; crags the color of liver; cliffs from old quarries' gashes, the soil's purulent crust an arid ecru.

Is this vast emptiness the view that I longed for? I reach out for the aluminum box. Its coldness seems to pierce through my gloves, like the solitude of this uninhabited landscape penetrating me to the bone. I search in the high frequency band until the speakers broadcast a well-known message:

"…you are not alone! We run a sanctuary near Cairo. We have medication, food, equipment. We offer help. Come at first morning light to the entrance of the Egyptian Museum or contact us in the following frequencies…"

While the voice repeats the message in Arabic, I transmit and wait. The unknown language sounds distant, forlorn.

"Hello, Nina! Have you checked in for today's flight?"

I sigh. Elpida used to say that I'm devoid of humor because I must've been cloned from a bone with low life current. "Actually, Uthman, right now I'm cruising at thirty-six thousand feet over…" Scattered swollen earthen tumors germinate out from the sea. "Over the Cyclades, probably."

"Oh, damn, Nina, that's great! And what about our passengers? The fish?"

It's not the right time to argue about species classification. "You mean the dolphins and the seals. They'll have coffee service in a while, I guess." Sometimes I try to mimic humor though. People seem to appreciate it.

"Okay, so, Nina, I've got a couple of aviation fans by my side, who would kill to be your first officers. I've also got three working trucks and volunteers to drive them to the vault after you land. It wasn't easy, you know. People around here value their survival more than the planet's gene heritage. Can't blame them, to be honest."

Yes, you can, but let's not get into that kind of conversation. Elpida said that she was lucky to bump into Uthman on the other side of the radio, as he was easy to convince—easier than me or the rest of our shelter's crew. Maybe it wasn't luck; maybe it took someone who could buy into saving animal genes, to keep radio watch for years. A dreamer. Someone who called the life currents, ghosts.

Then comes a bump again. Muffled through my mask, it sounds like the one I heard before takeoff. Perhaps another crate fell down? Or some screws have loosened and the pressure difference is stretching the fuselage?

"All right, Uthman, I've got some work to do. Talk to you later."

"Work? Doesn't the piece of junk you're flying have an autopilot?"

"You've caught me. I'd like to contemplate the landscape. I don't know when they'll roster me for another flight."

He cackles—Elpida would be proud of me. And I used to frown at her when she'd say that jokes can help you evade pointless chit-chat. "Nina, as soon as you land, you might as well apply for stand-ups. The council keeps nagging that we're short of comedians."

"I'll stick to the aviation business, thank you."

"That won't be easy, you know. You'd have to come up with a proper excuse…"

Another bump. My thought leaps to yesterday's clang in the aquarium. But this is different; this is a knock on wood, like someone rapping on a door. Someone or something is in the cabin.

The manuals have a definition for the moment you freeze after a failure or a shock: startle effect—

Knock.

The cockpit door is sturdy; I could proceed to my destination and find out what's going on when I'm safe on the ground. But my ride is smooth, Cairo is more than five hundred nautical miles away and I ache with curiosity.

"Nina, are you ok?" Uthman sounds worried.

"Yeah… Why?"

"Cause I've been talking to you and you don't answer."

"Well—"

Knock.

"Wait a minute, Uthman."

I unbuckle my seatbelt and my glance falls on the pedestal. "I'll be right back, baby."

As I open the cockpit door, I hear Uthman behind me: "Sure, Nina. Go on and send my regards to your fish. We wouldn't want to rebuild an earth without them, would we?"

Elpida never spoke of rebuilding the earth. She reckoned a visit from outer space more probable and wanted to make sure that cloning the extinct species from their bones would be possible. From her hopes placed on aliens and the lack of faith in humanity's own ability to recover, I shared only the second.

I leave Uthman's comment unanswered.

The beating of my heart shakes the cabin in a rhythmical turbulence. My trembling hand wriggles the aircraft's crash axe—I took it from its holster in the cockpit, you never know. I stand in the front galley, listening to my heavy breathing; the heat inside my suit and mask is building up. Three crates have collapsed and are piled in front of me. A *knock* and the box at the bottom jolts.

Ghosts are not supposed to communicate, let alone knock. Elpida was right, we shouldn't even call them ghosts; they're nothing more than some short of currents only good for cloning. *And we found a way to kill them too, with radiation, didn't we,* I think as I remove the two upper boxes. The nails on the remaining one's cover jut out like rusty stems. It's the one with the dolphin skull. I open it. A quick peek stimulates a second startle effect, way more physical than the first one: I stumble and fall back, the diapers scratching the roots of my thighs.

There are no skulls inside the crate. Just a tufted head and a skinny body draped in rags. A child, wearing no protective equipment at all.

The kid screams, springs up and darts to the aisle, scrambling over crates and seats.

"Wait!" I yell, but he gets to the aft galley and hides inside the lavatory.

I leave the crash axe where I dropped it—it's just a child—and scurry to the back, pushing crates out of the way.

I beat on the lavatory door. "Listen, kid… I'm not going to hurt you."

No answer.

"Look… I'm coming in now, all right?"

Silence. I open the door.

He's crouched on the toilet lid, knees to the chest and shivering. His torn jeans are wet at his thighs—if it wasn't for my mask, I bet this place would stink worse than an overused latrine.

"How did you end up here?"

No answer.

Back when Elpida and the rest of our crew were plowing southern Greece in search of bones with strong life currents, they had found evidence suggesting the existence of survivors. Maybe they had died recently or maybe they had modified a military camp's fallout shelter appropriately. Could this kid have escaped from such a place? A knot climbs up my throat; for how long has he been exposed to radiation? How much time left till the first blemish on the skin, the first vomit? Is he trembling because of the pain?

"I won't hurt you. Are you ok?"

The kid looks up; flaxen hair, sharp cheekbones, dry lips, huge eyes, the color of cobalt. She's a girl. Her starry gaze unlocks all protective instincts inside me with an almost perceptible *clack.*

Then she speaks.

"What?"

She speaks again. The language sounds Slavic and I don't understand a word, but maybe someone in Uthman's place does.

I extend my gloved hand. "Come."

The girl sits on the first officer's seat, scrawny arms coiled around knees, kinked like a clasp knife. She jolts at the voice coming from the speakers: "Nina are you there?"

I gesture at her to calm down, then I grab the microphone. "Yes, Uthman. Give me a minute."

According to the navigation display, acquiring position from the inertial reference systems, and my little knowledge of geography, we're now flying over Crete. The island, with its rugged, anhydrous ridges, is resting on the sea's surface like a gigantic crocodile cadaver.

I turn to the girl. "Are you ok?"

She waves her thumb at her mouth and stutters a word that I get: "voda."

I've brought no supplies; in case of an accident, I'd prefer to commit suicide before I suffer any symptoms

"Wait."

I find an old coffee pot at the front galley and put it under the espresso maker. I guess that she won't mind if the water has been deposited in the aircraft's unused tank for years. The first three spurts have a muddy hue but the fourth is almost clear. I fill the jug with boiled water and bring it back to the cockpit.

She grabs it with two hands.

"Careful. It's hot."

"Nina?"

"Yes, Uthman, sorry 'bout that. Seems that I've got a passenger."

She empties the aluminum jug with thirsty gulps.

"A… A cockroach or something?"

The myth of the cockroaches' survival. I remember a guy who was scared that sooner or later we would be devoured by a horde of them. I guess he wasn't the only one.

"A girl."

Silence. The vast Mediterranean Sea stretches in front of us.

"And no, Uthman, I'm not trying humor."

"How… How did that happen?"

"I don't know. She doesn't speak Greek, nor English."

"And… is she ok?"

"She looks fine, but she's not wearing any kind of protection. And judging by her rags, she must have been exposed for a long time."

"Poor child… maybe we can help her to a quick death after your arrival."

"I'm not sure if you'll have to."

"Wha… What do you mean, Nina?"

"Look, Uthman, do you have anyone who speaks Bulgarian or something?"

"Wait."

I point at the pot in the girl's hands. "Want a second one?"

She nods. I refill it and fetch it; now she waits for it to get cold.

"Hello?" New voice, Bulgarian accent.

"Hi."

"You must be Nina, yes? My name is Ivo. Where's the child?"

"Sitting right next to me. She can hear you."

He speaks, in Bulgarian obviously, and the girl jolts. She turns and looks at me puzzled. I bring the microphone to her mouth and press the button.

"Here."

They start talking. At every transmission his voice rises; he's now yelling, like he's cursing or threatening her. The girl pulls away from the microphone, tucks her hands into her armpits and looks at me, shaking her head.

I press the pushbutton: "what's going on here?"

"Well, Nina…" He sounds stupefied. "The girl is called Galina and she must be a compulsive liar."

"Why?"

"Cause what she told me makes no sense…"

What was his name again? Ah, yeah, "Ivo, be clear please."

"Yes, sorry… Look… She says that she used to live with her mom until she died… She mentioned a city called Sarisa?"

"Larisa. It was a city in central Greece."

"Okay. So, she claims that they lived there, outside. No fallout shelter, no cave… Nothing. And, supposedly, she walked all the way to Athens! Then she spied on you and hid inside the box."

And she threw that rock to get me away from my truck. Not a bad plan. But people living outside? This changes things.

"Nina, do you hear me?" It's Uthman.

"I do."

"Listen, we want you to bring her to us."

"Well," I start to speak, but the small box on the pedestal pulls my gaze and I don't utter that, sure, we're coming. Elpida's voice rings inside my head: what about the dolphins?

They're not real dolphins, Elpida. These are just their skulls. You can find skulls anywhere.

Sure, but what about their life currents, Nina? Radiation isn't evenly spread, you know that. Though it's supposed to finally subside in Africa, it must've already nullified most of the remaining bones there. You don't know how much time your skulls have left either, if they're left exposed.

Then what about the water? Surely some dolphin skulls will lie in the depths, safe from radiation.

And how long till they decompose, Nina? In the vault they'll be in sterilized conditions. Their life currents will linger for centuries to come.

A conversation repeated many times, ending usually with Elpida telling me it's fine if you

GALAXY'S EDGE

don't want to help, I'll just fly the plane by my-self, Nina.

I don't have time for this. This is no ghost I'm speaking to, no life current either. This is me talking to myself and I need to quit that and think.

"Nina?"

Uthman's voice stuns me for a second. "Yes."

"I was asking, where are you?"

"Hmmm... I've just crossed Crete. But I've got a little situation."

If I go on to Cairo, the girl will hijack everyone's attention in Uthman's shelter—a person who might be able to resist radiation reshuffles the deck. They might even postpone the whole mission; and even if they don't, I guess that I'd be lucky if they simply hurry to dump my load into the vault and seal it with cement.

"I said, what's wrong, Nina? Is the aircraft..."

"The aircraft's fine. But the girl... Galina was hiding inside the crate with the bones from the aquarium. And she has emptied it."

"So?"

"So, we're short on dolphin, seal and shark skulls."

Would they wait for me to fetch any of those? I could ask him, but he'll probably agree to anything just to make me stick to the plan. And when I get there, it might be too late for those species.

"And the easiest place where I can find those skulls is the aquarium back in Athens," I add.

Silence.

"No. The answer is no."

"I didn't ask, Uthman."

"Nina, listen to me, please. Risking your life over some fish is your own business... But now you've got a child who might have survived the radiation for years. So, first you'll bring her to us, and then you may go wherever you like."

"Uthman, you know, you're in no position to give orders."

"I know. Yet I'm appealing to your common sense. Think, Nina. This child could be our last hope. The animals' last hope! I know that you've lost your faith in humanity, but..."

"Spare me this conversation, Uthman."

This is not just about the missing skulls. Elpida had me promise her long before that landslide. Instead of exchanging melodramatic vows of eternal love, she used to ask me: what kind of Earth would it be without dolphins?

"All right. So, what are you going to do?"

According to my flight computer, I can land in Cairo with one and a half ton of fuel left. If I turn back now and fly back to Athens, I'll need to refuel which might require some effort. But if there's one place I can do this, this is Eleftherios Venizelos Airport.

Galina's glance swings from me to the jug. I feel a pang of guilt as I gesture at her to wait. But if she made it all the way to the zoo from Larissa, surely she can hold on for a couple of days in case I return to Athens. Plus, I've got some spare radiation suits in my shelter.

I sigh.

"Nina, you have to learn to answer out loud. But, believe in you. I know you'll make the right choice."

I reach for the autopilot panel. I pull the heading knob out and turn it, changing the aircraft's course by one hundred and eighty degrees. The wings start to bank—a loud bang and the hull judders violently; a second bang, and the aircraft starts to yaw. A chime rings repetitively, the left engines' indications turn red, the gauges begin a dance of fluctuations and there's a message in the upper display:

ENGINE ONE FAIL.

According to the manuals, I have to follow the procedure described on the upper display; retard the left engine's thrust lever, turn off its master switch, then turn it on again and hope for a relight. Meantime, the aircraft's nose gets higher while the speed decays. Galina is throwing horrified glances at me.

Startle effect, I have to get over it. Think; yes, know what's going on: the autopilot can't hold such a high altitude with one engine. I stop turning the aircraft—I'll work out my options in a while—and start to descend. After a few failed relight attempts I go on with the procedure: turn off the failed engine's master switch, push its fire pushbutton, select continuous ignition on the functioning one and open the fuel cross-feed valve to feed it.

I level off at twenty-five thousand feet; speed is stable, nose is not rising; the aircraft can maintain this altitude and I'm heading to Cairo.

62

I breathe out and pee in my diapers again. They're wet already, but, hey; I've just handled an engine failure on my first flight.

"What did you decide, Nina?"

"Well, it seems that I've lost an engine. And, no it's no joke, Uthman."

Silence. Then: "Okay, the guys in here ask if you've tried to relight it. And do you need any help?"

"Yes and no. The engine won't start up."

"So, can you get here?"

"Actually…" According to my flight computer, I should land in Cairo with… Minus two hundred kilos. Flying single engine at a lower altitude has increased consumption. "Maybe."

"Good. We'll be waiting for you."

"I didn't say I'm coming."

"What are you talking about?"

"I can go back to Athens as well, Uthman."

I bet that in the half minute of muteness, they're discussing ways to persuade me.

"What's wrong with you, Nina? Do those fish bones mean more than a child's life to you?"

"Off with that shit, Uthman. The child will be fine at my place."

"Then what about humanity, Nina?"

If I return to Athens, I can forget about this aircraft; I'll have to find another one and this might prove a hard task, since most of them were totally wrecked. Still, flying to Cairo might not improve my odds either. Even if I find an airworthy plane to fly from there, I'll have to convince Uthman's people not to seal the vault with cement and wait for me to fetch the rest of the bones.

"Nina, think… What if there's a way to survive radiation? Would you deprive humanity… Would you deprive *us* of our last hope?"

What Uthman ignores is that if this was a humanity versus bones argument then I would have already turned back to Athens without second thought. We had had our opportunities, we had had our warnings. We chose to fight against each other instead. I couldn't care less about giving humanity a second chance. What I do care about is my promise to Elpida, and my promise was giving a second chance to the rest of the species.

But I'm not dealing just with humanity in here. I've got a living girl on the first officer's seat beside me. And she might not speak Greek or English, but her eyes are fixed on mine, desperate for any kind of reassurance.

"Nina, I know you don't believe in God, but this is a sign. This could be your life's mission. Don't disdain it, I'm begging you."

I avoid Galina's gaze. What would Elpida do in my shoes? I close my eyes. The aluminum box feels smooth under my gloved fingertips. I rub it as if to warm it. I open my eyes and dare to meet Galina's stare. Then, I pull my hand away from the box.

This is not some vague concept of humanity as an ensemble that's guilty for destroying this planet. This is me and this is Galina. And her best chance—our best chance—lies ahead.

Elpida had said that humans tend to fixate on the positive outcome of a risk. I'd reply that this trait played a part in the mess that we made out of our planet and she'd say that perhaps humans never thought there was a risk.

Funny thing; I just did the same when I decided.

Less than half a ton of fuel remains inside my tanks, when Africa's coastline surfaces on the ulcerated horizon, a vague cinnamon stripe of fog rooting the firmament to the oceanic carpet. I could still divert to Alexandria but I've no idea of the runway's condition. I can only hope that I'll be able to glide my way to Cairo.

I'm not lying when I say to myself that I'll do my best to keep my promise to her. I won't let anyone seal the vault before I fetch the missing skulls. I'll fucking block them with my own body if needed.

But I need to land this aircraft first.

The layer of fog looks thinner when I fly above it; I can make out the River Nile and after a while some triangular caps: the pyramids. Then the second engine bangs and starts to shake, the chime jangles and finally I face the negative outcome of the risk I took:

DUAL ENGINE FAILURE.

Galina tries to jolt from her seat but I've got her buckled up. I go through the checklist's actions. I turn on the auxiliary power unit to recover all my electrics, air conditioning and the autopilot. Then I start a shallow descent.

"Okay, Uthman. I'm going down."

"Where are you?"

"Eighty nautical miles north of Cairo."

"Do you see any landmarks? Anything?"

"Not really. I'll let you know after the crash."

"All right, Nina. Good luck."

Sweat is fogging the bottom of my lens. The auxiliary power unit is too far back in the tail to be heard, but the aerodynamic noise and the air conditioning drone are deafening. A spark of regret: what would've happened if I had turned back to Athens? No use thinking about it now; I get closer and closer to the ground. Through the layer of dust, I make out a boulevard crossing the desert, ruined buildings scattered at both sides. Using it as a runway is not an option; it will be laden with traffic signs and electricity pylons—whatever is left of them anyway. However, if I find a nearby flat field and survive the crash, Uthman will locate us easily.

The engines are windmilling, powering up the hydraulic pumps, so I manage to lower the flaps. I pull out the knob on the pedestal—close to the aluminum box—turn it three times, and gravity extends the landing gear. I'm set for landing, though the aircraft's drag has increased immensely and it plunges in a steep dive.

I disconnect the autopilot and wiggle the stick a bit; the aircraft is responsive. The radio altimeter comes alive with a male mechanical voice: two thousand five hundred. The warning springs up on top of Galina's chanting of the same unknown words. She's trembling at the corner of my eye. Two thousand and the fog welcomes us in its bister haze, hiding the soaring terrain.

In a single moment, the sweat inside my suit freezes. I'm flying blind.

One thousand.

Something touches my right hand resting on the thrust levers; Galinas' palm. I clench it in my glove.

Five hundred. Fortunately, the ground materializes again, staunch and definite and dead as it always was. My choice is easy: there's a large patch of open land close to the highway.

Two hundred. Buildings and electricity pylons grow larger and they dash out of sight rapidly, as if I'm accelerating—the effect of flying low. Galina's grip tightens; she has quit praying.

One hundred.

I pull the stick aft to cut down the rate of descent. Fifty. Forty. Thirty. I hold the aircraft, the speed reduces. Thirty. Signs and road curves and the torn land hurtle back. Twenty. I pull the plane's nose higher—ten—and I fix my gaze at the hazy horizon. Ten. Breathless silence. Ten—again. Five.

The aircraft sinks abruptly and the main wheels bump down. I release the stick, the front wheel touches down too, and the aircraft starts to bounce on the rugged soil. I step on the brakes hard. From straight ahead a ditch charges headlong at full speed. I press harder and try to turn but it's too late; the plane falls in the ditch and the front panel thrusts to my forehead, once, twice; darkness.

I open my eyes and see everything through a coppery brume. The front panel has collapsed and is hanging in front of fractured displays, stained with a dark splotch. My aluminum box has somehow fallen on the floor between my legs. Everything is blotched, even the drab cloud that floods the cracked windshield, as if I've sunk in a sea of rust—no, the specks are on my lens.

A smell of sweat and dust and urine, unknown words. Galina scrambles on the pedestal and unbuckles my seatbelt. There's something about her squeals, an odd clarity. Has the crash sharpened my sense of hearing?

The tight suit adheres to my skin. A warm wetness on my forehead, an itch on my eyebrow. A deep breath, a mouthful of torrid air, crunchy, like a bite full of sand; I cough. Something's wrong, I fumble my lens…

I feel the sleek plastic of my glove on my skin. My mask is torn above my brow. I'm breathing unfiltered air. I nudge Galina away, reach for my rucksack, grope inside frantically until I find the duct tape. No, I need to wash my skin first, but water is not safe either. Fuck it, I swiftly tape my mask, smearing my gloves with blood—damn, my left glove's wrist is torn as well. I tape that too. I hop up from the chair—a stinging pain in my knee, I fall down. Did I break something?

I sit on the pedestal and go through the rest of my suit. Except for scratches and creases, it's intact. Yet, I've been exposed.

"Nina?"

Fuck you, Uthman. You and your shelter and this fool's errand. My stare stumbles on the box, fuck you too…

No. I pick it up and fondle its lid. I resist the temptation to check on it with the lammeter; crashes aren't supposed to affect a skull's current—a skull's ghost. Then again, screw that, I reach for my rucksack…

I hear Galina sobbing. She's cowering in a corner. "Nina?"

Uthman can wait; I open my arms. "Here… Galina…"

She rubs her face with the back of her palm.

"Come."

She stands up—cheeks and nose begrimed—and collapses in my arms. How long has it been since I hugged someone?

"Nina, are you ok?"

Kid nestled in my lap, I seize the microphone. "Yes, Uthman, I survived the crash."

"And… And the child?"

"Galina's fine."

The dust cloud settles in clusters of shriveling ochre cysts, like bunches of grapes drying up in fast-forward. No, wait, some shapes are conical and curved and protrude like fins emerging and sinking in again like… they're like a pack of dolphins riding a troubled amber sea! Like the ghosts of dolphins—no, my mind plays tricks on me. I blink, but they're still dancing. I blink again and now I see only fog thinning fast. And out of its dissipation, a cubic cement mass and a traffic sign slowly materialize.

"Listen, Uthman, I see a highway and a sign… Cairo, 5 km, Alexandria 170… Oh and there's also a destroyed mart or something—does the word 'Issam' ring a bell?"

"Wait…" Silence. "Okay, we know where you are, Nina. Stay put. We're coming to get you."

I walk around the white Airbus 320 and check on the wheels, the turbines and the fuselage with the blue-lined logo of Horus, the sky deity in Egyptian mythology.

Uthman waits for me under a brick building's hefty shade.

He had told me the truth. Their fallout shelter is huge, harboring more than two hundred people. A small group of scientists that they had assembled were all stunned to discover that radiation gradually faded out of Galina's body, leaving no detectable damage. Unfortunately, it didn't work the same way for me.

Dressed in a T-shirt and jeans, she stands with Ivo, the translator, close to Uthman, whose mask almost conceals a forced smile.

"Well, finally you found a reason to stick to the aviation business, didn't you?"

"Why not? The prospects are looking good lately."

He laughs. I'm keen to fly to Athens and back to retrieve the missing skulls instead of searching for a nearby aquarium, so I took at his word that radiation has killed all the ghosts on Africa's surface.

"So, I'll see you tomorrow, Nina. Don't worry. We're not burying any bones until you return. Just try to land on a runway this time."

I smile as we share a gloved handshake. Then I fondle Galina's hair.

I grope in my rucksack and take out the small box. I kiss it; I kiss *her*; through my mask, through the aluminum lid, through the silk pouch, through all the cold barriers that separate my lips from her.

"Soon," I whisper. Then I squat and hand it over to Galina.

"Can you hold on to this for me please?"

Ivo translates and Galina nods. A tear streaks down her cheek.

"You'll give it back to me tomorrow."

If I come back, that is. Luckily all the skulls survived the crush—some a bit cracked—and I've already instructed Uthman to bury it with them, in case I don't return.

Galina replies. The translator says: "She wants you to promise that you'll come back."

I smile. "I will. I do."

I get up. "Thanks for everything, Uthman."

"Don't thank me yet. Don't forget, our scientists need you as a test subject."

Harmless lies. I don't share their hopes of discovering a way to make the human body resistant to radiation. I can settle with less: Galina growing old, Elpida's skull buried in the vault among the dolphins and the rest of the animals; and perhaps, perhaps my own remains lying beside her.

Jean Marie Ward writes fiction, nonfiction and everything in between. Her credits include a multi-award nominated novel, numerous short stories and two popular art books. The former editor of CrescentBlues.com, she is a frequent contributor to Galaxy's Edge *and ConTinual, the convention that never ends. Learn more at JeanMarieWard.com*

COMPUTER SCIENCE, COMMERCIALS, AND KUNG FU: *GALAXY'S EDGE* INTERVIEWS WESLEY CHU

by Jean Marie Ward

Computer science professional, martial arts student, gamer, actor, stuntman, writer—Wesley Chu has led almost as many lives the eponymous, mind-hopping alien at the heart of Chu's award-winning debut novel, The Lives of Tao. These days, however, all those lives have been pressed into the service of his writing—a passion ignited when he first glimpsed the bright dragons, snakes, and swords adorning the covers of the science fiction and fantasy novels at a local bookstore. Fantasy was Chu's first love. But at the start of his writing career, it proved easier to translate the absurdist comedy of office life into the science fictional adventures of Roen, an ordinary guy possessed by a bossy alien determined to save the world. Chu wrote six novels in the universe of Roen and Tao, as well as a time-travel duology, an urban fantasy trilogy in collaboration with Cassandra Clare, and Typhoon, a Walking Dead tie-in novel set in China. Through them all, the desire to write a big fantasy like those that first inspired him remained undimmed.* Galaxy's Edge *caught up with Chu shortly before the release of* The Art of Prophecy, *the first book in* The War Arts Saga, *the character-driven, high-octane, kung fu epic he's been working toward since his life-changing visit to that Nebraska bookstore so many years ago.*

Galaxy's Edge: When did you realize you wanted to be a writer?

Wesley Chu: I answer that question differently now than four or five years ago, because I have a two- and

a five-year-old now. So, a lot of how I felt and how thought when I was a kid is viewed from a differen lens now that I have children.

I wanted to be a writer from the second or third grade; I think that was when I really discovered sto ries. I moved from Taiwan to Nebraska when I wa five years old, back in the early Eighties. My father i an English professor, which is why we moved. On of the things he did to help me learn English wa he took me to a bookstore, and he was like, "Picl a book." He was a Shakespeare professor. So, h wanted me pick up *Beowulf* or something like tha But instead, I beelined toward all the science fic tion books with the pictures of the dragons and th snakes and swords. I picked out two books. The firs one was *A Spell for Chameleon* by Piers Anthony, anc the second one was *The Misenchated Sword* by Law rence Watt-Evans.

I think *The Misenchanted Sword* was my gateway drug to fantasy. I learned English that way. I've al ways wanted to be a writer since then. In the third grade, I wrote this short story about the solar system and my father was impressed. He was like, "Thi does not suck," which in traditional Asian culture was actually a pretty good compliment.

I've always been a big reader, and when I was ap plying for college, I was like, "Dad, I'm gonna be ar English major, just like you. I'm gonna write book for a living, though."

His response was: "No, son, your wife will suffer."

So, I didn't. I went into computer science instead It took me about ten years to find my way back to writing after I had a whole other career in compute science and consulting, and I realized that it wasn' really making me happy.

I was thinking about this earlier when I saw tha question. When I was a kid, I wanted to be a whole bunch of things. I wanted to be a veterinarian, wanted to be like a firefighter, and I wanted to be a writer.

And I see what my kids like doing these days. Wha do they want to be? They talk about that kind of stuf

But what I don't see them do—which I also did as a kid—is follow up. I wanted to be a veterinarian, but it wasn't like I would go to the library and check out books on dog anatomy. There's a difference between wanting to do something and having a calling to do something. With writing, I wanted to be a writer and to support that I read more, I wrote some short stories. I followed up on things like that, which in hindsight, tells me now that maybe this was my calling because it was something more than just an impulsive desire.

GE: You mentioned your computer science background. How did that play into your first published book, *The Lives of Tao*?

WC: To be honest, I am not naturally a science fiction author. When I was a kid, and for most of my adulthood, I wrote fantasy. I wanted to be a fantasy author. I did not have any writing background or English background. No creative writing. So, when I started trying to write, my first book was this really, really terrible, low fantasy. It was the worst book ever. I always say it's my worst but also my most important book, because I made all my mistakes there. I cut my teeth learning how to write there.

When I finished that book, I trunked it. I realized that I wasn't at a level where I could write a fantasy novel competently and professionally. So, I did a little research, and I realized that "Write what you know" is one of those common tropes people use. And I wanted to write a story that I could handle where I was at. That became *The Lives of Tao*.

The Lives of Tao in many ways mirrored my own path. Roen became a super spy, but Roen's journey is the same as my journey, going from what I was doing to what I wanted to be and what I became. We followed mirrored paths, and because of that, I wrote what I knew, which was the corporate world, the martial arts, with some humor involved. It might have been a little bit too close, because when my father read an early draft of *The Lives of Tao*, he was like, "It's surprisingly good, son. But there's a problem with it. Your main character is likable but he's not that likable. Is he modeled after you?"

GE: Ouch.

WC: No, it's fine. I'll be honest, Roen is a little whiny, and Roen was real. He had all the annoying traits that real people sometimes have, that many times an author will not put into their characters, because first of all, they know better, but also because you need a main character that the reader can grasp upon. If you hate the main character, it's hard for you to like the book. So, on one hand, it was a risk to write him the way I wrote him. But on the other, it made him a lot more real and relatable.

GE: I didn't think he was too whiny.

WC: I made him less whiny because I had to find that balance, that humor.

GE: Was humor always part of the equation?

WC: Humor is kind of my natural style. I would say *The Lives of Tao* series is, probably up until this new book, my most real voice. I always tell people, "If you like me, you'll probably like *The Lives of Tao*. If you don't like me, you probably won't like *The Lives of Tao*." My personality, my sense of humor, the way I talk, to be honest, is similar to the narration for Tao.

GE: You also did something that absolutely terrifies me as an author: You let your dad read the manuscript and hammer on it.

WC: Yeah, that's a complicated relationship there.

When my father convinced me to go into computer science instead of becoming an English major, I did. If you ever look at engineers and people who do CS, you know we can't write worth shit. We're terrible at writing. Even our technical writing is often incoherent. When I pivoted to trying to write a book, it was my crutch, because after ten years of not writing full sentences, you kind of can't write full sentences, and now you're writing a book. My father taught ESL—he was a tenured professor, he taught Shakespeare, and in many ways, he was a grammar purist.

Back then, when I was a new writer, I didn't have experience. I believe very strongly that the purpose of grammar is not to be grammatically correct. The purpose of grammar is to support the story. It took me quite a few years to reach the conclusion that I can break these rules if it serves the story. But back then I didn't have the experience, I didn't have that skill set. So, my father, when he edited, would apply very strict grammar rules. It worked in a way, because sometimes it fixed a lot of my grammar problems, but also, sometimes it stilted the story. It was a good learning experience for me, because the answer is obviously somewhere in the middle. You want to be clear with the grammar, but you don't want the grammar to get in the way. So, it was definitely a good experience for me to have. These days, I don't ask my father to edit, not because he couldn't do, but because I'm now in the space where my grammar is strong enough. I also know when to break grammar to serve the story.

GE: I hope he still likes the stories.

WC: He reads every single one. I tell him not to buy any more copies, because they're expensive, especially the hardcover ones, but he keeps buying copies.

GE: I guess he likes you.

WC: Yeah, I keep the sales.

GE: Because of The Lives of Tao series, you're strongly associated with humor. But your second series, the Time Salvager series, was a hard turn into gritty, grimdark sci-fi. What prompted the shift?

WC: The truth is, when I first started writing *Time Salvager* I didn't even know what grimdark was. At the time, I was one of those guys where I read the ten authors that I loved. I wasn't as well-read. So, I didn't really know what grimdark was. *Time Salvager* definitely was a tonal shift that took some stretching. Part of it was because I wanted to stretch. I had just written three *Tao* books, and I had been in that voice for a while.

The concept for *Time Salvager* came to me through a dream. When I woke up, I was like, "Oh, my gosh, it's a great idea. It's a great concept. Now, let me explore the concept. Let me flesh it out and see what kind of story can grow out of it." The story that grew out of it was kind of dark. I think *Time Salvager* had moments of levity. But with what was happening with the characters, there wasn't as much room to be

funny because it got serious, and the main character was an alcoholic.

Once I got into that framework, that tonal shift just came naturally. When I write *Tao*, I don't intentionally try to be funny. It's the tone, it's that level, it's that frequency that my mind is operating at, and everything just comes out. When I wrote *Time Salvager* it was the exact same thing. I'm in this world now. I'm in these characters, and I'm trying to guide them through their decisions. I'd like to think that these people are organic, so when they make a decision I will honor that decision. When I follow their path, and they don't go towards levity, I don't do it. I view it as this is what's happening to them. This is what they're feeling and thinking.

GE: You've studied and worked in computer science. Now you write books. Most people who have that career path don't also include actor and stunt man in their resume. How did that come about?

WC: This will transition over to *The Art of Prophecy*. We moved from Taiwan to Nebraska when I was five years old. Nebraska back in the Eighties was super white. Super white. There were like five Asians in the whole state, and three of them were in my family. When you were an immigrant back then and didn't really speak English, your focus was a) to survive and b) you wanted to fit in. It was very much: "How do we be American? How do we exist and survive in this space?" Especially in the Midwest where there aren't that many Asians.

For me in many ways, the kung fu, the old samurai movies, the wushu genres were my bridge to my culture. I fell in love with the whole idea of kung fu and martial arts when I was a kid. As soon as I was old enough, I started training, and that really snowballed into everything else. At one point when I was training, a director came in looking for extras and stuntmen. This was for a low-budget movie, and I ended up getting cast as one of the main characters because when you do film, you can have as many takes as you want. You don't know how to act sometimes. I sort of learned to act afterward.

After I did that role, I took it more seriously. I became a [Screen Actors Guild] actor and got some stunt work on the side. In Chicago, though, most of it is commercials. There's a lot of commercial work, some features, some TV shows, but the majority of it is commercial work and independent stuff. That's how I got started. At one point, I was serious enough about acting that I thought I was going to move to LA. But then—this goes back to the idea of when you're a kid and you want to do something, how do you know if it's your calling? I enjoyed acting. I didn't love it. I thought it was cool. I thought it was interesting, but I wasn't a student of the craft. It was just a fun, cool thing to do.

That's when I realized that it wasn't my calling. While writing a book, it's *no matter what*. I'm one of those guys who will probably never retire. I will die at my desk when I'm eighty, ninety years old. I'll be in the middle of the act, writing a little bit of a chapter, and I'm just going to keel over. That's the difference from the relationship I have with these previous careers. I actually don't practice martial arts anymore, because after you do it for a long time, your body starts getting all busted up. But also, it's not where my passion is anymore.

GE: But you use it to augment your fight scenes and make sure they're realistic,

WC: Yes. I'm a big fan of having good fight scenes. That's one of the things I had to learn to pare down over the years. Learning to trim is very important for fight scenes.

GE: Do you still game?

WC: On the computer?

GE: Yeah.

WC: In the past, yes. It's weird because I used to play a lot of games, mostly PC games. I was a PC gamer. Around like the time I turned forty-two, forty-three—it might have been because that's when I had my first kid, to be honest—but when he turned two, I kind of stopped gaming, and not because I wanted to. Right now, I play online, games like *Magic: The Gathering*—card games. But it's been harder for me to play the games I used to play, like those open sandbox games, the shooter games. Part

of it is probably because all those kids are so good right now. All those damned twelve-year-olds are like kicking my ass. But it's also I've run out of patience. I just don't have the patience to sit down, kill nine boars and take their pelts. I spent a lot of time on *World of Warcraft*, but I just don't have the mental space to play that anymore.

GE: Somebody once told me the reason a lot of people can't write after work is that you can only make so many decisions a day. Writing is all about decisions, and gaming is all about decisions. So, you've got brain space to write, or you got brain space to game.

WC: I think when I had my day job, it actually helped me write more, because I kind of didn't like my day job. I had the inspiration to not do my day job anymore, which was a great reason to write. These days I'm a full-time writer, so that doesn't work for me anymore.

But there was a new game that came out like last month called *Elden Ring*. It's the one that George R.R. Martin is working on. It's one of those games which I knew I didn't have the patience for, where you're dying a thousand times. But I tried it anyway because it got great reviews. Then I realized, I'm maybe two, three hours in, and I'm like, "I'm not really having fun. It's beautiful, and the story's good, but I'm not really having fun." Then I asked myself, "Wouldn't I rather be working on my book than playing this game?" And it was kind of a toss-up. At that point, if it's a toss-up whether I'd rather be working on my book or playing this game, I should be working on my book.

GE: You've also done things like a *Walking Dead* tie-in and collaborations with Cassandra Clare. Are you planning to do more of these in the near future?

WC: Probably not. The thing about writing is it's also a business. There are advantages and disadvantages of doing tie-ins. On one hand, it's kind of cool to work in somebody else's world. It's cool to play with their toys. In some ways it's a little easier, because you're not starting from scratch. But from a business standpoint, with a tie-in, basically you're getting a salary. You're getting paid cash to do this pile of work. Usually, you don't get that much on the back end. No royalties, no percentages. That's just the business mode of tie-ins.

In this day and age, the day of streaming and multiple platforms, content is king. Intellectual property is king. So, there's something to be said about owning your IP. I think I told you earlier, all my books have been auctioned… So, there is a financial aspect to owning that IP you can never get with a tie-in. Also, usually, when you are doing your own IP, you are god of your universe. When you're doing a tie-in, you are a servant to the god of that universe. The freedom isn't there. It's something you have to accept.

When I did *The Walking Dead* book, the editor called me and said, "I want it to be set in Asia. Go." He gave me a blank check to do whatever I wanted. Even then, even though he let me do "whatever I wanted," I had to give him a ten-page outline on what I wanted that he had to sign off on before we went further. Then there were several layers that went all the way to Robert Kirkman to determine if everything in the story fit the tone of *The Walking Dead*. Does it fit the universe and physics of *The Walking Dead*? There are all these aspects that you have to know and make sure of, because you can't break the physics or the rules of this universe.

GE: These are great points, and I don't think anybody I've interviewed for *Galaxy's Edge* has talked about the issue of intellectual property, even though we've talked to a lot of writers whose works have been optioned. So, I'm glad IP got in there.

WC: I can talk all day about the business of writing. I actually enjoy talking about the business of writing more than the craft of writing.

GE: Well, we're going to get back to the craft of writing right now. You've mentioned in other interviews that you love history. What role did your readings in history play in the creation of your new book, *The Art of Prophecy*?

WC: *The Art of Prophecy* is a complete secondary world. The inspiration comes from a lot of wushu movies: *Once a Upon a Time in China*, *Fong Sai-yuk*, *Fist of Legend*, *House of Flying Daggers*. That's

the heart of the story. But one thing I became very fascinated about was from the era of *The Romance of the Three Kingdoms*. I read about the eunuchs and emperors, how that relationship coalesced, and then how it affected their relationship with the warlords.

There was a level of accepted corruption throughout ancient China which precipitated so many events. If you read it from a top level down, you're like, "Wow, that's, really messed up." But once you live it, once you put yourself in these people's shoes, you're like "I would totally do the exact same thing."

Obviously, I went through a lot of concepts. Back in *The Lives of Tao*, I talked about cause and effect, how certain actions, thoughts, and beliefs from certain parties cascade through everything else. I did the exact same thing with The War Arts Saga [the series beginning with *The Art of Prophecy*]. I remember I saw these very real focal relationships and stuff that happened. Then I put myself in the shoes of the characters. If I was a eunuch who was best friends with the child of the emperor, how would I take advantage of the situation? If I were these people, how would I live? And I would totally be the bad guy sometimes, because it's easy to be honorable when you're not the guy who has to make that choice.

So yeah, there were a lot of inspirations from 1000 AD to 1300 AD. Honestly, China's history is so fascinating. Some of their architecture is so cool—the ways they just break apart. The way the society has been structured over centuries is so unique. I just took everything that I thought was really cool, put it all together, and made sure that it still made sense for that universe.

GE: One of the interesting aspects of *The Art of Prophecy* is that the whole chosen one narrative is completely turned on its head. Could you talk a little bit about this? It sounds like it's the chosen one's teacher who's kicking butt.

WC: His master does kick butt. Taishi, who is his master, is probably my favorite character I've ever written. I really enjoyed writing her. I honestly like writing older people. I think they're so much more fun. There are so many more layers to play with, and they get to be their honest self so much more.

The chosen one trope is very commonly used, and it's kind of worn out. So, I'm glad that it's been flipped on its head in *The Art of Prophecy*. But that wasn't my goal. I don't start writing a book saying, "My intention to write this book is to subvert this." My intention is I want to tell a great story. I want the reader to read it and go, "Wow, that is really cool, and I'm gonna miss these characters."

I feel when you start your storytelling based on an ideology or an intention—like, my goal is not to tell this story, my goal is actually to expose this, or tell this, or whatever—you're limiting the story. If the story that you want to tell happens to do this, happens to subvert this trope, or whatever, that's great. But your goal should always be to serve the story. If your goal is not to serve the story, but to reveal this point or to do this, it can certainly be done. But I think you're limiting yourself.

I didn't mean it that way when I wrote *The Art of Prophecy*. I'm really glad I did, because that was a story that spoke to me. It's funny, when we took War Arts to the studios, one of the producers mentioned that a master-student relationship between an older woman and a younger boy is rare. In hindsight, it wasn't intentional. I just thought it would be a great relationship. But there aren't that many. I'm sure there have to be a few out there, but in stories and novels, TV and film, that relationship is relatively rare. But for me, it was: "That's the relationship I want to tell, and I think it would be super cool."

GE: So, it was all about the relationship. You thought it would be neat to have an older female character shaping a younger male character who had to do something important to save the world.

WC: Yeah. How do you make the chosen one when, basically, the chosen one is mediocre? He's spoiled. He can't take a hit. What do you do then? Let's find out.

I think so many times we put our heroes and chosen ones on a pedestal. The reason why the superhero genre isn't as popular in China is because there's a narrative of American exceptionalism—you know, hero ball, I call it hero ball. We have so many stories about these people who are unique and special and powerful. They alone can save the universe. They alone can fix the problem. I think it's a very unique Western kind of concept. Not that it's not in other cultures, but it's very strong in the West. So, when I wrote The War Arts Saga, I was like, "I want this kid who's has already been ordained as this special boy. I want him to earn it. I want him to struggle and earn it and fail. And I want him to know what it's like to be at the bottom."

GE: What is the most important thing you want readers to know about or to take away from The War Arts Saga?

WC: I think if I was to give a real answer, an honest answer, it would be I want them to finish the book, and I want them to miss the characters. I want them to consider these characters friends, and I want them to care about these people. When I first started writing *The Art of Prophecy*, a lot of my peers were writing what I consider really big, important books—books about culture, books about racism, sexism, identity, gender identity. They were writing science fiction and fantasies that were weaving in a lot of cultural issues that were important to them.

Then they would ask me, "Wes, what are you working on these days?" And I was like, "Well, I wanna write a kung fu book." Because that's what I want. That's what my heart wants to write. I want to write a kung fu book. They'd be talking about the environment and politics, and I just wanted to write a kung fu book. And at the end of the day, I want to write a kung fu book where readers would love the characters. That's the goal. I want them to read the story and be like, "I want to reread the story again, because I love hanging out with these people." Or: "I care about this person, and I hope he marries this girl, because I really hate that girl over there." I want them to come back saying, "These are people that are my friends. And I want to reexperience the adventure with them again. I want to see where they go next."

GE: What are you working on now?

WC: I'm working on book two of The War Arts Saga. I'm about two-thirds of the way through the book. It's due right when the first book comes out. And fantasies are big books. These are the biggest books I've ever written, and I'm like, "Wow, now I know why Neil Gaiman is smart writing 80,000-word books. Why am I not that smart?"

GE: Because the contract calls for 120,000 words. That's why.

WC: I think my contract is like 150,000. Even then, book one was about 180. Book two is going to be about 200. It's one of those things where people always say, "Oh, you should just kill more characters." And I'm like, "I like my characters, and they're necessary to do these things."

GE: Is there anything you'd like to add? Soapboxes provided free of charge.

WC: I think I'm good. I'm not a soapbox person. To be honest, I'm actually very much a soapbox person, but I'm doing my best to not be a soapbox person, because no good comes out of screaming into the internet about how right you are. There is a life coach I used to be friends with. Anytime somebody wanted to pick a fight with him, he would ask, "What do you hope to get out of this conversation?" And then he'd say, "I hope you get it, and I hope you attain what you're looking for." That's it. No soapboxes.

GE: Then how about this: Do you have any thoughts you want to share with the aspiring writers out there, or any goals that you'd like to admit to?

WC: I will say this: when it comes to writing, the more experience I get, the less confident I am as a writer. When I was writing The Lives of Tao, and when I was writing the book before it, I was so confident. Like, "This is an amazing book. And I'm such a great storyteller." But writing is one of those few careers where, as you get more experienced in your craft, it becomes harder.

When you're an engineer, when you're a doctor, when you're an attorney, the more you do your job, the better you get at it. You get more comfortable, more confident. You understand what you need to do. You know more.

I feel like when it comes to writing, it's the opposite. Because you know more, you have more options and you are less confident. And that's perfectly okay. I write a lot less per day now than I used to. Part of it's because every time I start crafting a scene, I subconsciously focus on many more variables. And because I'm writing more intentionally with more layers, it becomes more of a slog.

The funny thing about writing is, at least for me, I don't know if I'm writing good stuff. I don't know if the scene is good. I don't know if these words are good. I don't know if this sentence is making any sense. But what I do know is when something is not working. That's the one skill that I've honed as I've become more experienced as a writer. I absolutely know when something is not working.

And almost one-hundred percent of the time, when I know something's not working, the solution is to find out what's wrong with it. I mean, that's an obvious solution. But it's something I don't ignore any more, because if it doesn't serve the story, it's going to mean more work later on. So, I guess the advice would I give aspiring writers would be, if you don't know what you're doing, you're probably on the right track. If you're very confident you know what you're doing, that's when I'd worry.

Copyright © 2022 by Jean Marie Ward.

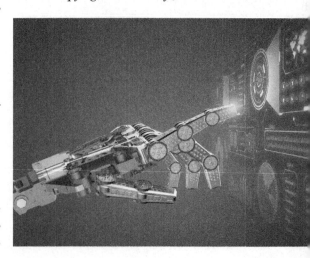

Richard Chwedyk sold his first story in 1990, won a Nebula in 2002, and has been active in the field for the past thirty-two years.

RECOMMENDED BOOKS

by Richard Chwedyk

PERFECTION AND ITS DISCONTENTS

Humans are perfectionists. Except when we're not. We're often ready to cut ourselves some slack. After all, no one is perfect.

However, we can be pretty picky when it comes to books. Especially thanks to platforms like Goodreads, everyone has become a book reviewer. Many of us are more than ready to lower the boom on one author or another, or one kind of book over another. It gives us a sense of power. And it also considerably shortens our "TBR" lists. Entire shelves of the library can be dismissed rather efficiently with the right pronouncement.

The trouble is that some of our most brilliant moments can be found amid a sea of imperfections. And at times our flaws are more revealing and perceptive than our most brilliant declarations. Those who write take chances, or should. And not every chance leads to success. I got into a discussion not long ago where so-and-so author was being excoriated because, even though that author wrote two or three brilliant volumes, there were a dozen or so books with that same author's name on them that were at best mediocre, at worst utter failures. At least in the eyes of these tough critics, that lowered the author's reputation. I told them that good authors risk failure. That the number of less-than-perfect books may only confirm that the author was willing to risk failure many times to achieve greatness. A baseball batter can strike out six times out of ten and still make it into the Hall of Fame. Why hold our authors to a greater standard?

Of the books reviewed below, none are near perfect, but each one of them is filled with valuable, entertaining and enriching things. The greater error would be to let them slip out of your book-friendly grasp.

◆ ◆ ◆

Worlds of Exile and Illusion
by Ursula K. Le Guin
Tor Essentials
March 2022
ISBN: 978-1-250-78126-0

I know these three early novels by Ursula K. Le Guin have been released before as an omnibus volume, but this Tor Essentials edition gives me the opportunity to mention how much I enjoy them, especially when read in sequence, as this compilation makes amply manageable. It also contains a touching and insightful introduction by Amal El-Mohtar.

It is not the Le Guin who would give us the masterworks *The Left Hand of Darkness*, *The Dispossessed* and *Always Coming Home*. It is Le Guin working out her craft and, as they say, finding her own voice and interests. It is Le Guin laboring in the fields of the science fiction of that era, the mid-1960s, and finding her own way between the established storytelling approaches and the New Wave experiments. And she was also working out how to write novels—to make something more of them than extended short stories or an omnium-gatherum of episodes.

Are they classics? Do they have to be? They are entertaining and fascinating at several levels. *Rocannon's World* because it is as much a heroic fantasy as it is a space opera (and using that term without disparagement). And with the creation of her protagonist, Gaveral Rocannon, we see the beginnings of some of those qualities she will later bestow upon Genly Ai in *The Left Hand of Darkness*—along with those she will jettison. *Planet of Exile* takes a shape more like the ones we'll find in her later works, and it brings her characters together in a more engaging ensemble. *City of Illusions* is the most challenging. It covers a great period of time and introduces the concept of memory transference, which presumes in some ways that humans or any other sentient beings are merely collections of memories housed in organic frames. The way she tries to convey this is sometimes difficult to follow, but in some ways it serves as a preface to what she'll work out more clearly in her non-Hainish Cycle novel, *The Lathe of Heaven.* But the greatest problem I had with this novel is a fault that is purely mine and for which Le Guin cannot be blamed: the flying machine hermit All-Allonio gives to protagonist Falk is called a "slider," and I cannot think of that name without imagining a White Castle hamburger.

In some ways (though not in others), these novels are like viewing the sketches that will eventually lead to the later masterpieces. The struggle with shape and proportion are evident, but there before us are all the essential qualities that will come to fruition in her later science fiction novels, and even in her Earthsea series.

As an added bonus, we get the invention of the ansible. How can you go wrong?

◆ ◆ ◆

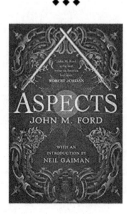

Aspects
by John M. Ford
Tor
April 2022
ISBN: 978-1-250-26903-4

Publishing the unfinished work of an author who has passed away can be a risky business.

Even though financial concerns may dictate the decisions of executors to make such a move, and fans of the late author may encourage publishers to make every last jot of that author's work available, an incomplete work-in-progress may potentially hurt the reputation of the late author. I remember an anecdote from Anne Lamott about how she lived in fear of being struck down by a car on her way back from a writer workshop. Someone would look at her critiqued work and think that she must have stepped in front of car to end her life. You want to go out on a high note.

And do you publish the unfinished work as is, or do you hire another author to complete it? Depending on who is chosen, fans of the later author might be gratified or horrified. We've seen the results of both outcomes in recent memory.

Whatever their reasons, I'm glad that Ford's estate has allowed Tor to publish the late John M Ford's last (or are there more?) unfinished manuscript. *Aspects* is such a pleasure to read. It is, with all due respect, like discovering the remains of an ancient civilization beneath an urban parking lot, something strange and magical under something familiar and mundane. He manages to mate steampunk with magic in a landscape at once familiar and strange. It reminds me a little of the Europe invented by Avram Davidson for his Dr. Eszterhazy adventures, with a little Anthony Hope and Jack Vance thrown in for good measure. Again, these comparisons fall short of conveying Ford's mastery of the narrative craft. He knows his story, and in what exists of it as he guides us with certainty and experience.

As in this moment with Varic, our hero, in the presence of mage-for-hire Agate:

> It came: power sheeting across him like hard driven rain through a suddenly opened door. Like rain, it soaked his skin but went no deeper; it drew warmth from him, but what was that? There was little enough to lose.
>
> He heard the crockery thud to the carpet, the curtain fold up with a groan of trapped air. Agate's head tipped forward, and her shoul-

ders slumped. He did not touch her for a full minima, until the small Craftlights ceased to shift around her eyes and fingernails.

So it was done again. Not so hard after all, nothing really required on his part except to sit still enough, to care little enough. A soul with any decent capacity for affection would have burned up.

There were legends about sorcerers remaining virgin for the sake of their Craft, and of the less resolute Archain drinking the—well, whatever—of their lovers. As with most good legends, there was a truth buried there.

We get the feeling that even though we've never been in this world before, Ford has long experience within it. We are in trustworthy hands, from the duel that begins the novel to the discussion of laws governing duels that dominates the fragment of Chapter Eight, where the manuscript ends:

> "The stakes are high enough when one has to steal one's dinner," Winterhill said, entirely without inflection.
> "That is of interest as well," Varic said. "Because people have had to steal their bread for as long as there has been bread to steal, no doubt the third loaf ever baked vanished when the baker turned away. It is a truth more important than any tablet of laws."

Another thing we can thank the editors of *Aspects* for are the five sonnets included after that last unfinished chapter breaks off. Ford was an accomplished poet, unashamed to write in traditional forms and traditional meter and rhyme schemes. Not many contemporary poets could pull off traditional sonnets in this day, but Ford did so not only with skill, but with that precious and elusive quality, grace.

Perhaps it is that grace which most marks Ford's work, completed or fragmentary, and why it seems so appropriate for this book to be released at this time.

◆ ◆ ◆

The Best Science Fiction of the Year, Volume 6
edited by Neil Clarke
Night Shade Books
February 2022
ISBN: 978-1-949102-52-9

The main imperfection here can be blamed on the supply chain breakdown that delayed the release of this volume. Neil Clarke edits the best "best of the year" science fiction anthology currently going. Not that there's that much competition, but it doesn't take away from Clarke and his team's hard work. It's well worth the wait.

I'm one of those folks (though I'm far from alone) who keep saying that the best science fiction can be found in the shorter forms. Primarily, I believe, that's because writers of short fiction are given greater freedom to try new things or to pursue less-traveled approaches to storytelling. The stakes are higher in novel writing, which makes publishers far more cautious in what they allow their authors to do. I know I've said this before, but it deserves repeating: if you really want to know what's new and interesting in the field, look at what's being done in short fiction.

The current volume has a great display of voices, thanks to Clarke's catholicity of taste and his eye for quality on a number of levels.

Not only do we have excellent examples from such reliable authors as Carrie Vaughn, Tobias S. Buckell, James Patrick Kelly, Nancy Kress, Matthew Kressel and Aliette de Bodard, but there's some outstanding work from voices new to me, most notably Arula Ratnakar, Nadia Afifi, Sameem Siddiqui, Julie Nováková, Bogi Takács and S.B. Divya.

My two favorite pieces here are Sofia Samatar's incredible "Fairy Tales for Robots" and Carolyn Ives Gilman's "Exile's End." Gilman and Mercurio D. Rivera, represented here with "Beyond the Tattered Veil of Stars," never cease to amaze and surprise me. I'm also glad to see Eleanor Arnason back, represented here with the brilliantly detailed "Tunnels." And M. Rickert has a short and deceptively powerful story, "This World is Made for Monsters."

Two authors better known for their much longer works (or three, since one is a pseudonym for two authors), Adrian Tchaikovsky and James S.A. Corey, contribute stories so impressive I really wish they would do more work of this length.

Two more stories I can't forget: "Yellow and the Perception of Reality" by Maureen F. McHugh and "Beyond These Stars Other Tribulations of Love" by Usman T. Malik.

There isn't a story within this book not worth reading, but those are the ones that stick with me most. Clarke's summary of the state of the field is perceptive and informative. The recommended reading list at the end is always worth reviewing to point you in the direction of more short fiction worth reading.

◆ ◆ ◆

This Weightless World
by Adam Soto
Astra House
November 2021
ISBN: 978-1-6626-0063-0

First off, you can always get my attention by starting a science fiction novel in Chicago—and depicting it ably. Adam Soto writes about the city as if he knows it, which I presume he does, though he currently re-sides in Austin, Texas. He also writes about Silicon Valley with equivalent authority, though I can vouch less for its accuracy. "Place" is important, though, and Soto gets that right.

And *This Weightless World* truly is a science fiction novel, though some contend otherwise (they always do). A decade ago, I was on a panel where one co panelist decried the state of what was then "current science fiction. She said something to the effect of "We've been invaded by the MFAs!" I questioned who "we" were supposed to be, and how "we" (science fiction? Collectively? Had someone taken a poll?) could be invaded as we don't have borders or boundaries and do not require passports. Later I wrote an article about how those new "invaders came more often from the sciences and other liberal arts disciplines, maybe somewhere around twenty percent coming from MFA in creative writing pro grams. But that was a decade ago. In any case, as I read this novel, I imagined that it was what that co panelist had in mind.

It is a first novel, and as such one can expect some of the imprecision that comes from taking one's first baby steps into an imposing arena. It stays too long in some places. In some places not long enough. I don't fault its subtle introduction of "big ideas" with almost a whisper, because that is often how big ideas get dropped into the stream of thought. Its char acters are beautifully drawn, and at times we may find them frustrating in their equivocation, but it's just that hesitancy which is at the heart of the novel Sevi, our main protagonist, and his girlfriend Ra mona, may want to shake things up and save the world from itself, but not at the cost of the little they have. This is the second recent science fiction novel (the other is Tochi Onyebuchi's *Goliath*) I've encountered that poses gentrification as a metaphor for what we're doing now—and doing wrong, for reasons both wrong and right.

The other big idea here is the idea that the dis covery of extraterrestrial beings will not be a "game changer," not after the novelty wears off. It reminds me that when the Air Force announced not long ago that they were going to release a ton of UFO-related documents heretofore top secret, an old journalist friend working on an article called me to ask why more people weren't excited by the news. In many respects, this novel provides a better answer than I was able to give my old journalist friend.

I'm always hesitant to compare authors with authors (though I still do so to an embarrassing degree), and I can understand how readers of more conventional science fiction novels will be frustrated that the themes of extraterrestrial life and artificial intelligence aren't more directly addressed, but at times while reading Soto's novel I found myself thinking that if C.M. Kornbluth had managed to live to what we'd now consider a "full" lifespan, he'd have written a novel much like this—only better. Which is not to say that Soto's novel is not worth reading—far from it. Kornbluth didn't make it. But we have Soto's novel, and though it may be a lesser vessel than what Kornbluth could have produced, it may be as much as we can hope for.

◆ ◆ ◆

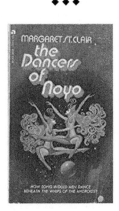

The Dancers of Noyo
by Margaret St. Clair
Ace
1973
No ISBN on the first paperback edition

Let us now praise Margaret St. Clair.

She was, like Robert F. Young, who I mentioned last issue, best known for her short fiction, which I read in the pages of *The Magazine of Fantasy and Science Fiction* and elsewhere. Under her own name and under the pen name of Idris Seabright which she often used for poetry, she was one of the authors, like Mildred Clingerman, Miriam Allen deFord, Doris Pitkin Buck, Zenna Henderson, Katherine MacLean, Kate Wilhelm, Karen Anderson and others, who assured me that science fiction and fantasy were not entirely a boys' club. For some reason, that was important to me at the time (as it is now). Women authors were still far outnumbered, but they were there, in the pages of the digests, next to the men, often writing the better stories—and earning a fraction of the acclaim.

Margaret St. Clair was a born storyteller. Her work could be both shocking and hilarious. If you read through a collection like *Change the Sky and Other Stories* you never got the feeling any of the stories were an "early" work or an experiment. They all had the same level of craft, intelligence and wit. And her perspective on any given subject was never the one you'd expect from her fellow authors, without regard to gender or to anything else. She was one of a kind. Seek out her stories like "The Man Who Sold Rope to the Gnoles," "Brightness Falls from the Air," "An Egg a Month from All Over," "Mrs. Hawk" and "Lazarus." You'll see what I mean.

Back then, I was unaware that she had also written a few novels. Eight of them, in fact. The last three supposedly form something of a loose trilogy, but the last, and the one I chose, *The Dancers of Noyo*, reads well enough as a standalone work. It incorporates her knowledge in classical studies, Wicca, and the culture of the indigenous Pomo people of California, along with some early notions of genetic engineering and climate change. Its protagonist, Sam McGregor, is sent off on a "Grail Vision" quest up the vestiges of Highway 101 in a plague-depopulated world. In 1973, when this first came out, much that occurs to Sam and those he meets throughout the vision quest must have struck readers as "freaky" or "psychedelic." After almost a half century, it takes on a wider meaning, much of it prescient, effectively communicated with an enviable clarity and evocative prose.

I picked this up for cheap in a convention dealers' room, and the reading of it has paid me back tenfold. It supports my secret (well, not so secret now) belief that often the best books of an era go undetected and neglected by contemporary readers, even by the most prestigious of the era's critics. Nobody's perfect. But time often unmasks our oversights.

We need to rediscover Margaret St. Clair and grant her work the respect and status it deserves.

Copyright © 2022 by Richard Chwedyk.

Gregory Benford is a professor of physics at the University of California, Irvine and the author of Timescape, *among other novels.*

THE SCIENTIST'S NOTEBOOK

by Gregory Benford

ALIENS WE CAN KNOW

On Columbus Day of 1992, five hundred years after the last man to discover America, the USA began its full-bore program of radio listening for other civilizations—the Search for Extraterrestrial Intelligence, SETI.

It was a big, media-savvy kickoff, made possible by adroit renaming, under Senate review, from SETI to a title invoking microwave research: Serious Science, see? That pried forth the necessary million or so dollars a year. The big van filled with electronics began eavesdropping at such speed that the program outdistanced all previous SETI observations in its first hour on the air. It was a satisfying moment, the culmination of thirty years of concerted, orderly dreaming.

When I visited the SETI office at the Jet Propulsion Laboratory in June, 1993, I was very impressed with the electronics and computers, allowing the astronomers to direct the antenna cupped skyward at Goldstone, California. That big dish was baking in desert heat, but the astronomers could study the microwave sky during office hours, from air conditioned comfort. Comfortable lodgings for the new Columbuses.

Don't expect results immediately. Two searches proceed in parallel, one peering intensely at nearby stars, the other methodically eyeing the whole sky. Both will take at least seven years to make a solid search, and then they can both expand the range of frequency, bandwidth, listening time, etc. for deeper scrutiny. I wish them well.

But sitting here in 2022, we see the sixth year of the Breakthrough Listen program, funded at $10million/year. They've listened for more time than the sum of all previous listening, in microwaves and optical, too. Still, no detections.

Still... Though I have known some of the principals in the SETI community for decades, I have always felt a bit displaced from their views. I am uneasy with the cast of our radio-listening ideas, because they are so human grounded.

Of course, in a deep sense they could not be otherwise. But many of our assumptions about aliens reflect our own recent development. I have a slide of a recently studied nebula in the Milky Way which illustrates this nicely. When I show it to audiences, ask them what they see.

Within ten seconds, most perceive a human face, complete with a Renaissance-style headband. After more study, they see two faces. Of course, nobody in the nebula is producing this to communicate with us; our eyes, intimately linked to our brains, pull the images out of a natural swath of gas and dust. We impose ourselves on the universe.

I do subscribe to the basic case for SETI, which envisions a plausible set of linked events. Life as we know it conjures up from carbon and water, abundant in the universe. Quite a few planets probably have these chemicals warmed by a nearby sun.

Life here blossomed in about half a billion years, perhaps less, suggesting that it's not a difficult trick for randomly colliding chemicals to do. Laboratory reproductions of such early conditions—a cocktail of ammonia, methane, water, molecular hydrogen laced by ultraviolet sunlight and zapped by lightning—readily yield amino acids, the precursor molecules for life as we know it.

After a fast start, life took a puzzlingly long time to build up interesting structure. 'Modern'-type multicellular organisms with complex structures took about a billion years to appear. Apparently there is something difficult about the first halting steps upward. On some worlds it may simply never happen. If the time varied by merely a factor of three life here would be still quite primitive.

Brains came along a full billion years after that, then land life a further two hundred million years and finally—us. In the fossil record there is only one category that constantly improved: brain size, implying that it has consistent survival advantage.

Will aliens evolve similarly? Our brains are ramshackle layers of complex cellular units, slapped together to give momentary advantage. Much of our mental processing is buried, unconscious, and hard to manage (emotions, for example). Evolution's twists and turns won't be the same elsewhere, so other minds will be vastly different. Will they have our astonishing capacity to chart the origin of the universe, frame a sonnet, sing and laugh and dare?

SETI must assume that they do share at least some of our habits of mind. SETI is not a science in itself, though it uses the methods and conclusions of science to frame its arguments. Instead, it is an agenda of second-hand exploration.

Science predicts, then checks; exploration ventures, expecting surprises. Many explorers had reasons that seem fanciful to us today. Ponce de Leon sought immortality in Florida, as did the ancient Chinese in the Pacific. Columbus ignored evidence that the Earth was three times larger than his charts and plans assumed, and was purely lucky that a whole unknown continent lay between him and his goal, China.

The basic trouble with making scientific-sounding estimates in support of SETI is that they finally rest upon an imponderable puzzle: us. We do not understand the imperatives driving our evolution and attitudes well enough to generalize beyond our noses.

Brian Aldiss once told me a story which neatly illustrates our problem. It seems an Oxford college received a bequest, and the senior fellows gathered to decide how to invest it. Their bursar felt they should sink the money into property, "After all, property has served us well for the last thousand years."

But then the Senior Fellow, voice shaking, replied, "Yes, but you know, the last thousand years have been exceptional."

Our entire experience of high technology has been exceptional—and exceptionally short, one hopes, if civilizations have much hope of enduring on the galactic stage. In selecting radio for SETI we advocate a technology less than a century old.

As a species, we turned at least three great techno-tricks. First came our invention of stone tools about two million years ago. We numbered perhaps a few hundred thousand then, spread out in tribes in Africa and perhaps across Asia. *Homo habilis* with a brain cavity of 750 cubic centimeters was plainly making simple chipped knives. Many paleontologists think

it was no coincidence that tools came along with rapid expansion of the cranial vault.

Archeological traces show a rise to several million of us when the next trick appeared, probably driven by the necessity of crowding our resources: agriculture. Cultivation drove the human population exponentially for several thousand years, though it hit a plateau until the industrial revolution, our most recent trick.

Most sf readers believe that one further, essentially open-ended trick remains: developing the resources of the solar system. Our numbers now edge above seven billion, with demographers projecting a world population peaking at between ten and twenty billion, if the low birth rates of the industrial world eventually become common everywhere. The opening of space could lead, by scaling from these earlier tricks, to a human population of perhaps a hundred billion scattered throughout the inner solar system. Centuries from now, of course.

Think of the SETI implications of such a society, which could easily afford to invest the energy resources of our entire current civilization in radio signaling. If this is a typical development for aliens, then the SETI dilemma—what if there are plenty of aliens, but everybody's taking the cheap way out, merely listening?—is solved.

But is this path of ever-widening resources, and the tools that can manage them, typical?

Much of what we believe about our upward trek from the neolithic is broad, often inaccurate generalization. For most of this century, archaeologists believed that the world's first potters were near eastern farmers. We now have even older pottery made by Japanese fishermen. A staple of our scenario for civilization is the importance of agriculture as a new, city-forming technology. Natives of what is now Mexico learned to cultivate corn, yet still remained essentially nomadic for three thousand more years. Similarly, early European farmers used slash-and-burn cultivation which forced them to move as the old fields wore out.

The sedentary, information-building habits of comfy villages (reading, writing, 'rithmetic) do not necessarily follow from agriculture, as long as there is plentiful land. Apparently, in the near east our species was simply too successful, our numbers rose, and we had to invent both fishing and stationary agriculture to feed ourselves, about eight to ten thousand years ago.

But even sitting still does not necessarily bring about an inevitable, triumphant upward march. The Maya of southern Mexico and Central America built a widespread empire with huge pyramids and developed written script, but never produced great cities.

The Incas of Peru did develop cities, roads and a vast political empire, without learning to write. Neither society discovered the wheel as a transportation tool, though they did use them on toys, and had rollers for carts. Without good roads, wheels aren't so effective.

Of course, many other civilizations did master more. Still, the diverse talents developed by our own ancestors point to a real possibility that an intelligent species does not necessarily have to eventually produce all the skills necessary to join the Radio Club.

Nor need they have our motivation. Most societies in human history have been disinterested in science and only grudgingly open to advances in technology. Many have avoided contact with outsiders, rather than seeking it, in the recent western model.

Witness the Chinese Ming Dynasty of over 500 years ago, which excelled the Europeans in deep sea craft. They explored throughout the Indian Ocean and reached Africa, perhaps even California. Dawning realization of the diverse cultures far over their horizon caused the rulers of this powerful navy to retreat, fearing invasion of mainland China by disruptive social forces. They broke down their largest ships and dispersed the seasoned crews who could have rounded Africa and reached Europe—or, going east, discovered the Americas.

This failure of nerve is a classic case of stepping back from opportunities, ventures which would open wide windows on vistas which many fear before they are even glimpsed. It's common, too. Only a minority of human civilizations have ever had the western sense of outward-directed, welcoming contact.

Many alien civilizations could harbor *no* such sentiments. In this case they will simply ignore the implications of radio, once they develop it.

This issue of motivation is, I think, rather more important than the astronomers have realized—probably because as a breed, they are voraciously curious. Perhaps the observable fact that most people are not inquisitive, but some are, has a deep origin.

Consider that until about ten thousand years ago, when we evidently exceeded the easily-gotten resources and settled down, all of us were hunter gatherers. We formed tribes of at most a few hundred, which is probably why we now organize our lives in overlapping 'tribes' of special interest, from local neighborhoods to a fondness for, say, science fiction. Tribes needed tight organization to survive at all, caroming around in spacious territory.

This shadow of our ancient social habits suggests that roving tribes had a recurrent problem—what to do when they met each other. They saw strange, ugly faces, bizarre customs, differently colored skin, odd eyes. Tribes which simply couldn't make themselves deal with alien tribes could either fight or flee. Either way, they couldn't get any help.

On the other hand, people who could tolerate the alien and come to understand them, often across a language barrier, could choose from a menu of choices. They could trade, or settle territory disputes, or delay a fight until they had the advantage or even set rules for war which minimized casualties. Anyone who could talk persuasively to aliens could probably also command an audience in his own tribe. She might well be chief. So alien appreciation might be written into our social and mental selves at a deep level. Such abilities sit in uneasy tension with tribal suspicion of outsiders, leading to ethnic frictions which will be with us forever, I suspect, often mis-labeled 'racism'.

Would alien societies resemble our social evolution in this way? Perhaps, if they were hunter gatherers. Many other strategies are available in our own animal kingdoms—herbivores, chipmunks monkeys that seldom leave the same stand of tropical forest. So radically different aliens are certainly plausible. On these grounds it may be quite unlikely that even technological aliens will be likely to want to talk—or listen.

And mere idle curiosity won't do. SETI has taken decades to get solid funding since the ideas first became widespread. Frank Drake and others who have been on board since the beginning suspect that the odds are low, so a search might last several more decades—and then will end because of diminishing probable returns, as we probe further away, listening for the whispering voice, faintly crying out in the background hiss.

This suggests that some genuine tenacity is necessary to fly across the vast parsecs on electromagnetic wings. How common might that determination be? Again, our origin as a species suggests pessimism. Our hunting strategy is very specialized. All evidence suggests that we hunted in groups, and were unafraid to take on quite sizable game, such as mastodons.

Our method, though, was not to rely upon brave displays of courage. Rather, we shout and wave sticks and run after the prey. Typical grazing animals spook easily, run well, then tire. They often stop within a fraction of a mile and go back to cropping grass. Most carnivores who fail to make a catch on their first lunge also lose interest, rest up a bit, and wait for another target to amble by.

We did not. Instead, we pursued the same prey to its next stop. Surprised it again. Ran it until it outdistanced us. How those grazers must have hated us!

We aren't particularly fast compared with, say, a cheetah, but we are the greatest distance runners in creation. (That's why the American Indians used men, not riders on horseback, to carry distant messages. The men held up better.) Eventually, we could run down the tired grazer: a guaranteed result, if we persisted.

In this tenacity lies our major difference from other omnivores, and certainly from carnivores. The dog family shares this trait. It's an odd adaptation. Most mammals cannot sustain aerobic work greater than ten times their basal metabolic rate for more than an hour or two. Olympic cross country skiers and the like reach about fifteen times their basal rate. Champion Alaskan sled dogs, incredibly, reach thirty times their base rate. They can run nearly a hundred miles in a day, pulling a sled in sub-zero weather, day after day. This makes marathons or iron-man trials look like a stroll in the park. Humans in good shape can out run a horse or cow, but try to out last a dog and you'll die trying while the dog just grins. Their cardiovascular systems have enormous reserve. They

got this capability by following the same strategy we did—running down herbivores.

We speak much of our brains, our delicious chattering, our opposable thumbs, our two-footed grace—but maybe stubborn perseverance is the key asset we or any alien will need to make SETI work. Maybe we should be looking for aliens with the psychology of dogs...

If so, such aliens are probably rare. Our strategy is shared by few other species here, despite ample opportunity to flourish. Does this mean octopus-like aliens who can manipulate objects but do not pursue game are out of the Radio Club? Or that herbivores generally are in the wrong business to begin with, hemmed in by short attention spans? Such thoughts imply skepticism about a galaxy packed with eager correspondents.

But what is persistence, after all? Basically, it means the ability to sustain effort over times significant to your own wellbeing —getting fed, in the case of hunting. Perhaps more germanely for a SETI project funded by a government with the attention span of a term in office, can we envision a species which nourishes efforts much beyond the life span of an individual?

Any truly long-lasting talk between the stars will require that. We have a few institutions which preserve historical continuity, the longest lived being the great religious bodies such as the Catholic church, which holds the record at about 2000 years.

But what is an individual life span? For humans in the famous Hobbesian state of nature, it was about 25 years on average. Excavations of ancient burials have shown that in prehistory we lived lives that may not have been nasty and brutish, but were indeed demonstrably short. No skeletons of those who reached age thirty did not have a major broken bone, and nearly all showed skeletal signs of vitamin deficiency.

But that's nasty old nature. We now live beyond 75 on average, with prospects of perhaps 125 within a century or so. (Since our average expectancy has increased by half again in a century, this isn't a crazy possibility.)

Is there some limit on the lifespans of aliens? Fundamental evolutionary reasons imply that mortality is built into most species. Creatures effectively enhance their ability to reproduce while young, by trading off against problems later in life. Evolution doesn't care if you die after you've passed on your genes.

So probably aliens will confront mortality as profoundly as we—unless their technology eliminates the problem. The experts on aging whom I know believe there is probably no solid limit on the human life span, given ever-questioning science and appropriate technology—or if there is, it is probably several centuries.

This suggests that 'high' civilizations of sophisticated technology may be very important for long-lived SETI. They will live long and prosper, with time to indulge such odd, expensive hobbies as SETI broadcasting. Many SETI enthusiasts harbor gloomy sentiments are that such societies will inevitably either incinerate themselves in wars, or drown in their own garbage, i.e., environmental catastrophe.

I suspect this is a hasty generalization from our current list of Big Problems. Consider how few of these ideas were current even a century ago. In a century or two more, we will probably have a different menu of worries. Projecting them into our SETI estimates is short-sighted.

SETI scientists estimate their chances using the famous 'Drake equation', which estimates the number of available technological civilizations in the galaxy. It contains astronomical estimates (probabilities of a star having habitable planets), biological ones (chances of developing highly intelligent forms), and finally social ones (chances of producing technology, and then wanting to do SETI).

By far the most sensitive factor of all is the lifetime of those communities, because we know absolutely nothing about it, beyond the fact that we have survived into our radio-emitting era only a bit more than sixty years, since the first radio telescope in 1931.

Many astronomers have taken their crack at the equation, estimating the various probabilities differently (much as considerable latitude enters in estimating the success of cryonics, as I discussed last time). Strikingly, most get a similar result: the number of currently active civilizations in our galaxy is of the same order of magnitude as the lifetime of

an average Radio Club candidate civilization, measured in years.

If the typical alien society lasts a million years then, there are about a million of them currently in the galaxy. Since the galaxy has about 300 billion stars in it, that means we would need to search 300,000 stars to find a Radio Club member, on average.

The typical separation of such members is about six hundred light years. Think of such societies sending messages back and forth, with about a thousand years needed for one round trip—say, a question and its answer. Then in the million year lifetime of the average civilization, there would be time for about a thousand exchanges.

These would be members of the Galactic Radio Club, slowly able to amass knowledge and history from others. A bit of arithmetic shows that there is a critical lifetime for societies which allows them to enter into this cross-talk. It works out to be about 3500 years. If the average civilization lasts less than this, then a similar society is too far away for a single exchange of messages.

If Club members live longer, though, they probably win big, experiencing an exponential benefit. Communication yields learning, which could affect the lifetime. High technologies would perhaps be spurred to interstellar travel, colonies, the whole Galactic Empire motif so beloved of science fiction. Such societies would then probably produce many radio-emitting sites.

My bias favors knowledge. Civilizations with more of it may well live longer. This means that the 3,500 year mark is a minimum down payment. Once met, I suspect societies live longer, and SETI gets easier.

Notice that this is unstable, driving lifetimes up. The galaxy then gains Club members, and the numbers change with time, keeping civilizations around longer so they are on average nearer. This favors societies which come along a bit later.

Our galaxy has been spinning about ten billion years. The first billion or two years probably laid the groundwork, literally, for life, by building up heavier elements that make for interesting life forms (iron, carbon).

Thereafter, perhaps another four or five billion years must pass before intelligence arises on the first-born worlds. That means that seven billion years into our galaxy's history, the Club could start to grow.

That was three billion years ago. An obvious question, first posed by Enrico Fermi, is *Where are they?* Shouldn't some have visited Earth by now? Or at least, how come the night sky is not full of Radio Club members?

A few decades of listening will comb through most of the choices—in radio frequencies, Doppler shifts of those frequencies by planetary motions, signal durations and pulse strengths—available to us. If the skies are still silent, then we will have to rethink our position.

That means looking not only outward, but backward—into time, into our origins. Maybe we really are quite special. Or maybe aliens are talking on some other circuit, one that will not seem natural to us.

For example, maybe radio is kid stuff. Consider if the ancient Romans had developed visual signaling to knit their empire together. Using mirrors to reflect sunlight to the next relay point on the horizon, the heliograph engineer could block and unblock the beam to carry a Morse Code-style message.

L. Sprague deCamp suggested this in *Lest Darkness Fall*. Now suppose light messages became the prevailing paradigm. Progressing through the Industrial Revolution, heliographs would use automated mirrors, electric arc lamps, moving on to lasers and fiber optics.

Why use radio? many would ask. Light can carry more information, in principle, since the message-bearing is proportional to frequency, and optical light beats radio by a factor of nearly a million. Sure, being limited to line of sight is a problem, but relay stations are no technical difficulty. While fog can block sunbeam signals, lightning interferes with radio.

Extending this argument to aliens, perhaps they do not use radio, preferring optical, maybe lasers. Then we should look for very fast signals, variations in amplitude or frequency in a range down to a billionth of a second. Their local sun would swamp the optical radiation, but that simply means a smart alien would use infrared lasers. That way, the signal would pop up above the star's rather weak emission in those wavelengths. Infrared lasers are cheap and easy to build, even for us radio addicts.

This reasoning implies a different SETI strategy. Instead of pricey radio telescopes, use an ordinary small telescope with some fast electronics attached. Such a rig costs a few tens of thousands of dollars. Amateurs could do it! There are many who might be so inclined, just as a corps of amateurs has discovered most of the asteroids in this century, through patient hours in back yards.

My larger point here is that social biases, tradition and culture shape technology. They always have. Consider nuclear technology, the Strategic Defense Initiative, and genetic engineering. The technologically unversed have greatly affected these technologies, usually impeding them.

Radio seems 'natural' to us, but really advanced aliens may use, say, neutrinos. After all, we in the American west no longer use the long-distance communication technology favored by the inhabitants of this region only a few centuries ago: smoke signals.

In that case, perhaps we should look for their accidental signatures—effects far outside the radio SETI paradigm.

For example, I have worked for some years on theoretical explanations of the dozens of mysterious long, luminous strands seen at our galactic center, which stand out so strikingly in the radio frequencies. Proceeding in conventional fashion, I calculated that they could be plasma discharges carrying huge currents—a kind of frozen lightning bolt. This is a strange, though acceptable, picture.

But suppose their structure—half a light year wide and hundreds of light years long—is not natural at all? If they serve some artificial end, what could it be? A transportation corridor, like a freeway? A power source? A religious monument?

As I'm fond of having my characters in sf novels remark, the thing about aliens is, they're *alien*. Maybe we can't guess such functions, even in principle. Perhaps noticing artificiality is the best we can manage.

But of course, our impulse as scientists is to find a natural model, even if it involves electrical discharges a hundred light years long. Indeed, we *prefer* such models. They are more 'scientific', and certainly they are less disturbing.

Or take another class of astronomical objects, the speeding neutron stars recently detected in several parts of the galaxy. The latest discovery stands revealed in a radio map on the cover of the March 11, 1993 *Nature*. A clear bow shock curls back from a tight point of radio emission. This knot is evidence of a compact source emitting relativistic electrons.

Underlying the cloud of electrons is a neutron star moving at above 800 kilometers per second. This is fast enough to let it escape the gravitational potential of the galaxy itself. We can measure the 0.68 second period of the radio pulsar and so know that a neutron star is powering this bright shock wave, which energizes electrons and makes them radiate.

But what of other such shock waves elsewhere in the galaxy, which we have seen without a pulsar? They look remarkably like the wakes of great vessels. Could they be some method of transport, starships winging their way?

Almost certainly not, but the fact that we can now see such relatively faint scratches across the radio-visible sky suggests that we should keep our minds open. A true starship would presumably be faster and fainter, unless the crew is fond of wasting a lot of energy in useless radio waves.

More generally, we should be alive to the possibility of accidental discoveries—and strange ones. Meanwhile, conventional SETI is the best bet. With steady funding as of now, it should show us within our lifetimes whether there is a Radio Club, or whether we are a rare breed.

Which will it be?

We are about to find out. Maybe…

Copyright © 2022 by Gregory Benford.

Alan Smale is the Sidewise Award-winning author of the Clash of Eagles trilogy, and his shorter fiction has appeared in Asimov's *and numerous other magazines and original anthologies. His latest novel,* Hot Moon, *comes out this month from CAEZIK SF & Fantasy. When he is not busy creating wonderful new stories, he works as an astrophysicist and data archive manager at NASA's Goddard Space Flight Center.*

TURNING POINTS

by Alan Smale

EARTHRISE

Welcome to the first in a series of columns discussing scientific, historical, and cultural turning points!

How will I be defining a Turning Point, for the purposes of this column?

Sometimes I'll talk about an invention, or a discovery, that led to a major change in our lives, or to our understanding of life, the universe, and everything. At other times the pivot point will be a battle, a revolution, a key death or birth, or some other seminal event in history. And occasionally—as with this first column—I might go with something more conceptual, perhaps almost intangible.

But, overall, I'll focus on changes with far-reaching consequences. Those twists and turns of science and history after which nothing was the same again … at least in one part of the world. (It's a big world.) I'll often try to choose turning points that might be less well known, and so perhaps more interesting and thought-provoking. And I'll be pointing out some of the cnnections to speculative fiction along the way.

Once in a while I might pick a topic that maybe *should* have been a turning point, but wasn't. From my interest in alternate history, I recognize a lot of potential points of departure that went unrealized but might have led to fascinating alternate timelines.

And some columns might be less portentous. We might get a bit playful here, once in a while, by way of light relief.

My credentials for this endeavor? My background is in science, and I've been a professional astronomer and science enabler for most of my working career. I earned a bachelor's in physics and a doctorate in astrophysics from the University of Oxford, in England. (One of my own pivotal Turning Points was being rejected the first time I applied to Oxford, which I think was the very best thing that could have happened to me at that time in my life. I might delve into that a little in a future column.) Shortly after, while still in my twenties, I moved to the US and have lived here ever since. I've also been a history buff all my life.

As for my writing career, I'm the author of over fifty pieces of published short fiction, most recently in *Asimov's*, and over the past fifteen years they've been almost entirely alternate history and historical fantasy. My *Clash of Eagles* trilogy (published by Del Rey, 2015-2017) postulates a Roman Empire that survived until the thirteenth century in its classical western form, which is now moving into North America (with substantial Norse help) at just the time when the Mississippian Culture is at its heyday. (Lots of scenes in Cahokia, a magnificent Native American city that will likely be the topic of a later Turning Point.) And I'd likely have never written the original novella, "A Clash of Eagles", that won the Sidewise Award and led to that trilogy, if I hadn't read *1491*, by Charles Mann, which had a chapter on Cahokia, and if I hadn't, much earlier, spent a lot of time studying and thinking about the Columbian invasions of North America, way back in that half-millennium-anniversary year of 1992. My most recent book *Hot Moon*, is an alternate-Apollo novel set in a timeline where the US continued with Moon landings after Apollo 17.

So in that vein, we'll start off this series with an easy" Turning Point: the Apollo 8 mission, and in particular the canonical Earthrise picture taken from lunar orbit by astronaut William A. Anders on Christmas Eve of 1968. This famous photograph shows the beautiful blue and white jewel of the Earth, streaked with cloud, against the jet black of the sky, rising above the barren gray lunar horizon. You see no national boundaries, no evidence of humanity at all. Just a unique, fragile oasis, surrounded by the bleakness of the void.

Today, we're so familiar with that view that it's become a cliché. Back then, it was a sensation. It's been described as "the most influential environmental photograph ever taken" by Galen Rowell, and was one of *Life Magazine*'s "100 Photographs that Changed the World." In July 2009, *the New York Times* claimed that the image kickstarted the environmental movement, and *The Guardian* (UK) made the same claim in December 2018. Emotional response to the image at the time was immediate and widespread across the United States and other parts of the world, along with an upsurge in environmental awareness. A huge number of people have spoken of their own shock and awe at seeing the picture for the first time, and it's been a clear inspiration to artists and activists everywhere. Most experts credit the establishment of Earth Day in 1970 and the growing focus and influence of the Club of Rome beginning in 1969 as direct consequences of the massive perception change stimulated by the Earthrise picture.

(An interesting sidenote is that Anders' spectacular shot wasn't actually the first image of the Earth taken from the Moon. In August 1966 the US Lunar Orbiter 1 probe had snapped a black-and-white image of the Earth seen "rising" over the Moon's limb, but it was kind of messy-looking, striped with raster lines, whereas the Anders picture is … extremely pretty, taken on standard 70mm color film by a rather snazzy custom Hasselblad 500 EL camera. Which just goes to show: presentation is everything.)

Although the crew of Apollo 8—Frank Borman, Jim Lovell, and Bill Anders—famously read passages from Genesis for a TV broadcast later that day, Anders has since said that the sight of the Earth from the Moon "really undercut my religious beliefs" and eventually swerved him into atheism. He also said, "We set out to explore the Moon and instead discovered the Earth."

Of course, Apollo 8 made history in many other significant ways. The mission achieved a bunch of knockout technical firsts. The first crewed launch of the Saturn V rocket. The first time humans had been out of the Earth's gravitational field, or in orbit around another celestial body (the astronauts circled the Moon ten times, at an altitude of sixty miles). In short, our first real trip to the Moon. And it was … uneventful, from a technical standpoint. Most everything worked as it was supposed to. It was a stunning engineering achievement, as well as a human victory. The success of Apollo 8 was its own turning point.

It wasn't supposed to be that way. Apollo 8 was originally intended to be a different mission entirely. But NASA was concerned that the Soviets would beat them to the punch, sending a cosmonaut around the Moon first, and they wanted to preserve that "first" for the US of A. This was a race, after all.

The Lunar Module wasn't ready in time for Apollo 8. It would fall to Apollo 9 to give the LM a workout in Earth orbit, and to Apollo 10 to take one into lunar orbit, where astronauts Stafford and Cernan climbed into it and sailed away from the Command Module, their lifeboat, their only route home. To break orbit and head down toward the Moon, but not quite get there. To blaze the trail. Or, in plainer words, do a full-up systems check to ensure the success of the later, Moon-landing Apollos.

In Robert Poole's 2008 book *Earthrise: How Man First Saw the Earth*, he writes that "it is possible to see that Earthrise marked the tipping point, the moment when the sense of the space age flipped from what it meant for space to what it means for Earth." In a similar spirit, Michael Collins made the point that if Apollo 11 was about arriving at a new place, Apollo 8 was about truly leaving the Earth. He came to the conclusion that both were equally significant.

Given everything *else* that happened in the 1960s and 1970s, and the great sea changes that were happening in society, it would be hard to prove beyond any doubt whatsoever that the progress of the environmental movement would have been substantially different without the Earthrise photo. But it has certainly achieved an iconic status, and spoken to people's souls. Other than the picture of Apollo 11 astronaut Buzz Aldrin standing on the lunar surface, it's difficult to think of a more popular photograph from the Space Race era. And in terms of what it embodies—the spectacular leap forward of the US Space Program, our understanding of the fragility of our planet, and the evocation of the joy and wonder that many of us feel about our world and our own place in it—it provides a magnificent visual representation of a turning point in history that has inspired us for generations.

Copyright © 2022 by Alan Smale.

L. Penelope is the award-winning author of the Earthsinger Chronicles and The Monsters We Defy (forthcoming from Redhook). Her first novel, Song of Blood & Stone, *was chosen as one of* TIME Magazine's *100 Best Fantasy Books of All Time. Equally left and right-brained, she studied filmmaking and computer science in college and sometimes dreams in HTML. She hosts the My Imaginary Friends podcast and lives in Maryland with her husband and furry dependents. Visit her at: http://www.lpenelope.com*

LONGHAND

by L. Penelope

THE WRITING PRACTICE

When does the work of writing begin and how or why does one invoke a writing practice? Writing is a discipline and like any discipline it requires practice. But unlike yoga or martial arts, simply showing up on the mat, or at the keyboard, is not always enough. Does the work of writing begin when you sit at the desk? When you boot up your computer? Open your writing software or your notebook and poise your fingers on the keyboard or grab your pen? Or does the work begin when you ready yourself to create, and if so, how do you achieve that state of readiness?

A ritual is defined as a religious or other solemn ceremony consisting of a series of actions performed according to a prescribed order. It's habit, elevated to the level of the sacred, and many writers have them. When looking for inspiration, we often seek it in learning about the rituals of great and beloved writers and artists. Ernest Hemingway claims to have written every day, as does Stephen King. Haruki Murakami, when at work on a manuscript, awakens at four o'clock in the morning to write, then runs six miles or swims 1,500 meters, or both. Dancer and choreographer Twyla Tharp famously begins every day with a trip to the gym and a two-hour workout. According to her, the ritual is not the exercise, it's getting into the cab.

Why do artists and writers need these rituals? For those like Tharp, the habitual, oft repeated act is much like Steve Jobs's repeated wardrobe—one less thing to think about. It's a way to avoid decision fatigue, which is a type of mental overload that occurs because we each have a limited capacity to make decisions each day. Try to make too many and you can become stressed and exhausted. Take away a choice and you remove a point of failure in your day, freeing up your mind for other tasks.

For many, the routines help them tap into creativity. Murakami has said that he keeps to his writing and exercise regimen every day. "The repetition itself becomes the important thing. It's a form of mesmerism. I mesmerized myself to reach a deeper state of mind."

Creating a habit, a sacred ritual, and then sticking to it normalizes the act of creation and forms a kind of muscle memory. This is very helpful for those struggling to find time to write and further their creative goals. When I decided I wanted to write novels seriously while still juggling running a business full time, I started waking at six o'clock every morning to get my words down. This (difficult for me) habit was key in not only finishing my first novel, but eventually in meeting aggressive publication deadlines set by my publisher.

Discovering the exact cocktail of activities, items, or customs you need to enter your practice is a process. We all cannot write daily. Few of us will run six miles a day. For many, coffee is a must have, for me it's tea, and for others nothing will get written without their favorite fountain pen. Just as with a religious or spiritual practice, our rituals are very personal and we must each find our own path forward.

Personally, I find I don't like to rely on anything too elaborate. I want enough flexibility that the lack of a specific item—like a certain brand of tea—will not stymie my progress. One of Maya Angelou's rituals was to go to hotel rooms to write. I find that an expensive proposition. I have considered going to a local coworking space to get my words, though my preference is to be in my own space. However, once I was in New York City with several hours to kill and dropped in with a day pass to a writer-specific coworking space. While in the writing area, everyone was required to be completely silent. The only talking allowed was in the common areas and kitchen. Working at a desk in a quiet space with dozens of other people all doing their own creative work was inspiring and energizing. I found that I was extremely productive in this environment and that knowledge has altered the way I approach my writing sessions.

Your ritual could include morning pages, tea, yoga, meditation, deep breathing, working at a specific time of day, or in a specific place, or the equipment that you use. My habit is to do first drafts of a manuscript on a specialized writing machine like an AlphaSmart or Freewrite. I know writers who draft entirely by hand and at least one who can only write her novels on her cell phone. Crystals and candles, a tarot spread, lighting incense, saying a prayer, or invoking the spirits are other examples of regular habits used to begin the work.

To find your own, think about your five senses. What would you like to see while getting the words in? Does that mean that location is important to you? Would a writing retreat be a good idea, or regularly changing locations—for instance, from a coffee shop to a library to a bookstore? My office looks out onto the wooded area behind my home and I find that view very calming and a great creative inspiration.

What would you like to smell? Would candles, incense, or even air freshener help set the stage? Are there special snacks that would get you in the proper mindset? My morning green tea turns to herbal lemon and ginger in the afternoons. What sounds do you find inspiring? Does music help? With lyrics or without? I have a friend who writes with the TV on and a twenty-four-hour news channel going on in the background. I'm a big fan of an app that plays coffee shop sounds. I've also used white noise generators to block out the outside world.

If you don't know what your ritual is, and you are struggling to complete your work or find yourself stuck and frustrated, then try experimenting with different tools and systems. Research what has worked for other writers and see if there is any inspiration to be found there. Writing sheds have become popular with certain folks who have the space and means to build or buy an entirely separate structure that's only used for writing. I have a standing desk and alternate sitting and standing during the day for health reasons.

Eliminating distractions can also be a reason for a ritual. The act of closing the door to your writing space or putting up a sign alerting the people you live with that important work is in process can signal the mindset shift necessary to begin the practice. Unplugging the router, or engaging a software tool that doesn't allow you on the internet are other ways to ritualize your focus.

Knowing when to rest is also just as important as pushing forward. The creative mind is like a muscle and sometimes it can be overused and requires recovery. In those times, reading and filling the creative well with other forms of media or entertainment can become part of the ritual. I make sure that I'm always reading something—often more than one something—because inspiration is part of the habit I've created.

Our rituals get us into the mindset. They may even mesmerize us, as Murakami says. Find yours and use it in your practice. However you come to it, the work of writing begins when your mindset is in place. When you show up to the mat, ready to work, you will find that the muse rewards your efforts and you will be well on the way to reaching your writing goals.

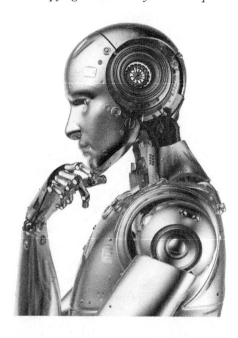

Nancy Kress is the author of thirty-four books and over one hundred short stories. Her work has won six Nebulas, two Hugos, the Sturgeon, and the John W. Campbell Memorial Award. Her most recent work is Sea Change, *a standalone novella from Tachyon and* The Eleventh Gate, *from Baen.*

ACT ONE

by Nancy Kress

BREEDING FICTION

Stories can grow out of anything: a fleeting thought, an overheard remark, a dream, a news item, a memory. Sometimes the writer has no idea where a particular story comes from. It just suddenly seems present, like air. Usually, however, stories grow from a combination of elements that arrive in the mind from different places and at different times. "Act One" is such a hybrid. Four germ cells cross-fertilized to produce it.

The first was my long-standing interest in genetic engineering, as well as a long-standing frustration that it is often written about so badly. Recombining genes will produce monsters without souls. No—it will produce supermen. No—it will produce a rigidly stratified society locked in by genetics, as in *Brave New World*. No—it will save humankind. No—it will be used for women to eliminate men, or blonds to eliminate redheads, or some mad scientist in a basement to eliminate everybody.

The much more likely scenario is that genetic engineering, like medicine and physics, will lurch forward in fits and starts. It will make some mistakes. It will create some benefits. It will have some unforeseen consequences. This is already happening, because a genome is not a destiny. A hundred other influences determine what turns genes on and off in a given individual, as the burgeoning science of epigenetics proves every day. So I wanted to write a story in which a deliberate change to the human genome results in ambiguous outcomes for multiple characters.

Such a goal is not a story, however. A story has specific characters and a specific situation. The second element that ultimately produced "Act One" was an image of two people groping their way down a grimy basement staircase. I didn't know anything about one of them, but I knew the second was a middle-aged woman of fragile beauty and iron will. She was an actress. I could see her quite clearly, although not why she was descending into that basement.

A few weeks later I was poking around the public library, scanning the shelf of NEW NON-FICTION. It held a book on dwarfism. The book seemed to be really well-written so I checked it out. After a few pages, I knew who the second person on the staircase was. Over the next few weeks I read two more books on dwarfism. Writers do this: read six times as much verbiage in research than the length of the eventual story. I read a book by a journalist, one by a dwarf, one by the average-sized father of a dwarf daughter. They were all fascinating.

The final piece of my story came during a chess match. I play a lot of chess, and I play it very badly. My usual chess partner, Marty, and I will play several games in a row, accompanied by chess trash talk ("Don't think that's a move that impresses me! You think I don't see the bishop moving up? In your dreams!") My toy poodle, Cosette, watches us distrustfully, and somehow she always knows when it's the last game of the evening, sometimes even before we do. How does she know? What clues is she reading?

Once Marty and I asked each other this question, the entire story of "Act One" solidified in my mind. I knew what genetic engineering change it would concern, to whom it would happen, why, and with what consequences. The actual writing then went swiftly.

Not all my stories are grown this way. Sometimes the soil is less fertile. Sometimes I just can't quite come up with enough inventive rain to keep the thing alive. Sometimes the result is puny and pale.

But, then, literary cross-breeding is just as chancy as the biological kind. And we lurch forward anyway.

✿

"To understand whose movie it is one needs to look not particularly at the script but at the deal memo."

—Joan Didion

✿

ACT ONE

I eased down the warehouse's basement steps behind the masked boy, one hand on the stair rail, wishing I'd worn gloves. Was this level of grime really necessary? It wasn't; we'd already passed through some very sophisticated electronic surveillance, as well as some very unsophisticated personal surveillance that stopped just short of a body-cavity search, although an unsmiling man did feel around inside my mouth. Soap cost less than surveillance, so probably the grime was intentional. The Group was making a statement. That's what we'd been told to call them: "The Group." Mysterious, undefined, pretentious.

The stairs were lit only by an old-fashioned forty-watt bulb somewhere I couldn't see. Behind me, Jane's breath quickened. I'd insisted on going down first, right behind our juvenile guide, from a sense of—what? "Masculine protection" from me would be laughable. And usually I like to keep Jane where I can see her. It works out better that way.

"Barry?" she breathed. The bottom of the steps was so shrouded in gloom that I had to feel my way with one extended foot.

"Two more steps, Janie."

"Thank you."

Then we were down and she took a deep breath, standing closer to me than she usually does. Her breasts were level with my face. Jane is only five-six, but that's seventeen inches taller than I am. The boy said, "A little way more."

Across the cellar a door opened, spilling out light. "There."

It had been a laundry area once, perhaps part of an apartment for some long-dead maintenance man. Cracked wash tubs, three of them, sagged in one corner. No windows, but the floor had been covered with a clean, thin rug and the three waiting people looked clean, too. I scanned them quickly. A tall, hooded man holding an assault rifle, his eyes the expression of bodyguards everywhere: alert but nonanalytic. An unmasked woman in jeans and baggy sweater, staring at Jane with unconcealed resentment. Potential trouble there. And the leader, who came forward with his hand extended, smiling. "Welcome, Miss Snow. We're honored."

I recognized him immediately. He was a type rampant in political life, which used to be my life. Big, handsome, too pleased with himself and his position to accurately evaluate either. He was the only one not wearing jeans, dressed in slacks and a sports coat over a black turtleneck. If he had been a pol instead of a geno-terrorist, he'd have maybe gotten as far as city council executive, and then would have run for mayor, lost, and never understood why. So this was a low-level part of the Group's operation, which was probably good. It might lessen the danger of this insane expedition.

"Thank you," Jane said in that famous voice, low and husky and as thrilling off screen as on. "This is my manager, Barry Tenler."

I was more than her manager but the truth was too complicated to explain. The guy didn't even glance at me and I demoted him from city council executive to ward captain. You *always* pay attention to the advisors. That's usually where the brains are, if not the charisma.

Ms. Resentful, on the other hand, switched her scrutiny from Jane to me. I recognized the nature of that scrutiny. I've felt it all my life.

Jane said to the handsome leader, "What should I call you?"

"Call me Ishmael."

Oh, give me a break. Did that make Jane the white whale? He was showing off his intellectual moves, with no idea they were both banal and silly. But Jane gave him her heart-melting smile and even I, who knew better, would have sworn it was genuine. She might not have made a movie in ten years, but she still had it.

"Let's sit down," Ishmael said.

Three kitchen chairs stood at the far end of the room. Ishmael took one, the bodyguard and the boy standing behind him. Ms. Resentful took another. Jane sank cross-legged to the rug in a graceful puddle of filmy green skirt.

That was done for my benefit. My legs and spine hurt if I have to stand for more than a few minutes and she knows how I hate sitting even lower than already am. Ishmael, shocked and discerning nothing, said, "Miss Snow!"

"I think better when I'm grounded," she said, again with her irresistible smile. Along with her voice that smile launched her career thirty-five years ago. Warm, passionate, but with an underlying wistfulness that bypassed the cerebrum and went straight to the primitive hind-brain. Unearned—she was born with those assets—but not unexploited. Jane was a lot shrewder than her fragile blonde looks suggested. The passion, however, was real. When she wanted something, she wanted it with every sinew, every nerve cell, every drop of her acquisitive blood.

Now her graceful Sitting-Bull act left Ishmael looking awkward on his chair. But he didn't do the right thing, which would have been to join her on the rug. He stayed on his chair and I demoted him even further, from ward captain to go-fer. I clambered up onto the third chair. Ishmael gazed down at Jane and swelled like a pouter pigeon at having her, literally, at his feet. Ms. Resentful scowled. Uneasiness washed through me.

The Group knew who Jane Snow was. Why would they put this meeting in the hands of an inept narcissist? I could think of several reasons: to indicate contempt for her world. To preserve the anonymity of those who actually counted in this most covert of organizations. To pay off a favor that somebody owed to Ishmael, or to Ishmael's keeper. To provide a photogenic foil to Jane, since of course we were being recorded. Any or all of these reasons would be fine with me. But my uneasiness didn't abate.

Jane said, "Let's begin then, Ishmael, if it's all right with you."

"It's fine with me," he said. His back was to the harsh light, which fell full on both Jane and Ms. Resentful. The latter had bad skin, small eyes, lank hair, although her lips were lovely, full and red, and her neck above the windbreaker had the taut firmness of youth.

The light was harder on Jane. It showed up the crow's feet, the tired inelasticity of her skin under her flawless make-up. She was, after all, fifty-four and she'd never gone under the knife. Also, she'd never been really beautiful, not as Angelina Jolie or Catherine Zeta-Jones had once been beautiful. Jane's features were too irregular, her legs and butt too heavy. But none of that mattered next to the smile, the voice, the green eyes fresh as new grass, and the powerful sexual glow she gave off so effortlessly. *It's as if Jane Snow somehow received two sets of female genes at conception*, a critic wrote once, *doubling everything we think of as "feminine." That makes her either a goddess or a freak.*

"I'm preparing for a role in a new movie," she said to Ishmael, although of course he already knew that. She just wanted to use her voice on him. "It's going to be about your… your organization. And about the future of the little girls. I've talked to some of them and—"

"Which ones?" Ms. Resentful demanded.

Did she really know them all by name? I looked at her more closely. Intelligence in those small, stony eyes. She could be from The Group's headquarter cell—wherever it was—and sent to ensure that Ishmael didn't screw up this meeting. Or not. But if she were really intelligent, would she be so enamored of someone like Ishmael?

Stupid question. Three of Jane's four husbands had been gorgeous losers.

Jane said, "Well, so far I've only talked to Rima Ridley-Jones. But Friday I have the whole afternoon with the Barrington twins."

Ishmael, unwilling to have the conversation migrate from him, said, "Beautiful children, those twins. And very intelligent." As if the entire world didn't already know that. Unlike most of The Group's handiwork, the Barrington twins had been posed by their publicity-hound parents on every magazine cover in the world. But Jane smiled at Ishmael as if he'd just explicated Spinoza.

"Yes, they are beautiful. Please, Ishmael, tell me about your organization. Anything that might help me prepare for my role in *Future Perfect*."

He leaned forward, hands on his knees, handsome face intent. Dramatically, insistently, he intoned, "There is one thing you must understand about the Group, Jane. A very critical thing. *You will never stop us.*"

Portentous silence.

The worst thing was, he might be right. The FBI, CIA, IRS, HPA, and several other alphabets had lopped off a few heads, but still the hydra grew. It had so many supporters: liberal lawmakers and politicians, who wanted the Anti-Genetic Modification Act revoked and the Human Protection Agency dismantled. The rich parents who wanted their embryos enhanced. The off-shore banks that coveted The Group's dollars and the Caribbean or Mexican or who-knows-what islands that benefited from sheltering their mobile labs.

"We are idealists," Ishmael droned on, "and we are the future. Through our efforts, mankind will change for the better. Wars will end, cruelty will disappear. When people can—"

"Let me interrupt you for just a moment, Ishmael." Jane widened her eyes and over-used his name. Her dewy look up at him from the floor could have reversed desertification. She was pulling out all the stops. "I need so *much* to understand, Ishmael. If you genemod these little girls, one by one, you end up changing such a small percentage of the human race that… How many children have been engineered with Arlen's Syndrome?"

"We prefer the term 'Arlen's Advantage.'"

"Yes, of course. How many children?"

I held my breath. The Group had never given out that information.

Jane put an entreating hand on Ishmael's knee.

He said loftily, hungrily, "That information is classified," and I saw that he didn't know the answer.

Ms. Resentful said, "To date, three thousand two hundred fourteen."

Was she lying? My instincts—and I have very good instincts, although to say that in *this* context is clearly a joke—said no. Resentful knew the number. So she *was* higher up than Ishmael. And since she sure as hell wasn't responding to Jane's allure, that meant The Group now wanted the numbers made public.

"Yes, that's right," Ishmael said hastily, "three thousand two hundred fourteen children."

Jane said, "But that's not a high percentage out of six billion people on Earth, is it? It—"

"Five billionth of one percent," I said. A silly, self-indulgent display, but what the hell. My legs ached.

She always could ad-lib. "Yes, thank you, Barry. But my question was for Ishmael. If only such a tiny percentage of humanity possesses Arlen's Advantage, even if the genemod turns out to be inheritable—"

"It is," Ishmael said, which was nonsense. The oldest Arlen's kids were only twelve.

"Wonderful!" Jane persisted. "But as I say, if only such a tiny percentage of humanity possesses the Advantage, how can The Group hope to alter the entire human future?"

Ishmael covered her hand with his. He smiled down at her, and his eyes actually twinkled. "Jane, Jane, Jane. Have you ever dropped a pebble into a pond?"

"Yes."

"And what happened, my dear?"

"A ripple."

"Which spread and spread until the entire pond was affected!" Ishmael spread his arms wide. The ass couldn't even put together a decent analogy. Humanity was an ocean, not a pond, and water ripples were always transitory. But Jane, actress that she was, beamed at him and moved the conversation to something he could handle.

"I see. Tell me, Ishmael, how you personally became involved in The Group."

He was thrilled to talk about himself. As he did, Jane skillfully extracted information about The Group's make-up, its organization, its communications methods. Resentful let her do it. I watched the young woman, who was watching Ishmael but not in a monitoring sort of way. He couldn't give away really critical information; he didn't have any. Still, he talked too much. He was the kind of man who responded to an audience, who could easily become so expansive that he turned indiscreet. Sooner or later, I suspected, he would say something to somebody that he shouldn't, and The Group would dump him.

Ms. Resentful wasn't anything near the actress Jane that was. Her hunger for this worthless man was almost palpable. I might have felt sympathy for her pain if my own wasn't increasing so much in my legs, back, neck. I seldom sat this long, and never on a hard chair.

My particular brand of dwarfism, achondroplasia, accounts for seventy percent of all cases. Malformed bones and cartilage produce not only the short limbs, big head and butt, and pushed-in face that all the media caricaturists so adore but also, in some of

us, constriction of the spinal canal that causes pain. Especially as achons age, and I was only two years younger than Jane. Multiple excruciating operations have only helped me so much.

After an hour and a half, Jane rose, her filmy skirt swirling around her lovely calves. My uneasiness spiked sharply. If anything was going to happen, it would be now.

But nothing did happen. The masked boy reappeared and we were led out of the dingy basement. I could barely walk. Jane knew better than to help me, but she whispered, "I'm so sorry, Barry. But this was my only chance."

"I know." Somehow I made it up the stairs. We navigated the maze of the abandoned warehouse where The Group's unseen soldiers stayed at stand off with our own unseen bodyguards. Blinking in the sunlight, I suddenly collapsed onto the broken concrete.

"Barry!"

"It's...okay. *Don't.*"

"The rest will be so much easier...I promise!"

I got myself upright, or what passes for upright. The unmarked van arrived for us. The whole insane interview had gone off without a hitch, without violence, smooth as good chocolate.

So why did I still feel so uneasy?

✿

An hour later, Jane's image appeared all over the Net, the TV, the wallboards. Her words had been edited to appear that she was a supporter, perhaps even a member, of The Group. But of course we had anticipated this. The moment our van left the warehouse, the first of the pre-emptory spots I'd prepared aired everywhere. They featured news avatar CeeCee Collins, who was glad for the scoop, interviewing Jane about her meeting. Dedicated actress preparing for a role, willing to take any personal risk for art, not a personal believer in breaking the law but valuing open discourse on this important issue, and so forth. The spots cost us a huge amount of money. They were worth it. Not only was the criticism defused, but the publicity for the upcoming movie which started principal photography in less than a month, was beyond price.

I didn't watch my spots play. Nor was I there when the FBI, CIA, HPA, etc. paid Jane the expected visit to both "debrief" her and/or threaten her with arrest for meeting with terrorists. But I didn't need to be there. Before our meeting, I'd gotten Jane credentials under the Malvern-Murphy Press Immunity Act, plus Everett Murphy as her more-than-capable lawyer. Everett monitored the interviews and I stayed in bed under a painkiller. The FBI, CIA, HPA wanted to meet with me, too, of course, once Jane told them I'd been present. They had to wait until I could see them. I didn't mind their cooling their heels as they waited for me, not at all.

Why are you so opposed to genemods? Jane had asked me once, and only once, not looking at me as she said it. She meant, *Why you, especially?* Usually I answered Jane, trusted Jane, but not on this. I told her the truth: *You wouldn't understand.* To her credit, she hadn't been offended. Jane was smart enough to know what she didn't know.

Now, on my lovely pain patch, I floated in a world where she and I walked hand in hand through a forest the green of her filmy skirt, and she had to crane her neck to smile up at me.

✿

The next few days, publicity for the picture exploded. Jane did interview after interview: TV, LinkNet, robocam, print, holonews. She glowed with the attention, looking ten years younger. Some of the interviewers and avatars needled her, but she stuck to the studio line: This is a movie about people, not polemics. *Future Perfect* is not really about genetic engineering. It will be an honest examination of eternal verities, of our shared frailty and astonishing shared strength, of what makes us human, of blah blah blah, that just happens to use Arlen's syndrome as a vehicle. The script was nearly finished and it would be complex and realistic and blah blah blah.

"*Pro or con on genemods?*" an exasperated journalist finally shouted from the back of the room.

Jane gave him a dazzling smile. "Complex and realistic," she said.

Both the pros and the cons would be swarming into the theater, unstoppable as lemmings.

I felt so good about all of this that I decided to call Leila. I needed to be in a good mood to stand these calls. Leila wasn't home, letting me get away with just a message, which made me feel even better.

Jane, glowing on camera, was wiping a decade years of cinematic obscurity with *Future Perfect*. I couldn't wipe out my fifteen years of guilt that easily, nor would I do so even if I could. But I was still glad that Leila wasn't home.

✿

Jane had promised that Friday's role-prep interview would be easier on me. She was wrong.

The Barrington twins lived with their parents and teen-age sister in San Luis Obispo. Jane's pilot obtained clearance to land on the green-velvet Barrington lawn, well behind the estate's heavily secured walls. I wouldn't have to walk far.

"Welcome, Miss Snow. An *honor*." Frieda Barrington was mutton dressed as lamb, a fiftyish woman in a brief skirt and peek-a-boo caped sweater. Slim, toned, tanned, but the breasts doing the peek-a-booing would never be twenty again, and her face had the tense lines of those who spent most of their waking time pretending not to be tense.

Jane climbed gracefully from the flyer and stood so that her body shielded my awkward descent. I seized the grab bar, sat on the flyer floor, fell heavily onto the grass, and scrambled to my feet. Jane moved aside, her calf-length skirt—butter yellow, this time—blowing in the slight breeze. "Call me Jane. This is my manager, Barry Tenler."

Frieda Barrington was one of Those. Still, she at least tried to conceal her distaste. "Hello, Mr. Tenler."

"Hi." With any luck, this would be the only syllable I had to address to her.

We walked across through perfect landscaping, Frieda supplying the fund of inane chatter that such women always have at their disposal. The house had been built a hundred years earlier for a silent-film star. Huge, pink, gilded at windows and doors, it called to mind an obese lawn flamingo. We entered a huge foyer floored in black-and-white marble, which managed to look less Vermeer than checkerboard. A sulky girl in dirty jeans lounged on a chaise longue. She stared at us over the garish cover of a comic book.

"Suky, get up," Frieda snapped. "This is Miss Snow and her manager Mr., uh, Tangler. My daughter Suky."

The girl got up, made an ostentatious and mocking curtsey, and lay down again. Frieda made a noise of outrage and embarrassment, but I felt sorry for Suky. Fifteen—the same age as Ethan—plain of face, she was caught between a mother who'd appropriated her fashions and twin sisters who appropriated all the attention. Frieda would be lucky if Suky's rebellion stopped at mere rudeness. I made her a mock little bow to match her curtsey, and watched as her eyes widened with surprise. I grinned.

Frieda snapped, "Where are the twins?"

Suky shrugged. Frieda rolled her eyes and led us through the house.

They were playing on the terrace, a sun-shaded sweep of weathered stone with steps that led to more lawn, all backed by a gorgeous view of vine-yards below the Sierra Madres. Frieda settled us on comfortable, padded chairs. A robo-server rolled up, offering lemonade.

Bridget and Belinda came over to us before they were called. "Hello!" Jane said with her melting smile, but neither girl answered. Instead, they gazed steadily, unblinkingly at her for a full thirty seconds, and then did the same with me. I didn't like it, or them.

Arlen's Syndrome, like all genetic tinkering, has side effects. No one knows that better than I. Achondroplasia dwarfism is the result of a single nucleotide substitution in the gene FGFR3 at codon 380 on chromosome 4. It affects the growth bones and cartilage, which in turn affects air passages, nerves, and other people's tolerance. Exactly which genes were involved in Arlen's were a trade secret, but the modifications undoubtedly spread across many genes, with many side effects. But since only females could be genemod for Arlen's, the X chromosome was one of those altered. That much, at least, was known.

The two eleven-year-old girls staring at me so frankly were small for their age, delicately built: fairy children. They had white skin, silky fair hair cut in short caps, and eyes of luminous gray. Other than that, they didn't look much alike, fraternal twins rather than identical. Bridget was shorter, plumper, prettier. From a Petri-dishful of Frieda's fertilized eggs, the Barringtons had chosen the most promising two, had them genemoded for Arlen's Syndrome, and implanted them in Frieda's ageing but still ser-

viceable womb. The loving parents, both exhibitionists, had splashed across the world-wide media every last detail—except where and how the work had been done. Unlike Rima Ridley-Jones, the Arlen child that Jane had spoken with last week, these two were carefully manufactured celebrities.

Jane tried again. "I'm Jane Snow, and you're Bridget and Belinda. I'm glad to meet you."

"Yes," Belinda said, "you are." She looked at me. "But you're not."

There was no point in lying. Not to them. "No, particularly."

Bridget said, with a gentleness surprising in one so young, "That's okay, though."

"Thank you," I said.

"I didn't say it was okay," Belinda said.

There was no answer to that. The Ridley-Jones child hadn't behaved like this; in addition to shielding her from the media, her mother had taught her manners. Frieda, on the other hand, leaned back in her chair like a spectator at a play, interested in what her amazing daughters would say next, but with anxiety on overdrive. I had the sense she'd been here before. Eleven-year-olds were no longer adorable, biddable toddlers.

"You'll never get it," Belinda said to me, at the same moment that Bridget put a hand on her sister's arm. Belinda shook it off. "Let me alone, Brid. He should know. They all should know." She smiled at me and I felt something in my chest recoil from the look in her gray eyes.

"You'll never get it," Belinda said to me with that horrible smile. "No matter what you do, Jane will never love you. And she'll always hate it when you touch her even by mistake. Just like she hates it now. Hates it, hates it, hates it."

✿

It started with a dog.

Dr. Kenneth Bernard Arlen, a geneticist and chess enthusiast, owned a toy poodle. Poodles are a smart breed. Arlen played chess twice a week in his Stanford apartment with Kelson Hughes from Zoology. Usually they played three, four, or five games in a row, depending on how careless Hughes got with his end game. Cosette lay on the rug, dozing, until checkmate of the last game, when she always began barking frantically to protest Hughes's leaving. The odd thing was that Cosette began barking *before* the men rose, as they replaced the chessmen for what might, after all, have been the start of just another game. How did she know it wasn't?

Hughes assumed pheromones. He, or Arlen, or both, probably gave off a different smell as they decided to call it a night. Pheromones were Hughes's field of research; he'd done significant work in mate selection among mice based on smell. He had a graduate student remove the glomeruli from adult dogs and put them through tests to see how various of their learned responses to humans changed. The responses didn't change. It wasn't pheromones.

Now not only Hughes but also Arlen was intensely intrigued. The Human Genome Project had just slid into Phase 2, discovering which genes encoded for what proteins, and how. Arlen was working with Turner's Syndrome, a disorder in which females were born missing all or part of one of their two X chromosomes. The girls had not only physical problems but social ones; they seemed to have trouble with even simple social interactions. What interested Hughes was that Turner Syndrome girls with an intact paternal X gene, the one inherited from the father, managed far better socially than those with the maternal X functioning. Something about picking up social cues was coded for genetically, and on the paternal X.

Where else did social facility reside in the genome? What cues of body language, facial expression, or tone of voice was Cosette picking up? Somehow the dog knew that when Hughes and Arlen set the chessmen in place, this wasn't the start of a new game. Something, dictated at least in part by Cosette's genes, was causing processes in her poodle brain. After all, Hughes's dog, a big dumb Samoyed, never seemed to anticipate anything. Snowy was continually surprised by gravity.

Arlen found the genes in dogs. It took him ten years, during which he failed to get tenure because he wouldn't publish. After Stanford let him go, he still didn't publish. He found the genes in humans. He still didn't publish. Stone broke, he was well on the way to bitter and yet with his idealism undimmed—an odd combination, but not unknown among science fanatics. Inevitably, he crossed paths with people even more fanatical. Kenneth Bernard Arlen joined forces with off-shore backers to open a fertility clinic that created super-empathic children.

Empathy turns up early in some children. A naturally empathic nine-month-old will give her teddy bear to another child who is crying; the toddler senses how bad the other child feels. People who score high in perceiving others' emotions are more popular, more outgoing, better adjusted, more happily married, more successful at their jobs. Arlen's Syndrome toddlers understood—not verbally, but in their limbic systems—when Mommy was worried, when Daddy wanted them to go potty, that Grandma loved them, that a stranger was dangerous.

If his first illegal, off-shore experiments with human germ lines had resulted in deformities, Arlen would have been crucified. There were no deformities. Prospective clients loved the promise of kids who actually understood how *parents* felt. By six or seven, Arlen's Syndrome kids could, especially if they were bright, read an astonishing array of nonverbal signals. By nine or ten, it was impossible to lie to them. As long as you were honest and genuinely had their best interests in mind, the children were a joy to live with: sensitive, cooperative, grateful, aware.

And yet here was Belinda Barrington, staring at me from her pale eyes, and I didn't need a genetic dose of super-empathy to see her glee at embarrassing me. I couldn't look at Jane. The blood was hot in my face.

Frieda said, sharply and hopelessly, "Belinda, that's not nice."

"No, it's not," Bridget said. She frowned at her sister, and Belinda actually looked away for a moment. Her twin had some childish control over Belinda, and her mother didn't. "Tell him you're sorry."

"Sorry," Belinda muttered, unconvincingly. So they could lie, if not be lied to.

Frieda said to Jane, "This is new behavior. I'm sure it's just a phase. Nothing you'd want to include in your project!"

Belinda shot her mother a look of freezing contempt.

Jane took control of the sorry situation. Sparing me any direct glance, she said to Belinda, "Did anybody tell you why I want to talk to you girls?"

"No," Belinda said. "You're not a reporter."

"I'm a movie actress."

Bridget brightened. "Like Kylie Kicker?" Apparently Arlen's Advantage did not confer immunity to inane kiddie pop culture.

"Not as young," Jane smiled, "or as rich. But I'm making a movie about the lives that girls like you might have when you're grown up. That's why I want to get to know you a little bit now. But only if it's okay with you."

The twins looked at each other. Neither spoke, but I had the impression that gigabytes passed between them. Frieda said, "Girls, I hope you'll cooperate with Miss Snow. She—"

"No, you don't," Belinda said, almost absently. "You don't like her. She's too pretty. But *we* like her."

Frieda's face went a mottled maroon. Bridget, her plump features alarmed, put a hand on her mother's arm. But Frieda shook it off, started to say something, then abruptly stood and stalked into the house. Bridget made a move to follow but checked herself. To me—*why?*—she said apologetically, "She wants to be alone a little while."

"You should go with her," Belinda said, and I didn't have to be told twice. These kids gave me the creeps.

Not that even they, with their overpraised empathy, could ever understand why.

In the foyer, Suky still lay on the chaise longue with her comic book. There was no sign of her mother. The other chairs were all mammoth leather things, but a low antique bench stood against one wall and I clambered painfully onto it and called a cab. I would have to walk all the way to the front gate to meet it, but the thought of going back in the flyer with Jane was unbearable. I closed my eyes and leaned my head against the wall. My back and legs ached, but nothing compared to my heart.

It wasn't the words Belinda had said. Yes, I loved Jane and yes, that love was hopeless. I already knew that and so must Jane. How could she not? I was with her nearly every day; she was a woman sensitive to nuance. I knew she hated my accidental touch, and hated herself for that, and could help none of it. Three of Jane's husbands had been among the best-looking men on the planet. Tall, strong, straight-limbed. I had seen Jane's flesh glow rosy just because James or Karl or Duncan was in the same room with her. I had felt her hide her recoil from me.

"*Sticks and stones can break my bones but words can never hurt me.*" How often as a child had I chanted that to myself after another in the endless string of bullies had taunted me? *Short Stuff, Dopey, Munchkin, Big Butt, Mighty Midget, Oompa Loompa, cripple....* Belinda hadn't illuminated any new truth for anybody. What she *had* done was speak it aloud.

"*Give sorrow words*"—but even Shakespeare could be as wrong as nursery chants. Something unnamed could, just barely, be ignored. Could be kept out of daily interaction, could almost be pretended away. What had been "given words" could not. And now tomorrow and the next day and the day after that, Jane and I would have to try to work together, would avoid each other's eyes, would each tread the dreary internal treadmill: Is he/she upset? Did I brush too close, stay too far away, give off any hurtful signal... *For God's sake, leave me alone!*

Speech doesn't banish distance; it creates it. And if—

"Bitches, aren't they?" a voice said softly. I opened my eyes. Suky stood close to my bench. She was taller than I'd thought, with a spectacular figure. No one would ever notice, not next to the wonder and novelty of the twins.

In my shamed confusion, I blurted out the first thing that came into my mind. "Belinda is, Bridget isn't."

"That's what you think." Suky laughed, then laid her comic book on the bench. "You need this, dwarf." She vanished into some inner corridor.

I picked up the comic. It was holo, those not inexpensive e-graphics with chips embedded in the paper. Four panels succeeded each other on each page, with every panel dramatizing the plot in ten second bursts of shifting light. The title was "Knife Hack," and the story seemed to concern a mother who carves up her infants with a maximum amount of blood and brain spatter.

Arlen's Syndrome kids: a joy to live with, sensitive and cooperative and grateful and aware.

Just one big happy family.

But sometimes the universe gives you a break. The next day I had a cold. Nothing serious, just a stuffy nose and sore throat, but I sounded like a rusty file scraping on cast iron, so I called in sick to my "office" at Jane's estate. Her trainer answered. "*What?*"

"Tell Jane I won't be in today. Sick. And remind her to—"

"I'm not your errand boy, Barry," he answered hotly. We stared at each other's comlink images in mutual dislike. Dino Carrano was the trainer-to-the-stars-of-the-moment-before-this-one, an arrogant narcissist who three times a week tortured Jane into perfect abs and weeping exhaustion. Like Ishmael, he was without the prescience to realize that his brief vogue had passed and that Jane kept him on partly from compassion. He stood now in her deserted exercise room.

"Why are you answering the phone? Where's Catalina?"

"Her grandmother in Mexico died. Again. And before you ask, Jose is supervising the grounds crew and Jane is in the bathroom, throwing up. Now you know everything. Bye, Barry."

"Wait! If she's throwing up because you pushed her too hard again, you Dago bastard—"

"Save your invective, little man. We haven't even started the training session yet, and if we don't train by tomorrow, her ass is going to drop like a duffel bag. For today she just ate something bad." He cut the link.

My stomach didn't feel too steady, either. Had it been the Barrington lemonade? I made it to the bathroom just in time. But afterward I felt better, decided to not call my doctor, and went to bed. If Jane was sick, Catalina would cancel her appointments. No, Catalina was in Mexico… *not my problem.*

But all Jane's problems were mine. Without her, I had my own problems—Leila, Ethan—but no actual life.

Nonetheless, I forced myself to stay in bed, and eventually I fell asleep. When I woke, six hours later, my throat and stomach both felt fine. A quick call discovered that Catalina had returned from Mexico, sounding suspiciously unbereaved. But she was efficient enough when she was actually in the country, and I decided I didn't need to brief Jane on tomorrow's schedule. That would buy me one more day. I would take a relaxing evening. A long bath, a glass of wine, another postponement of talking to Leila. The industry news on *Hollywood Watch.*

The local news came on first. Ishmael's body had been found in a pond in the Valley.

"…and weighted with cement blocks. Cause of death was a single gunshot wound to the head, execution style," said the news avatar, a CGI who looked completely real except that she had no faulty camera angles whatsoever. I stared at the photo of Ishmael's handsome face on the screen beside her. "Apparently the murderers were unaware that construction work would start today at the pond site, where luxury condos will be built by—"

Ishmael's name was Harold Sylvester Ehrenreich. Failed actor, minor grifter, petty tax evader, who had dropped out of electronic sight eight months ago.

"Anyone having any information concerning—"

I was already on the comlink. "Jane?"

"I just called the cops. They're on their way over." She looked tired, drawn, within five years of her actual age. Her voice sounded as raspy as mine had been. "I was just about to call you. Barry, if this endangers the picture—"

"It won't," I said. Thirty years a star, and she still didn't understand how the behind-the-scenes worked. "It will *make* the picture. Did you call Everett?"

"He's on his way."

"Don't say a word until both he and I get there. Not a word, Jane, not one. Can you send the flyer for me?"

"Yes. Barry—was he killed because of my interview?"

"There's no way to know that," I said, and all at once was profoundly grateful that it was true. I didn't care if Ishmael was alive, dead, or fucking himself on Mars, but Jane was built differently. People mattered to her, especially the wounded-bird type. It was how she'd ended up married to three of her four husbands and the fourth, the Alpha-Male Producer, had been in reaction to the second, the alcoholic failed actor. Catalina, Jane's housekeeper and social secretary, was another of her wounded birds. So, in his own perverse way, was her trainer.

Maybe that was why Jane had ended up with me as well.

But I could tell that neither me nor Belinda's cruel words were on Jane's mind just now. It was all Ishmael, and that was good. Ishmael would get us safely past our personal crisis. Even murder has its silver lining.

✿

As the flyer set down on Jane's roof, I saw the media already starting to converge. Someone must have tipped them off, perhaps a clerk at the precinct. An unmarked car was parked within Jane's gates, with two vans outside and another flyer approaching from L.A. Catalina let me in, her dark eyes wide with excitement. "*La policia*—"

"I know. Is Everett Murphy here?"

"Yes, he—"

"Bring in coffee and cake. And make the maids draw all the curtains in the house, *immediately*. Even the bedrooms. There'll be robocams." I wanted pictures and information released on my schedule, not that of flying recorders.

A man and a woman sat with Jane and Everett at one end of her enormous living room, which the decorator had done in swooping black curves with accents of screaming purple. The room looked nothing like Jane, who used it only for parties. She'd actually defied the decorator, who was a Dino-Carrano-bully type but not a wounded bird, and done her private sitting room in English country house. But she hadn't taken the detectives there. I could guess why: she was protecting her safe haven. Catalina rushed past me like a small Mexican tornado and dramatically pushed the button to opaque the windows. They went deep purple, and lights flickered on in the room. Catalina raced out.

"Barry," Jane said. She looked even worse than on comlink, red nose and swollen eyes and no makeup. I hoped to hell that neither cop was optic wired. "This is Detective Lopez and Detective Miller from the LAPD. Officers, my manager Barry Tenler."

They nodded. Both were too well-trained to show curiosity or distaste, but they were there. I always know. In her sitting room Jane kept a low chair for me, but here I had to scramble up onto a high black sofa that satisfied the decorator desire for "an important piece." I said, "You can question Miss Snow now, but please be advised that she has already spoken with the FBI and HPA, and that both Mr. Murphy and I reserve the right to advise her to not answer."

The cops ignored this meaningless window dressing. But I'd accomplished what I wanted. Dwarfs learn early that straightforward, multisyllabic, take-no-shit talk will sometimes stop average-sizers from treating us like children. Sometimes.

Officer Lopez began a thorough interrogation. How had she arranged the meeting with The Group? When? What contact had she had between the initial one and the meeting? Who had taken her to the meeting? Who else had accompanied her? When they found out that it had been me, Lopez got the look of a man who knows he's screwed up. "You were there, Mr. Tenler?"

"I was."

"You'll have to go with Officer Miller into another room," Lopez said. He stared at me hard. Witnesses were always questioned separately, and even if it hadn't crossed his mind that someone like me was a witness, he suspected it had crossed mine. Which it had. If law-enforcement agencies weren't given to so many turf wars, the LAPD would already know I'd been in that grimy basement. Or if Lopez hadn't fallen victims to his own macho assumptions. *You? She took a lame half-pint like* you *to protect her?*

"Everett is my lawyer, too," I said.

"You go with Officer Miller. Mr. Murphy will join you when I'm finished with Miss Snow." Lopez's formality barely restrained his anger.

Following Officer Miller to the media room, it occurred to me—pointlessly—that Belinda would have known immediately that I'd been withholding something.

It seemed obvious to me, as it probably was to the cops, that Ishmael had been killed by The Group. Narcissistic, bombastic, unreliable, he must have screwed up royally. Was Ms. Resentful dead, too? The bodyguard with the assault rifle? The boy who'd guided us through the warehouse?

The Group was trying to combine idealism, profit-making, and iron control. That combination never worked. I would say that to Officer Lopez, except that there was little chance he would take it seriously. Not from me.

✿

The media spent a breathless three or four days on the story ("Famous Actress Questioned About Genemod Murder! What Does Jane Know?") Then a United States senator married a former porn star named Candy Alley and the press moved on, partly because it was clear that Jane didn't know anything. I'd positioned her as cooperative, concerned, committed to her art, and bewildered by the killing. Opinion polls said the public viewed her favorably. She increased her name recognition six hundred percent among eighteen-to-twenty-four-year-olds, most of whom watched only holos and had never seen a Jane Snow picture. Publicity is publicity.

She got even more of it by spending so much time with the Barrington twins. Everybody liked this except me. Frieda liked the press attention (at least, such press as wasn't staking out the senator and his new pork barrel). The twins liked Jane. She liked caring for yet more wounded birds, which was what she considered them. Her thinking on this escaped me; these were two of the most pampered children in the known universe. But Jane was only filling time, anyway, until the script was finished. And to her credit, she turned down the party invitations from the I'm-more-important-than-you A-list crowd that had ignored her for a decade. I'd urged her to turn down social invitations in order to create that important aura of non-attainable exclusivity. Jane turned them down because she no longer considered those people to be friends.

As for me, I worked at home on the hundreds of pre-photography details. Before I could finally reach Leila, she called me.

"Hey, Barry."

"Hey, Leila." She didn't look good. I steeled myself to ask. "How is he?"

"Gone again." Exhaustion pulled at her face. "I called the LAPD but they won't do anything."

"He'll come home again," I said. "He always does."

"Yeah, and one of these days it'll be in a coffin."

I said nothing to that, because there was nothing to say.

Leila, however, could always find something. "Well, if he does come home in a coffin, then you'll be off the hook, won't you? No more risk of embarrassing you or the gorgeous has-been."

"Leila—"

"Have a good time with your big shot Hollywood friends. I'll just wait to hear if this time the son you deformed really is dead."

She hung up on me.

✧

Leila and I met at a Little People of America convention in Denver. She was one of the teenage dwarfs dancing joyously, midriff bared and short skirt flipping, at the annual ball. I thought she was the most beautiful thing I'd ever seen: red hair and blue eyes, alive to her fingertips. I was eighteen years older than she, and everyone at the convention knew who I was. High-ranking aide to a candidate for the mayor of San Francisco. Smart, successful, sharply dressed. Local dwarf makes good. More mobile then, I asked her to dance. Six months later we married. Six months after that, while I was running the campaign for a gubernatorial candidate, Leila accidentally got pregnant.

Two dwarfs have a twenty-five-percent chance of conceiving an average-sized child, a fifty percent chance of a dwarf, and a twenty-five percent of a double-dominant, which always dies shortly after birth. Leila and I had never discussed these odds because, like most dwarfs, we planned on the *in vitro* fertilization that permits cherry-picking embryos. But Leila got careless with her pills. She knew immediately that she was pregnant, and even before the zygote had implanted itself in her uterus wall, testing showed that the fetus had a "normal" FGFR3 gene. I panicked.

"I don't want to have an average-sized kid," I told Leila. "I just *don't*."

"And I don't want to have an abortion," Leila said. "It's not that I'm politically opposed to abortion. I'm glad to have the choice, but… Barry, I…I just can't. He's already a baby to me. Our baby. Why would having an Average be so hard?"

"Why?" I'd waved a hand around our house, in which everything—furniture, appliance controls, doorknobs—had been built to our scale. "Just look around! Besides, there's a moral question here, Leila. You know that with *in vitro,* fewer and fewer dwarfs are having dwarf children. That just reinforces the idea that there's something wrong with being a dwarf. I don't want to perpetuate that—I won't perpetuate that. This is a political issue! I want a dwarf child."

She believed me. She was twenty to my thirty-nine, and I was a big-shot politico. She loved me. Leila lacked the perspicacity to see how terrified I was of an average-sized son, who would be as tall as I was by the time he was seven. Who would be impossible to control. Who might eventually despise me and his mother both. But Leila really, really didn't want to abort. I talked her into *in utero* somatic gene therapy in England.

In those days I believed in science. The som-gene technique was new but producing spectacular results. The British had gotten behind genetic engineering in a big way, and knowledgeable people from all over the world flocked to Cambridge, where private firms tied to the great university where turning genes on and off in fetuses still in the womb. This had to be done during the first week or ten days after conception. The FGFR3 gene stops bones from growing. It was turned on in babies with dwarfism; a corrective genemod retrovirus should be able to turn the gene off in the little mass of cells that was Ethan. The problem was that the Cambridge biotech clinic wouldn't do it.

"We cure disease, not cause it," I was told icily.

"Dwarfism is not a disease!" I said, too angry to be icy. Waving high the banner of political righteousness. It wasn't a good idea, in those days, to cross me. I was the high-ranking, infallible campaign guru, the tiny *wunderkind*, the man who was never wrong. Fear can present itself as arrogance.

"Nonetheless," the scientist told me in that aloof British accent, "we will not do it. Nor, I suspect, will any clinic in the United Kingdom."

He was right. Time was running out. The next day we went off-shore, to a clinic in the Caymans, and something went wrong. The retrovirus that was the delivery vector mutated, or the splicing caused other genes to jump (they will do that), or maybe God just wanted an evil joke that day. The soma-gene correction spawned side effects, with one gene turning on another that in turn affected another, a cascade of creation run amok. And we got Ethan.

Leila never forgave me, and I never forgave myself. She left me when Ethan was not quite two. I sent money. I tried to stay in touch. I bore Leila's fury and contempt and despair. She sent me pictures of Ethan, but she wouldn't let me see him. I could have pressed visitation through the courts. I didn't.

My gubernatorial candidate lost.

✪

"Barry," Jane comlinked me the night before the first script conference, "would you like to come to dinner tonight?"

"Can't," I lied. "I already have dinner plans."

"Oh? With whom?"

"A friend." I smiled mysteriously. Some inane back-in-high-school part of my brain hoped that she'd think I had a date. Then I saw Bridget Barrington scamper across the room behind Jane. "Are those kids at your place?"

"Yes, I couldn't go there today because Catalina is sick and I had to—"

"Sick? With what? Jane, you can't catch anything now, the first reading is tomorrow and—"

"I won't catch this—*I* gave it to *her*. It's that sore throat-and-stomach thing we both had. Catalina—"

"You're not a goddamn nurse! If Catalina is ill—give me credit, I didn't say *actually ill instead of faking the way she fakes relatives' deaths every fifteen minutes*—"

"—then hire a nurse or—"

"She's not sick enough for a nurse, she just needs coddling and orange juice and company. It's fine, Barry, so butt out. I'm actually glad of the distraction, it keeps me from thinking about tonight. Oh, meant to tell you—I talked Robert into couriering the script to me tonight! I wanted to read it before tomorrow. He sounded weird about it, but he agreed."

My radar turned on. "Weird how?"

"I don't know. Just weird."

I considered all the possible "weirds" that the producer could be conveying, but I didn't see what I could do about any of them. I settled for, "Just don't catch anything from Catalina."

"I already *told* you that I won't."

"Fine. Whatever you say."

And it was fine. She was treating me the way she always did, with exasperated affection, and I was grateful. Belinda's poison, flushed out of our working relationship by the flood of feeling about Ishmael's murder, hadn't harmed us. I wouldn't lose the little of Jane that I had.

And the picture was going to be a blockbuster.

✪

…continued in issue 58

"I LOVED IT."
—*Larry Niven*

"A NAIL-BITING THRILLER."
—*Publishers Weekly*

"WILL DELIGHT AND ENTHRALL."
—*Library Journal*

"A PROVOCATIVE SCIENCE FICTION NOVEL."
—*Foreword Reviews*

JULY 26, 2022. Pre-orders available now

www.CaezikSF.com

Printed in Great Britain
by Amazon